A Love So Sweet

Sweet with Heat: Weston Bradens

Addison Cole

ISBN-10: 1-948868-12-1
ISBN-13: 978-1-948868-12-9

This is a work of fiction. The events and characters described herein are imaginary and are not intended to refer to specific places or living persons. The opinions expressed in this manuscript are solely the opinions of the author and do not represent the opinions or thoughts of the publisher. The author has represented and warranted full ownership and/or legal right to publish all the materials in this book.

Cover Design: Elizabeth Mackey Designs

WORLD LITERARY PRESS
PRINTED IN THE UNITED STATES OF AMERICA

A Note to Readers

Treat Braden and Max Armstrong have a very special place in my heart. Their love story is the beginning of my beloved Braden series, and introduces you to some of my favorite characters, and to a family that has become so real to me, I feel like they're always by my side. I hope you fall in love with them all just as I have.

For readers who enjoyed the Sweet with Heat: Seaside Summers series, you might remember meeting Dane and Lacy, and hearing about Savannah and Jack. As you read each of the Braden family love stories, you will see how each couple met and fell in love.

About Sweet with Heat Books

Addison Cole is the sweet-romance pen name of *New York Times* bestselling author Melissa Foster, and Sweet with Heat titles are the sweet editions of Melissa's award-winning steamy romance collection, Love in Bloom. Sweet with Heat novels conveys all of the passion you'd expect to find between two people in love without any graphic scenes or harsh language (with the exception of an occasional "damn" or "hell"). If you're looking for a more explicit romance, pick up the steamy edition of this title, *Lovers at Heart, Reimagined*, written by Melissa.

Within the Sweet with Heat series you'll find fiercely loyal heroes and smart, empowered women on their search for true love. They're flawed, funny, and easy to relate to. Characters from each series appear in future Sweet with Heat books. All Sweet with Heat books may be read as stand-alone novels or as part of the larger series.

Sign up for Addison's Sweet with Heat newsletter to be notified of the next release:
www.Addisoncole.com/Newsletter

For more information on Sweet with Heat titles visit
www.AddisonCole.com

Chapter One

TREAT BRADEN DIDN'T usually charter planes. It wasn't his style to flash his wealth. But today he needed to be anywhere but his Nassau resort, and missing his commercial flight had just plain pissed him off. He owned upscale resorts all over the world, and he'd been featured on travel shows so many times that it turned his stomach to have to play those ridiculous media games. The pomp and circumstance surrounding him had begun to irk him in ways that it never had before meeting Max Armstrong. It had been several long, lonely weeks since he'd seen her standing in the lobby of his Nassau resort, since his heart first thundered in a way that threw him completely off-kilter—and since they'd spent one incredible evening together. Treat wasn't a Neanderthal. He'd known he had no claim on her, even after their intimate evening. But that hadn't stopped his blood from boiling or kept him from acting like a jerk the next morning when he'd seen her with another man in front of the elevators, wearing the same clothes she'd had on when Treat had left her the night before.

He hadn't been able to stop thinking about Max since the moment he'd first met her, despite the uncomfortable encounter, but he'd been burned before, and he wasn't into repeating his mistakes. Getting away from resorts altogether and spending a weekend with his father at his ranch in Weston, Colorado, a small ranch town with dusty streets, too many cowboy hats, and a main drag that had been built to replicate the Wild West, was just what he needed.

His rental SUV moved at a snail's pace behind a line of traffic that was not at all typical for his hometown. It wasn't until he crawled around the next curve and saw balloons and banners above the road announcing the annual Indie Film Festival that he realized what weekend it was. He wasn't in the mood to deal with crowds.

His cell phone rang, and his sister's name flashed on the screen. Before he could say hello, Savannah said, "I can't believe you didn't tell me you were coming to town."

"Hi, sis. I miss you, too." The only girl among his five siblings, Savannah was a cutthroat entertainment attorney, but to Treat she'd always be his baby sister.

"When will you get into town?"

"I'm here now, sitting in traffic on Main Street." He hadn't moved an inch in five minutes.

"I'm at the festival with a client. Come see me."

All he really wanted to do was reach his father's two-hundred-acre ranch just outside of town, but Treat knew that if he didn't see Savannah right away, she'd be disappointed. Disappointing his siblings was something he strived not to do. Having lost their mother when Treat was only eleven and his youngest sibling, Hugh, had been hardly more than a baby, his siblings had already faced enough disappointment for one lifetime.

"You're with a client. Sure you can get away?" he asked.

"For you? Of course. Besides, I'm with Connor Dean. He

can handle things for a little while. Come in the back gate. I'll wait there." Connor was an actor who was quickly climbing the ranks of fame. Savannah had been his attorney for two years, and whenever he had a public engagement, he brought her along. It wasn't a typical attorney-client relationship, but for all of Connor's bravado, he'd been slandered one too many times. Savannah kept track of what was and wasn't said at most events—by both Connor and the media.

"I'll be there as soon as traffic allows." After he ended the call with Savannah he called his father.

"Hey there, son."

Hal's slow, deep drawl tugged at Treat's heart. He'd missed him. Hal had always been a calming influence on Treat. After his mother passed away, his father had pulled him and his siblings through those tumultuous years. But Hal wasn't a coddler. He had instilled a strong work ethic and sense of loyalty into their heads, and that had enabled each of them to be successful in their endeavors.

"Dad, I'm here in town, but I'm going to stop at the festival first to see Savannah, if you don't mind."

"Yup. Savannah called. She misses you, and I'd venture a guess that you could use a little extended family time, too."

He could say that again. Anything to keep his mind off Max.

TREAT PULLED UP to the rear gate behind a mass of media surrounding a number of cars. He rolled down his window and was met with too many shouts to decipher. It was obvious no one was going anywhere anytime soon. He pulled into the parking lot outside the fence and decided he'd run in, say hello to Savannah, and tell her he'd catch up with her later at their father's ranch. The last thing he needed was to deal with this type of headache.

He heard his sister's voice and swiftly scanned the crowd. If anyone was giving her a hard time, he'd set them straight. Savannah was standing with her body out of a limousine's sunroof, shouting who knew what as the media hollered questions at Connor through the slightly open tinted limousine window.

Treat leaned against the entrance to the gate, crossed one foot over the other, and watched his little sister in action. Her long auburn hair looked like fire against her serious more-green-than-hazel eyes. She'd inherited their mother's spitfire personality and was the only one to have their mother's coloring, while he and his brothers took after their dark-haired father.

Savannah's gaze shifted in his direction, and her scowl morphed into an excited smile as she hoisted herself through the sunroof like she climbed mountains for a living.

Treat pushed away from the fence and headed toward his sister in full protective mode. She might be tough, but those media animals pushing their way forward could easily injure her. He plowed through the crowd. His six-foot-six frame naturally commanded more space, and the sea of paparazzi parted for him. He gently persuaded the few that remained in his path with a domineering stare—a stare he hadn't needed to rely upon since Savannah was a teenager, when he and his brothers had spent countless hours keeping horny boys away from their precious sister.

He reached up and caught Savannah as she jumped down from the roof of the limo. He spun her around and, as he lowered her to the ground, his eyes landed on a woman standing at the front of a line of cars waving her hands. Her dark hair was pulled back in a ponytail, her red-framed glasses perched on her perky nose. She looked fierce and beautiful, and Treat's breath caught in his throat. *Max.*

MAX ARMSTRONG STOOD beside her car waving her hands, hoping to create a long enough break in the excitement to gain control of the crowd. Chaz Crew, Max's boss and founder of the Indie Film Festival, had created so much buzz over the past few years that they were expecting more than forty thousand attendees. The festival grounds covered one hundred acres a few blocks from Main Street and boasted five new theaters, restaurants, gift shops, and a high-class hotel. Hotels in neighboring towns were booked a full year in advance of the festival. Whether there were twenty thousand or fifty thousand attendees, Max was ready. She'd been handling the festival sponsors and logistics for almost eight years, and nothing could throw her off her game. Not even the ruckus between the celeb's entourage and the media, which was creating a tornado of confusion.

Photographers surrounded Connor Dean's limousine and the two accompanying SUVs. Max should have known this might happen. Dean was a local actor turned millionaire whose reputation had exploded since they'd booked him ten months earlier. She'd been wrong to think the Hulk-like security guards could manage a little drama. Shouts and threats were tossed around like candy to children, and no one was making any headway. *What on earth is that woman doing with her body halfway out of the sunroof on that limo? And what is she shouting? Legal jargon?*

The heck with this. It was time for Plan B. She climbed onto the roof of her car, which she'd strategically parked in front of the first SUV. *This* was why she wore jeans and her usual festival T-shirt. Because anything could happen at festivals.

With a quick flip of a switch on the control panel on her belt, she turned on the intercom mounted above the gate. "Okay, the show is over." Her voice boomed from the loudspeakers. "Let's give Mr. Dean some space to continue driving through. He'll be signing autographs and answering questions after his appearance." She scanned the area, her gaze landing on a man towering above the crowd with a gorgeous woman in his arms. He spun the woman to the side and his face came into view.

Max froze.

Treat?

Her pulse soared, and the butterflies in her stomach she thought she'd annihilated weeks ago swarmed to life with a vengeance. She had worked with Treat's assistant, Scarlet, for months coordinating logistics for Chaz's double wedding, which had taken place at Treat's Nassau resort. The other groom in the wedding was Treat's cousin, Blake Carter. She'd dealt with Treat so many times over the phone that he'd become the object of her late-night fantasies. But even her fantasies hadn't prepared her for meeting the impossibly tall, darkly handsome god that was Treat Braden, with his seductive voice and the way every inch of him screamed of adrenaline-pumping, heart-fluttering masculinity. She'd thought herself unflappable, but Treat had proved her wrong.

Her stomach clenched just thinking about the magical evening they'd spent in each other's arms. She could still feel his warm, sensuous lips on hers and see him gazing at her as though she were the only woman on earth. He hadn't even pushed when, after hours of dancing and walking on the beach, kissing like they'd been lovers forever, she'd turned down his offer to return to his suite and extend their evening into morning. Seeing him now, she had a hard time reconciling that incredibly romantic, thoughtful man with the arrogant one who had blown her off the next morning. Sure, she'd been in the same clothes she'd worn the night before, and yes, she'd been out for the remainder of that evening with a man named Justin, but Treat's assumption about what they'd done pissed her off. And the look he'd given her was too reminiscent of the painful relationship she'd escaped years earlier to chase him down and explain. She had every right to do whatever she wanted to do with whomever she wanted, without judgment. Even if she hadn't done anything at all.

She shouldn't care what he thought.

But she did, and that hurt because that awful look he'd given her was in such stark contrast to the impeccable manners he'd otherwise exuded, holding doors, thinking of the needs of her and his other guests before himself, taking extra steps to ensure that every little detail of his cousin's wedding had been taken care of. The truth was, she'd fallen hard for Treat within a few hours of being with him. But Max knew she shouldn't let those feelings sway her resolve. She'd been mistreated, demeaned, and judged by a previous boyfriend, and she swore she'd never go down that road again—not even for too-sexy-for-his-own-good Treat Braden.

She stumbled backward. One of the security guards reached for her across the roof of the car, and she grabbed his arm, finding her footing.

"Max! You okay?"

The security guard's voice wrenched her back to the ensuing chaos. She tore her eyes from Treat and whoever the woman was that he was holding as if she meant everything in the world to him and tried to blink away the unexpected sting of hurt slicing through her.

"Clear a path or you'll be removed from the premises for the rest of the festival." Even she could hear the difference in her voice, the weakness. Her gaze darted back to Treat, who was staring at her with an incredulous expression. Suddenly painfully aware of her jeans and T-shirt, the ponytail in her hair—and how she must look like a crazy woman standing on top of the car—she clambered down to the ground as the crowd surprisingly obeyed her orders and began to dissipate. Threats of eviction usually worked.

She turned off the intercom and fumbled for her keys. Treat was heading her way, but she didn't want to speak to him, couldn't speak to him, after the way he'd looked at her.

"Max," he called.

His rich, deep voice was enough to make her body ache. She cursed under her breath as she started the car and navigated around the crowd. She glanced in her rearview mirror. Treat stood alone in his dark suit, staring after her, while his beautiful companion looked on with a confused expression on her face. Max's hands trembled as she grasped the steering wheel tighter and drove away. Damn him for having this effect on her.

Chapter Two

"WHAT THE HECK was that all about?" Savannah asked.

Treat couldn't believe his eyes. *Max*. After all this time, he'd thought he had squelched the needs she stirred within him, but seeing the petite brown-haired beauty standing on that car like she could command the world brought all those urges rushing back. He saw right through her ponytailed persona to the sexy woman she tried so hard to ignore. What was Max doing at the festival standing on top of a car? Of course she was there, he realized. She worked for Chaz Crew, the festival's founder. One phone call would have told him everything he'd ever wanted to know about Max, but he hadn't made that call. His only goal had been to forget her—and he'd failed. *Epically*.

Savannah was looking at him like he'd lost his mind, and he wasn't so sure he hadn't.

"Nothing," he finally answered. How could he have been so stupid to have looked at Max so callously that morning at the resort? He'd been a jerk, regardless of how he'd been burned before. He clearly wasn't over her, and something told him he might never be.

"That was more than *nothing*." Savannah flashed a sly smile. "Let me tell Connor I'll catch up with him later, and we'll go grab some coffee and chat."

Treat couldn't put anything in his stomach if he wanted to. It took every bit of his willpower not to run after Max's car. He didn't want to make a scene, and it was obvious that she didn't want to talk to him, but the rush of emotions consuming him were too strong to ignore. With the hope of forgetting her gone, he accepted what he'd feared all along—he never should have let her go.

TREAT BRADEN. HOLY smokes, Treat Braden. Max drove as fast as she could into the underground garage reserved for the festival's staff. She slammed her car door shut and paced the concrete floor. *What is he doing here?* She thought she had become immune to even the sight of him. But the way her heart melted with one look from his piercing dark eyes convinced her she was wrong. Boy, was she wrong.

She needed to get a grip, because Max Armstrong did *not* lose control. She didn't melt, or pine, or otherwise fall apart over a man.

Or at least I never have. Until Treat.

A voice came through her earpiece. "Max, I need you by Marquee One."

Darn it, Chaz. Now? "Be right there," she said into the headset. There were thousands of people milling about. What were the chances she'd run into Treat again? Pretty low, she decided. She felt a pang of disappointment, and immediately chided herself for it.

She grabbed her planner and hurried out of the parking garage, flipping through her checklists to make sure there were no issues with that theater that she hadn't yet taken care of. She found Chaz staring up at the large sign.

"Max, come here." Chaz motioned her over with a flash of his pearly whites. His hair had lightened from the sun during the summer, and he sported a deep copper tan, giving him the look of a twentysomething surfer rather than the thirtysomething millionaire. "Look at that. What do you think?"

She squinted at the sign, having no idea what she was supposed to see. Maybe she just couldn't focus because her heart had yet to settle down. "What?"

"That there." He pointed again.

"Chaz, sorry, but you've lost me." She shifted her headset to answer another request. "Yes, no problem, Grace. Sure."

Chaz pointed to the sign. "I think we can have Joey maneuver something right along that wall, in that divot of the sign, to create another major sponsor location. I looked at both sides and they match. What do you think?"

Leave it to Chaz to find more opportunities for sponsorships in the middle of the festival, when Max would give anything to hide beneath a rock. There he stood, smiling and pleased with himself at the chance to sell more sign space and bring more funding to the festival. Max could easily be annoyed with him for his bad timing, but she had no siblings and he'd become the brother she'd always wished she had. After so many years of working together, they bickered like she imagined siblings would and cared just as deeply about each other. Chaz's wife, Kaylie, had become one of Max's closest friends when they were planning the destination wedding for her and her older sister, Danica, who married Blake Carter.

"I think you're a pain for calling me out here for something like this." She smiled, and he crossed his arms, trying his darnedest to look angry. "You know I'm right. Why are you even looking at this stuff right now?"

The screening had just ended, and people streamed out of the theater entrance. Max and Chaz stepped to the side, listening to the patrons as they talked among themselves.

"Incredible," an older woman said.

"Loved the dramatic flair of that one character. Winston?" said another.

"Oh, I hated him. Too full of himself," a short, stocky woman said with a wave of her hand.

"Hot, though. And talk about commanding an audience! That Connor Dean is amazing."

They could have just as easily been talking about Treat. Just the thought of him made Max's mind ache. Why was she torturing herself like this? She should just disappear into the office and stay there until there was a real emergency.

"Hey, Max, look!" Chaz waved across the street to Treat and his beautiful companion. "Treat! Over here. Hey, buddy. How are you?"

Oh no. No, no, no. This could *not* be happening. Max turned away, frantically running through excuses to hightail it out of there. *Sick? Need to go help the crew. Lighting, yeah, that could work.* She turned with her excuse at the ready, opening her mouth to speak. Treat's eyes locked on hers, and her mouth went dry.

"Chaz, Max, how are you?" Treat asked in that deep, sexy voice that made her legs turn to wet noodles.

Chaz said something, but it was all she could do to stare at the woman who had her hand on Treat's shoulder. She was gorgeous, with a friendly smile. Of course she had a friendly smile. She had Treat! Max hated the green-eyed monster clinging to her shoulders. She wasn't used to it, and she didn't like the way it made her feel.

"Hi. I'm Savannah." The woman extended her hand in greeting.

Savannah. What kind of name is that? She must be a model or something with those long legs and slim body. Max looked at Treat in his expensive suit and finely pressed shirt. Then she glanced down at her own less-than-glamorous attire. She absently touched her efficient ponytail, and cringed.

"Hi. I'm Chaz Crew." He shook Savannah's hand. "And this is Max Armstrong."

Max gave Savannah's hand a quick shake and tried her best to smile, then buried her nose in her planner before the woman—or Treat—could strike up a conversation.

While Chaz and Savannah talked, Treat moved to her side, bringing a wave of the spicy, masculine cologne she smelled in her dreams. "Max. How have you been?"

Too frazzled to face him, she kept her eyes trained on her planner. "Fine, thanks."

"I'm glad we ran into each other. I've been thinking about Nassau."

Giving me that look wasn't enough? You needed to flaunt another woman in front of me just to show me what I already know? That you could have anyone you want?

"Max," he said a little quieter. "I'm sorry for what happened there."

She wanted to dislike him, to run away and never look back, because that look he'd given her had been too reminiscent of the ex-boyfriend she'd spent years trying to forget. But the sincerity in his voice brought her gaze to his, and Treat was looking at her like he had in Nassau, as if she was all he saw. Memories tumbled in, one after another—their incredible kisses, the feel of his strong arms around her, his sweet whispers in her ear…

Those intimate memories were like an addictive cocktail, and she reveled in their intoxicating sweetness. She should not be thinking about them, and *he* should not be looking at her like that when he was with his ridiculously gorgeous girlfriend.

Unwilling to put herself in a position to be hurt again, and hanging on to that resolve by a thread, Max said, "I have no idea what you're talking about."

Hurt and confusion rose in his eyes, fraying that thread to near breaking.

"Come on, Treat," Savannah urged. "Let's get some coffee and catch up."

Treat held Max's gaze a beat too long, and she felt her cheeks flush with desire. She wanted to tell him it was okay—even though it wasn't—to take his handsome face between her hands, and kiss his luscious lips one more time. Why were her feelings for him so overwhelming? She'd never believed in love at first sight, and certainly not with a man who could be so quick to judge her, but her heart was racing the way it had the first time she'd seen him in Nassau.

"Treat?" Savannah's eyes darted curiously between Treat and Max.

"Right," Treat said sharply. "Max, may I call you?"

How can you ask me that with your girlfriend standing right there?

"You have a date with Dad, remember?" Savannah said in a singsong voice.

"Dad?" The word slipped from Max's lips before she had a chance to stop it.

"Yes. I'm here to visit with my father," Treat said. "Savannah hijacked me on the way to his ranch."

There was that look again. Not the one he'd given her, but the way he looked lovingly at Savannah. "Nothing like being hijacked by a beautiful woman," Max said a little too snarkily. Jealousy was not a pretty thing.

Amusement rose in Treat's eyes. "She's beautiful, yes, but she's also my younger sister."

Savannah crinkled her nose at him in a cute, sisterly way. "He's *so* not my type, all suited up and proper. Hey, Max, why don't you and Chaz join us for coffee?"

Max was too embarrassed about her misconception and was still struggling with too many emotions to be clear-headed. "I have to be on-site to field any problems that come up, and I have so much to do—"

"Go, Max. You deserve the break," Chaz urged. "She works like a maniac sunup till sundown. Max, just keep your earpiece on in case there's an emergency." He turned to the others and said, "Sorry, guys. I appreciate the offer, but I've got to run to a meeting. Max, don't forget to ask Joey about that sign when you have a chance."

She watched Chaz walk away and quickly remembered the list of excuses she'd already thought up. "I actually have some lighting issues that I need to attend to."

"Are you sure?" Savannah arched a brow in her brother's direction.

"Max, I would be honored if you'd join us."

The disappointment in Treat's expression was palpable. She was this close to changing her mind. Every bit of her— especially those naughty parts that she was trying so hard to ignore—screamed, *Yes! Yes! Go!* But Max was too confused by his showing up and his apology to think straight. "I'm sorry, but

I really can't."

Treat took her hand and brought it to his lips. She closed her eyes as his lips warmed her skin, bringing another rush of emotions.

"May I call you?" Treat asked again.

Still lost in that single kiss, thinking about what she'd like him to kiss next, Max had to shake her head to pull herself back to the conversation. She tapped her earpiece, hoping to pass off her zoning out as a technical issue. She was acting like those brainless bimbos she hated. Max couldn't believe Treat was laying it on so thick in front of his sister, but maybe Savannah was used to seeing this side of him. He *was* a billionaire who owned properties all over the world. He probably treated all single women this way.

If she believed that, why was she tearing a piece of paper from her planner and writing her phone number on it? And why was she staring at his butt as he walked away, hoping he'd call?

Chapter Three

HAL BRADEN'S CROWDED driveway told Treat that the rest of his siblings, or at least most of them, had come to see him. He stepped from the SUV as Savannah parked her car. She had peppered him with questions when they'd had coffee, and he'd tried to downplay his feelings about Max and simply said she'd worked with Scarlet to help organize their cousin's wedding. He thought he'd seen a hint of disbelief in Savannah's eyes, and the last thing he wanted to deal with was more questions—especially in front of his siblings.

"This was supposed to be a relaxing getaway, not a party," Treat said as Savannah looped her arm through his.

"It's not a party. Everyone's schedule was clear, so we thought…"

Treat sighed at the thought of a chaotic visit, but it would be good to see his family all in one place again. They each had built successful careers that had made them very wealthy—but kept them too busy for regular get-togethers.

They climbed the porch steps of his childhood home, and the familiar scents of fresh-cut wood, steak on the grill, and too much testosterone wrapped around him like a warm embrace. It was good to be home.

"There's my boy," his father called from the living room. He stood from his favorite leather recliner and hugged Treat. At six foot six, Hal Braden stood shoulder to shoulder with his eldest son, his broad chest and arms still solid and strong from years of toiling on the family ranch. His thick black hair now had patches of gray around his temples, hints of his age Treat liked to ignore.

"Hi, Dad."

"It's good to see you, son." His father drew Savannah into his arms. "Sweetie, did you have a nice afternoon with your big brother?"

"Yes. I always do."

The way Savannah's eyes lit up when they walked out to the backyard to greet three of their brothers told Treat of her adoration for each of them. He hoped that never changed, but had Savannah known how he'd looked at Max that morning at the resort that adoration would have quickly withered away.

Savannah headed for Josh, who was grilling at the other end of the yard, a few feet from where Dane was busy texting. Rex was walking toward Treat. Rex worked on the ranch with his father, and his muscular physique was proof of the rigorous physical labor he endured. Like their brother Dane, who spent his days trying to save the lives of sharks, Rex sported a year-round tan.

Rex hesitated for just a second before saying, "Treat, glad to have you back, man."

"How's he holding up?" Treat shifted his eyes to his father. His father was sixty-five years old and still strong as an ox, but that didn't keep Treat from worrying about him. Since their mother had died when Treat was at an age when every kid believes their parents will live forever, he counted every day with his father as a blessing.

"He's good." Rex ran an assessing eye over Treat. "You okay?"

Treat was close to all his siblings, but each relationship was different. Rex was three years Treat's junior, and as such, the competitiveness Treat felt with Dane, who was just a year and a half younger, had never been present in his relationship with Rex. But Rex carried a chip on his shoulder about the family business and was careful not to get too close to Treat.

"Yeah. I needed a break. Got a little burnt out." Treat watched Rex's eyes narrow. He knew his brother wasn't buying his excuse, but he wasn't ready to expose his feelings for Max just yet. He'd come here thinking he'd escape his feelings, but now they were in full force. He should be focusing on his family, when all he wanted to do was call her.

"Yeah? You sure?"

"Of course," Treat assured him. "I'm fine. Really."

"Can we have him back now, Rex?" Dane asked with a grin. He was three inches shorter than Treat and every bit as dark and handsome, the only difference being Dane's eyes always seemed to dance with optimism, while Treat's often appeared more serious, contemplative.

Rex feigned a punch to Dane's gut as he walked past.

Dane embraced Treat and said, "You should have seen the girl I was with last night."

Treat laughed at their running joke. In reality, Dane was more likely to be chasing big fish than bedding women. "I already had her mother," Treat joked, but this time their old joke tasted wrong as it rolled off his tongue. He glanced at his father, whose dark eyes had harbored the pain of missing his wife for countless years, and he once again felt the draw of wanting to experience the love his parents had shared—the draw that he'd begun to recognize when he'd met Max.

Dane pulled away, laughing. "You always were the king."

Treat went to the stone barbecue pit, where Josh was tending to steaks and baked potatoes, and put an arm around his shoulder. He was the leanest and least aggressive of the Braden crew. With a love of fashion since the day he could pick out his own clothes, Josh lived in New York City, was a designer to the stars, and owned several high-end fashion boutiques.

"I hear you're wiping Vera Wang off the map." Treat was proud of his brother's accomplishments.

He shook his head. "One day."

"One day you'll let that humble nonsense go and boast about your success. Got a girlfriend yet?" Josh had always been tight-lipped about his female conquests, even about the heart-quaking crush he'd had on their childhood friend Riley Banks when he was younger—the crush that everyone knew about but that Josh thought he'd hidden.

"Haven't you read the gossip magazines? Apparently I'm going out with three different women."

"Sounds like you're having fun, then. Where's Hugh?" Hugh was their youngest brother and the biggest risk taker of them all. He was supremely self-centered, which at times rubbed Treat the wrong way, and his career as a race-car driver was a testament to the way he lived his life, indulging in fast cars and even faster women.

Josh shrugged. "Race, maybe? Steaks are ready."

Treat took off his jacket and carried the platter of steaks Josh handed him to the table. His father had one arm around Savannah and the other around Dane as they went to sit down. Man, he'd missed these guys. Treat spent most of his time traveling and living out of a suitcase. He didn't usually mind his lifestyle. In fact, there had been a time when it was all he wanted. But lately he'd found himself contemplating a more settled life.

He set the platter of steaks in the center of the table alongside the salad, wine, beer, vegetables, and three types of sliced bread—typical Braden fare. Most family gatherings were centered around a barbecue of some sort.

"You started without me?" Hugh barged into the yard with his arms open and a grin on his face. His thick, wind-tossed hair gave him a youthful appearance. "Treat, you've graced us with your presence after all."

"Good to see you too, Hugh." Treat stood and wrapped an arm around him.

Hugh sat down and was the first to help himself to a steak from the platter, snagging the largest one.

Treat shook his head. "So, Dad, are you ever going to let me pay for that stone patio you keep talking about?"

"He doesn't need your money, Treat," Rex said roughly. "He needs my time."

"I didn't mean anything by it," Treat said.

"We've been busy running the ranch," Rex said with a hefty amount of attitude. "I haven't had time to get started. But I'll take care of it."

"I could bring in a crew to help you out," Treat offered.

"Are you the crew?" Rex asked pointedly.

Treat stared him down.

"Boys, settle down. I need a patio like I need a hole in my head," their father snapped. "Tell me about your latest acquisitions, Treat. What did you decide about Thailand?"

Treat had been negotiating for a resort in Thailand when

he'd first met Max. The justice of the peace who was supposed to preside over Blake's wedding in Nassau had fallen ill, and Treat had canceled his trip to Thailand and stepped in to officiate. He'd put the acquisition on hold after that weekend. But two days ago he'd received an email from his long-time friend Bill Harkness, the owner of the resort, advising him they had received another offer and honoring their verbal agreement of first right of refusal. Treat was best when he had a challenge, and Thailand would be just that. Taking over the resort would consume all his time and energy for at least three months.

"It's a solid resort and the numbers work," he explained. "I told them I'd submit an offer within two weeks." Unable to stop thinking about Max, he'd figured, after this trip home, three months away might be just what he needed. Now he wasn't so sure.

"He's in Max mode," Savannah added.

Treat glared at her.

"Who's Max?" Josh asked.

"Some hot girl who works at the festival and has Treat all googly-eyed," Savannah said.

"Hm. Max is a woman?" Josh arched a brow and grinned.

"Yes, she's a woman, and no, I'm not in Max mode." Treat bit into a hunk of steak, wishing Savannah had never seen her. Max's number had been burning a hole in his pocket ever since she'd given it to him, and it was all he could do not to get up and call her right that second.

"Treat, googly-eyed? You gotta be kidding me. The man eats women for breakfast," Hugh said with a deep laugh. He was always quick to throw a barb and just as quick to return to whatever he was doing for himself beforehand—in this instance, he turned his attention back to his plate of food and speared a forkful of potato.

Treat threw his napkin on the table. "Cut the crap, okay?"

He knew he was overreacting, and he knew Hugh was only stating what had once been the truth. Bile rose in his throat just thinking of himself in that player role. Yeah, he'd been with a lot of women, but he'd never found anyone who made him want more.

Hugh shrugged off his roar. "I won today. First place."

"Good job, son." His father raised his beer bottle. "To Hugh."

"To *Huge!*" the boys said in unison.

Savannah shook her head. "Idiots."

AFTER DINNER TREAT, Dane, and Rex cleared the table and did the dishes while Savannah visited with her father and Josh and Hugh talked about Hugh's race.

"Something you want to tell us?" Dane asked once they were safely in the kitchen, away from the others.

"I have no idea what you're talking about." Treat busied himself digging in a drawer for a dish towel.

"Is that the same Max from Blake's wedding?" Dane asked.

"How would you know Max from Blake's wedding? You never even met her." Dane had shown up for the wedding, but he had been called away for an emergency before the ceremony.

Dane cringed under his scrutiny.

"You're seeing Lacy, aren't you?" Lacy was Blake's wife's half sister. He had met her at the wedding. Treat had almost forgotten that Dane had given him a message to pass on to Lacy after he'd been called away.

"Nope." Dane focused on scrubbing a plate.

"Then how do you know Max?" Treat briefly wondered if Dane had somehow met and hit on her. Dane had slept with one of Treat's girlfriends when he was visiting Treat at college, and it had taken them months to move past what they now called the Mary Jane incident and get on solid ground again. Mary Jane had tried to reconcile with Treat, but any girlfriend who would sleep with his brother was not a girlfriend he needed. He'd gone out and hooked up with the most beautiful girl on campus the next night—right after sending Dane back home. He trusted Dane now, but even still, thinking about that incident brought it all to the forefront of Treat's mind.

"Dane?" he asked with a fisted hand. He and his brothers had come to blows many times over the years, but it had been forever since Treat had felt the urge to punch anyone. Max wasn't even his to claim, but he couldn't stop his protective claws from coming out.

"Leave him alone, Treat." Rex planted himself between them.

Treat stared at Dane until he relented and said, "I talked to Lacy a few days later, to apologize for not being at the wedding. She told me about Max coordinating the event, and that you two left together one evening, and...I know she hooked up with Justin, and I just assumed..." Dane shrugged.

Fire exploded inside Treat. He grabbed Dane, but Rex batted his arm away. Treat wasn't about to stand down. He drew his shoulders back, eyes locked on Rex, and stepped closer.

Rex crossed his arms, a formidable barrier.

Vaguely aware of his sister entering the kitchen, Treat spoke through gritted teeth. "Step aside, Rex."

"What are you doing?" Savannah looked from one brother

to the other.

"Dude's out of control," Dane said, taking a step back. "I don't think I've seen you this jealous since Mary Jane."

"Dane! Rex, get him out of here," Savannah ordered.

Treat held Dane's glower. It wasn't Dane's fault he was frustrated over Max. "Sorry, Dane. I don't know what's got into me." He straightened his shirt and cleared his throat as Rex and Dane left the room. "Sorry, Savannah. I'm just on edge."

"Why did he bring up Mary Jane?" she asked.

The worried look in Savannah's eyes pulled Treat from his angst. She was particularly sensitive to her brothers being at odds, and even though it had been years since they'd fought over a woman, he knew she worried about him and Dane falling right back into that awful place and time.

"I'm fine. He was just egging me on," Treat answered.

"Yeah, well, you all can be jerks at one time or another," Savannah said, fixing his collar.

Dane and Rex came back into the kitchen carrying more dishes.

"Is it safe?" Rex asked.

Treat locked eyes with Dane in a silent warning not to talk about Max and Justin in the same breath again.

"Yes, it's safe," Savannah insisted, glaring at Treat. "Treat, you have to go out with me and Hugh tonight."

"What are we, second rate?" Rex asked.

Savannah rolled her eyes. "You're anything *but* second rate. That's the problem. I don't want to spend the evening beating women away with a stick because you two look at them like you want to devour them. Treat has more couth. It's the festival after-party. Hugh has a date and two extra tickets." She raised her brows and said, "Max might be there."

The mention of Justin and Max had made his blood boil, and he wasn't sure he could even look at Max without feeling it rip through him again. "I'm beat," he lied.

"Yeah? Well, wake up," Savannah said. "You're going."

"She made it pretty clear that she wants distance from me. I can't push myself on her."

"Treat, you're such a fool. All men are. No matter what we women say, we want the knight in shining armor. We want Richard Gere riding up in his white limousine. We want Leonardo DiCaprio to tell us that he'll never let us go."

"I don't know about that," Treat said. "Don't they want us to respect their space when they make it clear they want it?" Savannah's energy was finding its way into his body, and he was actually wondering if he was wrong and should go after Max.

"Nope," she said. "We want you to read between the lines."

"She didn't leave much for interpretation."

"Trust me, big brother," Savannah said. "Every woman wants her man to read between the lines, and because of that, she leaves a bread-crumb trail for you to find her."

"I'm a pretty wise man. If there were a bread-crumb trail, I'd have seen it before she even realized she left it." He had dissected every word Max had said, and beyond the way she looked at him—like she wanted to kiss him as she had that night—there wasn't a hint of an open door. Was that the trail? Or had he conjured it in his mind with wishful thinking?

"Don't fool yourself. You're wise when it comes to business, but maybe not so much when it comes to the mysterious ways of women. Be ready for the party at seven. You're going with me."

Chapter Four

WHY THE HECK had Max given Treat her number? More bothersome, why hadn't he called? She had taken out her battery and rebooted her phone twice and had been checking her messages like she had OCD. She didn't know why she even hoped he'd call. He was a man with many resources. He could have tracked her down any time after she left the resort, and he hadn't. She was a fool to have played right into his hands again, sweet apology or not. He was in town to visit his father. Chances were he'd forgotten about Max the minute he'd walked away. *The same way he did after Nassau.* Maybe seeing her had simply sparked a memory, and he felt guilty for judging her. Well, she'd take that guilty apology over nothing any day, even if she hadn't been ready to accept it.

Now, if she could only stop thinking about him.

"Max, you've done it again," Chaz said as they left the festival that evening. They had reviewed the day's financial reports, and it was obvious that he was still thinking about their overwhelming success. It was only the first day, and they had already almost matched the previous year's total festival revenue.

"Not me, boss. *We* did it. At least the first day went off without a hitch." She'd been sure Chaz would say something about how weird she'd acted around Treat, but he hadn't mentioned him at all. Maybe she'd gotten lucky and no one else had noticed how uncomfortable she'd been, either.

"Don't forget, you said you'd do the after-party swing tonight. I can't wait to go home and see Trevor and Lexi. It's been a long day." Chaz and Kaylie had been married for just shy of two months, but their twins were two years old.

The after-parties were one of the highlights of the film festival, where locals and fans could mingle with celebrities, dance the night away, and take home expensive swag to boot. But Max wasn't the partying type, and tonight of all nights, she wasn't in the mood to pretty herself up and play nice. Maybe she could get out of it.

"Aren't the kids asleep by now?"

"Yes, but I still like to peek in on them. Besides, they're *asleep*." He raised his eyebrows. "We're still newlyweds, after all."

"Come on, Chaz," she pleaded. "You know I hate these things."

"It'll do you some good. You spend too much time working and not enough time socializing. Get out there, Max, and have some fun. Meet a nice guy and let him wine and dine you."

"I'd rather wine and dine myself while reading on the comfort of my own couch."

"Max…"

He gave her his I'm-counting-on-you look. The one she'd never been able to deny. "Fine! But you owe me one."

"Add it to the other million I owe you," he said as he walked away.

MAX STOOD IN her bedroom staring at her closet, which looked more like a teenager's than that of an almost-thirty-year-old woman, with too many T-shirts, sweatshirts, and jeans and not nearly enough grown-up clothes. She inspected the few dresses she owned, then selected two short black numbers and hung them on the closet door. One was tight fitting with a plunging neckline, leaving very little to the imagination, while the other was more conservative with a ring neck and slit pockets at the hips. Kaylie had convinced her to buy the one with the plunging neckline before the wedding, and when she and Treat had first met, she couldn't wait to wear it for him. But the hours they'd spent in each other's arms had come with no warning. She hadn't even had time to change out of her jeans when he'd dragged her out of the restaurant and swept her away for the next several hours. Even though they were the most incredible few hours of her life, when he'd invited her to his room, she'd held back, afraid of the overwhelming emotions that had swamped her. A few hours later, he'd seen her with Justin, and the desire to look sexy had disappeared.

Maybe she should have run after him, cleared up the situation right away. But the awful look he'd given her had thrown her right back to the boyfriend she'd thought she'd known who had turned on her with a vengeance. Max was brave, but she wasn't brave enough to walk directly into potential fire. She needed to remember that now, as she romanticized Treat and his apology.

Her cell phone rang, and for the second time that day, Max froze.

Her phone sat in the middle of her bed, lighting up like a beacon. Her traitorous heart went wild, hoping it was Treat. The incoming phone number came up as *restricted*. Her mind raced through scenarios. What would she say if it was Treat? What would *he* say? What if he asked her out? Should she go? She wanted to go, despite everything. He'd apologized, hadn't he? Even if she'd pretended she didn't know what he was talking about.

She stared at the ringing phone as if it were a land mine. Her mind reeled, but she couldn't hold back. As she'd done the night she'd fallen into Treat's arms, she threw caution to the wind and dove for it, quickly pushing the green icon. "Hello? Hello?"

She was met with dead air.

Max ended the call and banged her head against the mattress. She waited for her message light to blink, and when it didn't, she pushed to her feet with disgust.

"You're such a fool," she said to her reflection in the mirror. She stripped off her clothes on the way to the bathroom and stepped angrily into the shower. "An idiot, a *chicken*." She scrubbed her scalp so hard she was sure she was leaving scratches.

By the time she dried off, she'd calmed down a little and thought maybe it was better this way. No hard decisions to make, no trying to figure out if he was going to be like her ex, sweet one minute and crazy the next. She dried her hair and fluffed it into a sultry style around her face, then assessed herself in the mirror. She looked pretty good.

Max hadn't been on a date since her night with Treat. Not that she dated much anyway. She'd been denying her sexual urges for years—*literally*—because of the frightening scenario that had unfolded in the bedroom with her ex, Ryan Cobain.

She could do better than a man who would judge her, and as an idea formed in her head, a hopeful grin lifted her lips.

Maybe it was time she broke that wretched streak and forgot Treat altogether. It wasn't in her nature to pick up a man, and even the thought of it petrified her. But a distraction from her past, and from Treat, was just what she needed to move on. She was confident in every aspect of her life except the one Ryan had ruined for her, and she hated that. Though she wasn't sure how to get past it.

Everything started with baby steps, right? If she could get out there and flirt a little, she'd have people other than Treat to think about. That was a good place to begin. First she needed to look *hot*, not just good.

She turned on some music and danced as she got ready for her big night. She went heavy on the makeup, which took some time since she hardly ever wore any, and stepped into one of the few lace thongs she owned, feeling naughty and a little uncomfortable. She wanted to feel sexy, and this would help. At least that's what Kaylie always said. *Sexiness is a state of mind and starts with what nobody else sees.* She slithered into the skintight dress with the plunging neckline and spun around as the tunes escalated, slipping her bare feet into a pair of efficient black heels. She stood before the mirror, surveying herself from top to bottom. Her dark eyeliner said, *Take me*, her body screamed, *Touch me*, and her crimson lips whispered, *I'm in control*, but the total package, including the efficient heels, shouted, *Faker!*

She kicked off her heels and stared at her other footwear options with a frown. *Efficient, efficient, efficient.* No matter which dress she chose, she'd feel like a fake. *How on earth did I make it this far?* She snagged her phone from the bed and texted Kaylie.

Can I borrow your high black heels?

Her phone vibrated seconds later. *High black heels? lol. You mean the take-me-now heels?*

Max rolled her eyes and texted back. *I guess.*

Kaylie's text came fast. *Who's the guy?*

She responded, *Festival after-party. Yes or no?*

A minute later her answer arrived. *Yup. Babies are sleeping. I'll leave the heels on the porch.*

Max squealed, immediately worrying that maybe she'd interrupted a private moment between Chaz and Kaylie since Kaylie said she'd leave the heels on the *porch*. Oh well, what was done was done. She couldn't worry about that now. She spritzed on her sexiest perfume, put on her flip-flops, grabbed her purse and keys, and headed for Kaylie's house.

Twenty minutes later she was walking up Kaylie's front steps. As promised, the black stilettos were on the front porch.

"I can't believe you didn't tell me about Treat!"

Max gasped. "*Kaylie!* You scared the daylights out of me!"

Kaylie came out of the dark garage and into the light of the porch. Her blond hair was tousled, and she wore a nighty that barely covered her underwear—at least Max hoped she was wearing underwear—and fuzzy slippers.

"Sorry, but if you're borrowing my heels, I want details."

Max wished she had some to share. "I'm not seeing Treat. I'm going to the after-party because your husband wanted to spend time with you."

"Aw, he's so romantic. Chaz said Treat showed up today. Did he call you? I knew there was something going on at the wedding."

Max heard a faint ringing. "There was nothing going on at the wedding, and he didn't come to see me. He's in Weston visiting his dad, and it was just a coincidence that he was at the festival." *I wish he'd been there to see me. No. I wish he'd come to see me weeks ago.*

"Danica would tell you that there are no coincidences in life," Kaylie said. Her older sister was more like Max than Kaylie. "Hey, is that your phone ringing?"

"I thought it was the house phone," Max answered.

Kaylie shook her head. "We turn off the ringers when the kids go to bed."

Max ran for her car and tugged the door open, but her phone had already stopped ringing. She checked the missed call log and saw the restricted number had popped up again. She let out a breath and felt the confidence she'd bolstered begin to deflate.

"Sorry, Max. Were you expecting him to call?" Kaylie asked.

Max couldn't hide her disappointment. "Not really. He asked for my number, but you know how that goes."

"Sometimes men suck," Kaylie said. "Oh, Max. Look at you. I didn't even notice how gorgeous you look. Girl, if he is at that after-party, he won't be able to keep his eyes—or his hands—off you."

"Thanks. I'm sure he won't be there." Treat didn't seem like the partying type, which was one of things that had attracted her to him. He was strong and confident, but not showy or arrogant. *Until that look. The look he already apologized for.* If anything, she needed to apologize to him for acting rude when she was flustered this afternoon.

With a sigh, she said, "I'm not like you, Kaylie. This would be so easy for you. I had to talk myself into dressing like this, and I still feel like I'm playing dress-up. All I wanted was to look sexy and flirt a little to get my mind off of..."

"Well, you sure fooled me into thinking you were confident about how you looked. Listen, this is all there is to it. Flirting, meeting guys, it's all a game. It's them against you, and usually you both have the same agenda—to get the sexiest one into bed."

"Kay—"

"Save it, sister. And trust me, okay? I know what I'm talking about. The next time you see Treat, you act as if you're the sex-starved man, like you can't keep your eyes or hands off him. That'll knock him off his game, and you'll start to see the *real* him."

"I don't know if I can do that." *A sex-starved man?*

"If you want to win him over, then you have to. Then, when he thinks he's going to get you into bed, you pull back. Remember, *you* control the strings. Think of him as a marion-ette and yourself as the puppet master." Kaylie looked up at the dark sky. Her eyes sparkled with excitement. "Hey, that's good. I just made that up." She looked at Max and said, "Anyway, when you're in control, you'll totally knock down his defenses and it'll be more comfortable—for both of you."

Max shook her head. "I don't know if I can play games, Kaylie."

"Listen, Max. At that point, you won't have to *do* anything. You pull away and he sees you as the queen of seduction. You follow through and you're a sexual tigress. Win-win." Kaylie shrugged.

"What if I want to be with him and he turns me down?"

"Any man who turns you down isn't worth it." Kaylie must have seen Max cringe, because she quickly added, "No way. Did he turn you down at the wedding?"

Max shook her head. "No, but I turned him down when he asked me to go back to his room, and then we had a misunder-standing the next morning when he saw me with Justin." Kaylie had been in the elevator when Max had gotten on the next morning wearing the same clothes as she'd had on the day before. Kaylie had teased her about her walk-of-shame outfit, but she hadn't known about Max and Treat's evening together. She'd only assumed, as Treat had, that Max had slept with Justin.

"Oh, Maxy. You said you didn't hook up with Justin." Kaylie pulled her into a hug.

"I didn't, but Treat assumed I did." She'd never told Kaylie about Ryan, or what she'd been through with him, and she didn't want to get into that now. It was too private, too embarrassing.

"Well, trust me. He won't hesitate after you do this. Win-win. You remember that." Kaylie ran her eyes over Max and said, "More importantly, remember that you are in control of your own emotional state. I learned the hard way that misunderstandings can spread like weeds if you let them. So if you really care about Treat, you might bring some Emotional Roundup with you, so you can nix any more of them."

"Emotional Round Up," Max repeated.

Maybe she *could* pull this off after all.

Chapter Five

HUGH AND HIS date, Nova Bashe, a comically tall, impossibly skinny Swedish swimsuit model, were flanked by photographers as they made their way into the party. Hugh looked back with a shrug and a wave at Treat and Savannah. Treat was glad to be out of the limelight. The last thing he wanted to do was hang out with drunken celebrities. He planned to hide in the shadows and keep an eye on his sister.

"Thanks for coming with me," Savannah said as he handed her a drink. "I knew I could count on you."

"Why aren't you with Connor tonight?" Treat asked, swirling the liquor in his glass.

"Are you kidding? He'll have a whole entourage. I'm off duty when he's out drinking. I can't be held responsible for his liquored-up state, even if that's when he gets in the most trouble. He gave me tickets, of course, but I gave them to the girls in my office. Now, *they're* the kind of girls who love this stuff."

"Then why did you get all dolled up in that gold minidress and want to come so badly?"

Savannah looked around and then pointed across the room.

There, in the dimly lit nightclub, outshining all the other

women with her natural beauty, was Max.

"See you later, big brother." Savannah kissed his cheek and disappeared into the crowd.

Max was gorgeous no matter what she wore, but she looked stunning with her smoky eyes, her hair sexily framing her face, and a little black dress that hugged all her curves. His fingers itched to touch her, his body ached to discover how she felt lying beneath him. He stopped himself from taking that thought any further. He wanted much more than sex with Max. He'd blown it once, and he wasn't going to blow it again.

She lifted her face, and their eyes connected like metal to magnet. The air sizzled and popped as he crossed the dance floor, eating up the space between them. He ignored the gyrating bodies and seductive glances from women. The only woman he wanted was right there in front of him, and he never took his eyes off her, afraid if he did, she might not be there when he looked again.

She held a drink between her hands, her gaze flitting nervously away, then skittering back again as he approached. She was breathing harder, and she bit her lower lip. His body heated up when she released her lip and ran her tongue along the corner of her mouth, exhaling a ragged breath. He remembered those ragged, nervous breaths as they lay on the sand kissing, their hands roaming over each other's bodies.

Two more steps and he'd be close enough to touch her. In the next breath her sweet scent permeated his senses. His body thrummed as memories of their steamy night came rushing back. It had been years since Treat had spent time only kissing a woman, and with Max, he'd wanted to savor every second. It had been enough all those weeks ago. At least it had been when he'd imagined they'd have many more nights to find their way to darker pleasures.

"Hello, Max."

She didn't lower her eyes in the tentative way she had in Nassau. Her eyes narrowed enticingly behind her glasses, which gave her a smart appearance. He drank in her revealing dress, the way it hugged her hips and plunged so deeply between her breasts it made him want to—

"Treat," she said with a sultry tone. She sipped her drink, then licked the alcohol from her lips, holding his stare. "I didn't expect to see you here."

What happened to the shy girl who couldn't hold my gaze?

He had adored the careful woman he'd spent time with in Nassau. She'd been a refreshing change to the women he was used to being with, but the hungry look in Max's eyes, and seeing her sweetness all sexed up, made him want to forget his good intentions.

"My brother had extra tickets. I came with Savannah."

She looked around the room. "Savannah's here?"

"She's mingling." He stepped closer, enjoying the hitch in her breathing, the darkening of her eyes. Wearing that delectable dress and with the way she was visually devouring him, she was begging to be touched. Several weeks was a long time to think about a woman. An even longer time to refuse himself anyone else. "I don't want to talk about who I came with or why I'm here. I'd much rather talk about us."

She inhaled another uneven breath, revealing a hint of the woman he'd known. She quickly wiped away that image by boldly running her finger down his chest. "I'm glad you're here."

Man, she was killing him. He wanted to pull her into his arms and kiss her right then and there until all that nonsense from Nassau was forgotten.

She tugged his tie playfully, and Treat swore it had a direct line south.

She looked up, her eyes suddenly innocent again, making him want to take her in his arms to protect her and love her at once.

TREAT BRADEN HAD the conflicting effects of a tornado on Max by first knocking the strength from her knees, then gathering her into the center of the storm and buffering her from everything else. That's how he'd made her feel that night in Nassau. After sweeping her off her feet, he made her his sole focus, and she felt safe and special, like she could let her guard down. She couldn't afford to be knocked off-balance by him again with so much riding on her shoulders. She straightened her spine, forcing herself back into the sexy-girl persona she'd momentarily slipped out of. She'd liked the way she'd felt seconds earlier, so different from her normal self—from the seductive glances to the words that expertly slipped off her tongue. The minute their eyes had connected, she'd known it was now or never, and she still couldn't believe she was pulling off all the things Kaylie had suggested. *And they were working!* He was putty in her hands. The problem was, she would be putty in his the minute the tables turned. But when she was in that powerful position, she could almost pretend they didn't have anything to overcome, that Ryan hadn't ruined her for all men and her painful past didn't exist.

She'd planned on finding a stranger to distract her from thoughts of Treat, but now that he was right there before her, she knew a stranger wasn't the answer.

There was no forgetting Treat Braden.

In this new, daring headspace she possessed, she didn't want to hold back. Treat took her drink and set it, along with his, on a table, and without a word, he placed his hand on her lower back and led her to the dance floor. In the next breath she was in his arms, desire washing over her as she sank into his broad, hard frame. The scent of musk and spice with undertones of virility embraced her. He was more refined than any man she'd ever met, the perfect blend of sensitivity and strength. He put all other men to shame. How could he have thought she'd leave his arms and race into the bed of another man?

"You wouldn't listen before," he said into her ear, "but you need to hear me now. I was wrong to look at you the way I did in Nassau."

Max held her breath. She'd spent the last several weeks as consumed with Treat as she was with the way he'd looked at her that night.

"After spending that incredible evening together, I wanted to be the guy you were with. I wanted to be yours and for you to be mine. It didn't matter that we hadn't slept together, or that we'd known each other only by phone for months before finally landing in each other's arms."

He gazed into her eyes, and the honesty and emotions she saw made her heart tumble.

"Max, when I saw you with Justin that next morning, wearing the same clothes you'd had on when we were together the night before, I assumed you'd spent the night with him, and I realized I'd lost my chance. You saw an ugly, jealous, petty side of me that I haven't felt since college, and I'm sorry. You didn't deserve that."

"Since college?" slipped out before she could stop it.

His jaw clenched and his hand slid up her back, keeping her close. "It's embarrassing to admit, but when I was in college, my brother Dane came to visit and he slept with my girlfriend."

How was it possible for them to have so much in common that they were both hurt at the same time in their lives? "Oh my gosh, Treat. That's awful."

"It was not fun," he said, half laughing, half scoffing, but the truth shone in his soulful eyes. "It took a long time for Dane and me to move past that. But, Max, I wasn't your boyfriend. I had no claim on you, no right to look at you or judge you."

"Exactly," she said too sharply.

"I let my pain guide me, and I never should have. I've regretted it since the very second I saw the hurt in your eyes. I didn't know what to do with the magnitude of emotions I was feeling. There's no excuse for what I did, and if you'll let me, I'd like to try to make it up to you."

"I should have accepted your apology earlier today. I'm sorry I was too overwhelmed to think straight." Her heart ached for both of them. "I had a horrible experience in college, too. A boyfriend I trusted and thought I loved changed radically and really hurt me. When you gave me that look, it brought all that fear rushing back. If you had done that to any other woman, she probably would have chased you and explained, but I was too scared to put myself in that position again."

"Max, I..." He held her tighter, crushing her to him, and when he drew back again, his eyes were as fierce as they were loving. "I will never, *ever* put you in that position again."

"Thank you, but you also need to know that I didn't sleep with Justin."

His brows knitted. "Max, I might have acted like an idiot,

but you don't have to try to make me feel better. We're both adults. We both have pasts."

If he only knew the truth. "I'm afraid my sexual past isn't very exciting. The truth is, just as it was for you in Nassau that morning, my heart was controlling everything in me. And my heart wanted you. After we said good night I went up to my room alone, but I couldn't stop thinking about you, so I went down to the beach to look for you. When I didn't find you there, I checked the bar, the restaurant, *everywhere*...I finally gave up looking, and I went back out to where we'd sat by the water, and it was there that I met Justin, and we talked."

As she gazed into his eyes, feeling the vibrations of the music, vaguely aware of couples dancing around them, she thought about how she'd wished it was Treat she'd been talking with that night by the water. "We talked about you and the way you'd turned my heart inside out. I never told him who I was talking about, but he was a good listener. He was kind, and he had just come off a bad relationship. He said we gave him hope that he could find someone special one day, too. I didn't sleep with him, Treat. The kiss you saw him give me by the elevator was on my cheek, and it was a thank-you kiss. He was a *filler*. He filled the gap you had created."

"I probably shouldn't feel the amount of relief I do over that." He touched his forehead to hers and said, "I've been thinking about you for so long. I've tried to put you out of my mind, but I can't, Max. And I no longer want to try."

His gaze moved over the crowded room, and then his smoldering eyes landed on her again, and her heart went a little crazy.

"Let's get out of here," he suggested.

As he guided her toward the exit, she became aware of envious glances from other women. She lifted her chin, proud to be with him. Even more so now that they'd cleared the air. Her pulse spiked as she thought about what it would feel like to kiss him again, to have his hands on her bare skin.

When they stepped through the doors and into the cool night air, Max crossed her arms against the chill. She'd been in such a hurry to go to Kaylie's, she'd forgotten to bring a jacket. Treat gathered her in his arms again. He felt safe and warm, and the way he was looking at her sent her mind reeling.

"I want to take you someplace special." The sensuousness of his tone mixed with the seductive glimmer in his eyes, sending shivers down her spine.

The valet brought his SUV, and Treat helped her into her seat and then settled in behind the wheel. She nervously rubbed the goose bumps from her arms.

"Let me warm you up," he said with a husky tone.

She licked her lips, readying for the kiss she'd been craving. And, boy, was she ready. His arm stretched across her, bringing his magnificent lips a whisper away from hers. She slowed her breathing, her lips parted in anticipation, and he pushed a button on her door.

"Heated seats," he said as he sat back in his seat.

Max thought her heart might explode. *Really? I should have leaned in and taken the kiss. Next time...*

He reached for her hand, squeezing it gently as he leaned closer and said, "Ready, beautiful?"

Ready? Was he kidding? The way her heart raced and her mind played with thoughts of kissing him, she didn't know if she'd ever be ready for the whirlwind Treat caused inside her, but she sure as heck wanted to try.

Chapter Six

TREAT SENT A quick text, and fifteen minutes later they were in a dark, nearly empty parking lot. He shifted mischievous eyes to Max and said, "Be right back, sweetness."

Sweetness. That's what he'd called her in Nassau.

He left the engine running, and Max watched as he strode toward another SUV. A tall man stepped out, and the two men disappeared behind the vehicle. She didn't know what was going on, but it made Treat even more mysterious. She played with ideas that made her laugh about the clandestine meeting, picturing him as a drug lord or a mobster, neither of which could be true. But the amusement helped ease her nerves.

When the two of them reappeared, Treat held a large bag in each hand. The other man slapped him on the back and climbed into his truck. Treat put the packages in the back seat and climbed back in behind the wheel.

"Sorry about that," he said, and drove out of the parking lot.

"Aren't you going to tell me what that was all about?"

He put his hand on hers and asked, "What do you think it was about?"

"I came up with some pretty funny ideas. Drug deal, talking

about where you'll hide my body. You know, normal stuff."

Treat's low, sexy laugh rumbled through her, tugging at all the parts of her that had longed for him. How could she have missed his *laugh*?

"That was my brother Josh. He's visiting from New York, and I asked him to bring us a few things since the stores are closed."

He turned off the main road and drove down a number of dark, narrow streets. She wondered where they were going and what he could have possibly asked for to fill two large bags. She didn't have much experience with men, and she didn't want to make a fool of herself, but she felt a little out of her league and her confidence was slipping away.

As if Treat could read her mind, he brought her hand to his lips and kissed it. "I'm so glad I came home today." He rubbed the back of her hand against his cheek and said, "I remembered how soft your skin was. I missed it, Max. I missed *you*. How is that even possible after one night?"

He lowered her hand to his thigh and covered it with his own. She tried to keep her hand from trembling, but she had no idea how to respond.

"Thank you?" *Ugh.* Max could coordinate tens of thousands of people, she could multitask like a pro, negotiate with sponsors and always come out on top, but she had so little experience with seduction she should have had Kaylie give her CliffsNotes.

"Thank *you*"—he glanced over with a serious look before returning his attention to the road—"for giving me another chance."

"I think we're giving each other another chance." That earned her the sweetest, sexiest look she'd ever seen. She was about to ask where they were going when the SUV climbed a steep hill, and he pulled over on the side of the dark road.

"Um…Treat?" she asked as he cut the engine and darkness fell upon them. "Please tell me we're not going with the hide-the-body scenario."

"I'd love to hide something in *you*, Max." His voice was like liquid fire. "And I can assure you, getting rid of your body *isn't* on my mind."

Max. Couldn't. Breathe.

Rivers of desire flooded her as he came around to help her out of the truck. She wasn't a fall-into-bed type of girl and never had been. But when Treat opened her door, looking like a dream come true, it was too hard to wait for their first kiss after finally clearing the air and knowing he'd felt just as much for her that night at the resort as she had for him. Max turned and stepped onto the runner. He took her hands to help her down, and instead of stepping off, she leaned forward and pressed her lips to his. His hands moved to her waist as the kiss turned deep and sensual, and he drew her body against his. Max's arms circled his neck as he lifted her, and she wrapped her legs around his waist. He grasped her thighs, kicking the door closed as he intensified the kiss. One of his hands traveled up her back and into her hair, just like she remembered. His lips were soft yet firm, his hold confident and possessive. She wanted to kiss him all night, right there beneath the stars, with her legs around his middle and his phone ringing endlessly.

Phone?

Max pulled back, the ever-efficient side of her breaking through. "Your phone."

With a hand on the nape of her neck, he drew her lips to his again and said, "*Kiss me.*"

"It might be important."

"Nothing is more important than you."

He pressed his lips to hers, and her heart soared. His phone stopped ringing, and she surrendered to their passion, giving herself over to kiss after toe-curling kiss.

Sometime later, five minutes, maybe an hour, she had no idea, lights broke through her reverie, and they drew apart again as a car climbed the dark road.

"Oh gosh," she said breathlessly.

He set her gently on the ground, pressed his lips to hers again, and said, "Perhaps we should get away from the street."

He took off his jacket and tie and laid them neatly across the seat of the truck. Max liked his careful nature. It mimicked hers so perfectly. He grabbed the bags, carrying both in one hand, and put his other arm around her waist. He must have sensed her nervousness as they walked down a dark path through the woods, because he leaned closer and said, "Don't worry, sweetness. There will be no body hiding tonight. Promise."

Moonlight rained down on them through the umbrella of trees, guiding their path up a hill to a clearing. At the edge of the woods, two trees with long branches arched over the grass like gates to a private oasis.

"This is where I used to come to think when I was a teenager," he said as they walked into the clearing, presenting her with a breathtaking view of Weston.

"I've never seen anything like this," she said as he spread out a blanket.

A sea of sparkling lights lit up like diamonds against the landscape. Roads snaked through neighborhoods, partially hidden behind bands of trees. She could make out the vicinity of the fairgrounds and main streets through town. The mountains stood sentinel in the distance against the midnight-blue starry sky.

Treat wrapped his arms around her from behind and kissed her cheek, bringing his intoxicating scent with him. "It's almost as gorgeous as you."

She put her hands over his, weak-kneed by the rush of emotions coursing through her.

"How did you ever find this place?" she asked.

"I was knocking around with my cousin Pierce one afternoon. He lives in Reno now, but he grew up in Trusty." Trusty, Colorado, was a small town located just to the east of Weston, while Allure, where Max lived, was on the west. "Pierce has a big family, like I do, and we were out one afternoon looking to get away from everything. We parked and just blew through the woods. We figured we'd find a boulder and sit for a while. Then we found this spot. I don't know if Pierce ever came back, but I spent many hours here. Honestly, though, I haven't even thought about this place in years."

Treat turned her in his arms, and her heart skipped a beat. He'd hung lanterns from the branches of the trees. A bottle of wine and wineglasses sat upright in a small picnic basket beside a few throw pillows. He sat on the blanket and brought her down beside him.

"You had your brother do all of this for us?"

"I would have done it myself had I known I'd see you tonight." Treat smiled, and it reached his eyes, making him even more devastatingly handsome. "Although I have to admit, Josh did a better job than I could have. He's a fashion designer and has a knack for perfect presentations."

"It wouldn't have mattered if we were sitting on the grass

with none of this. Just the idea that you thought to bring me here is romantic. Why did you decide to bring me here?"

He filled the wineglasses and handed her one. "Believe it or not, even though I have properties all over the world, I don't own any in Weston. I prefer to stay with my father when I'm in town. I didn't have a house to take you to, and I wanted to take you someplace special. This was the first place that came to mind." He lifted his glass in a toast and said, "To new beginnings."

She sipped the delicious wine, feeling his presence like a torch beside her.

"Tell me something about yourself that I don't know," he said.

She had no idea what to say and was too inexperienced to come up with a quick, sexy answer. Where were those CliffsNotes when she needed them?

"I'll start," he offered. "My favorite place in the world, besides right here next to you, is Wellfleet, Massachusetts."

"You travel all over the world and your favorite place is a little town in Massachusetts?" She laughed, which helped ease her nerves.

"Yes. I have a little house on the bay. It's quiet, and has sentimental value. We vacationed there a few times when I was younger."

"That sounds nice. I've never traveled much."

"I'd like to change that." He put his hand on her leg, nudging those butterflies into flight again.

She downed half her wine trying to think of something else to say before she leaned forward and planted her lips on his. "What gets your juices flowing?" she asked, immediately realizing she deserved the amorous look he was giving her. "I mean, outside of...*this*."

"That's easy. My work. I get a thrill out of taking a resort from nonexistent in the eyes of travelers to world-renowned. I love every bit of the process. Even the negotiations are exciting. When I walk into a room and know the people on the other side of the table want something I'm not willing to give, just being able to turn it around is the biggest high I've found."

"I see it in your eyes. That's how I feel about my job, too. It's the same. I mean, not on the same scale, but I definitely feel a thrill with each piece of the puzzle coming together, and then seeing it to fruition. It's unreal."

He ran his finger down her cheek. "What else?" he asked in a seductive voice.

I want to kiss you right this very second. "I love sweets," she said quickly. "Chocolate mostly. And I hate jelly." *Jelly? I'm so lame. I'll tell you anything—just kiss me already.*

"Okay, no jelly." He smiled, resting his hand on her thigh again. "My favorite color is blue. Yours?"

My favorite color is your hand on my body. "Lavender," she managed. "Favorite scent?" *Scent? This is not good. Please just put me out of my misery before you laugh in my face and trade me in for a woman who knows how to act sexy.*

She downed the rest of her wine, and he set both glasses aside.

He slid his hand beneath her hair, cupped the back of her head, and brushed his cheek over hers. He'd done that when they were in Nassau, and she'd never forgotten the way it sent heat pinging through her from head to toe.

"Toasted almond ice cream," he said softly.

A hazy, lusty fog enveloped her mind, and it took her a minute to remember she'd asked him a question. "Ice cream has a scent?"

"A *delicious* one." He touched his lips to her cheek in a feathery kiss. "Tell me something you love," he asked in a voice full of desire.

She could taste his minty breath as he spoke. She curled her fingers into the blanket beneath them, sure that if she didn't, she'd pounce on him like a lioness on her prey and devour him in ways that made her blush to think about. She wasn't sure she was ready for that, no matter how much she craved him. *Something I love. Think, Max. Think.*

"My favorite flowers are Knock Out roses. I've never seen them in person, only in pictures."

"KNOCK OUT ROSES," Treat whispered, brushing his lips over hers. He'd told himself to go slow with Max, but weeks of thinking about her, wanting her, drove his need. "I'll show you Knock Out roses one day." He pressed a kiss to the corner of her mouth, testing the waters. "Tell me to stop, Max, and I'll stop."

"Don't stop," she pleaded.

His mouth came greedily down over hers. Her kisses were sweeter than sugar and so hot she made him ache with desire. He'd wanted to make love to her right there by the road when they were kissing. To lay her down on the back seat and show her how much he'd missed her. He'd never had sex in a vehicle. *Ever. That's* how much he craved her. But Max was *not* a one-night stand, and if his racing heart was any indication, she was destined to be so much more than any woman ever had.

He lowered her to the blanket, kissing her until he felt the tension ease from her body. She felt so good, so right, her delicate fingers clinging to his arms as he poured weeks of repressed desire into their kisses. But it wasn't enough. Would anything ever be? She was finally in his arms again, and he needed more of her. He ran his hands along her waist, up her ribs, and she arched beneath him. He kissed the edge of her jaw, the dip above her chin, and then he tasted her neck in a series of sensual kisses.

"Treat," she said breathlessly. "I want to touch you."

The plea in her voice sent fire through his veins. She reached for his pants, and he took her hand in his. "Not yet," he said. "Let me cherish you first. Is it too cold out here? Do you want to go back to your place?"

"No. I don't want to stop." She took off her glasses and set them aside.

He took her in another passionate kiss, earning a stream of sexy sounds, and they both went a little wild, groping and kissing. He wanted to savor this moment, and drew back just enough to see her sweet face in the moonlight. She was exquisite, and it took all his resolve to try to take it slow, pushing past the intoxicating rush of the innocence that softened her sexuality, setting her apart from anyone else.

He kissed the tender skin beside her ear and whispered, "I've dreamed of being close to you for so long."

He brought his mouth to hers again, taking her in a long, slow kiss as he caressed her thigh. Her skin was smooth and soft. *Perfect.* He rained kisses along her neck, across her breastbone.

"I love your kisses," she panted out.

He continued moving south, kissing her belly through her dress, and when he reached her legs, he pressed his lips just above her knee and glanced up to make sure they were still on the same page. Her eyes were closed, so he reached for her hand, wanting to be even more connected.

"Are you okay?" he asked.

"Yes," she whispered.

He pressed several kisses along her leg and ran his hands up her outer thighs, beneath her dress, feeling her tremble. He drew back again and noticed her clutching at the blanket harder than before. A pang of worry pierced his heart. He moved swiftly over her so he could look directly into her eyes, and she began fumbling with the buttons on his shirt.

He pressed his hand over hers, holding it against his chest. "Max, slow down."

Moonlight reflected in her eyes. Her skin was flushed, her lips pink from their kisses. She was so incredibly feminine, contradictory to the woman who'd been standing on the car, taking charge of the world before her. All hints of the vixen that had tried to seduce him were gone. Her gorgeous eyes brimmed with inescapable desire, but he couldn't deny the trepidation warring alongside it, and his protective urges charged forth again.

"We need to stop."

Max shook her head, but the fear in her eyes told him otherwise.

"We're stopping, Max." He righted her dress and helped her to a sitting position. Cradling her face in his hands, he gazed deeply into her eyes and said, "I shouldn't have gotten carried away. I'm sorry. I just feel so much for you."

"Sorry?" Her brow furrowed. The hurt in her eyes was all consuming as she put her glasses back on. "This is *my* fault. I'm the broken one, not you."

He gathered her in his arms and held her, feeling her heart

beating frantically against his. "It's not your fault. Don't ever say that. What we do together is both of us, and if I pushed too far—"

"You didn't."

Max tried to turn away, but he continued holding her, unwilling to let another misunderstanding come between them. "If this is about what happened at the resort—"

"It's not," Max insisted. "I feel so connected to you, and I *want* to be closer to you. It's all good. It's not you. It's..." She inhaled deeply, then pressed her lips together, as if she was trying to hold back her words. "I haven't been with a man in that way since..."

In that second, he knew in his heart what she was going to say. He pressed a kiss to her cheek and said, "Since the guy who hurt you in college?"

She nodded and closed her eyes.

"Sweetness, it's okay. I understand."

"Understand?" She opened her eyes, embarrassment evident in them even as she avoided looking directly into his eyes. "You can have any woman you want. You don't need one you have to try to *understand*. Can you please take me to get my car?"

Now he was the one filling his lungs with brisk air, gathering the courage to put his foot down on a sensitive situation. "Yes, I'll take you to your car, but can we talk first, please?"

Her eyes flicked up to his. "Treat..."

"I'll tell you what. You don't have to talk. Please just listen. Everyone has something to overcome. I don't care if it's the prince of Egypt or the first lady. We all have broken pieces, and we have choices to make. We can either tiptoe around those pieces forever and let them guide our happiness, or if we're lucky, we can find someone who has a broom, a dustpan, and a bottle of glue, and try to make it work."

Max smiled, and a soft laugh fell from her lips, warming him to his toes.

"When I first saw you at the resort, Max, I felt something so strong, it scared me."

"Scared you? You expect me to believe that? A man like you?"

"Of course I don't expect you to, but I hope you will. I didn't know what to do with my instant attraction to you. I mean, I've been attracted to women before, but with you it was different. I wanted to take care of you. I wanted to lo—"

Max closed her eyes, and he lifted her chin with his finger and said, "Please open your eyes. Hear me out. No more misunderstandings. If you walk away from us, I want you to do it with your eyes open."

She swallowed hard, barely breathing, and finally met his gaze.

"I had never felt anything so powerful," he confessed. "Then, before I had a chance to even process what I was feeling or why, I thought I lost you. I have shattered pieces too, Max. Lots of them. I'll bring the broom and dustpan. Hell, I'll even bring the glue. Just meet me halfway."

"I'm so embarrassed," she said. "All I want to do right now is bury my face in a big chocolate cake and forget this ever happened."

"That's funny, because I never want to forget a second of it."

Chapter Seven

TREAT'S CELL PHONE rang at eight o'clock the next morning. He fumbled with it and answered without looking at the number. "Hello?"

"Since when do you leave your little sister at a party?"

Savannah. She was trying to sound annoyed, but Treat knew her better than that. She was really fishing for information. "Hugh was there to drive you home."

"Hugh? He was too busy with *Supernova* to even think about me. Lucky for you, Connor's driver was free."

"I'm sorry, but you dragged me there hoping I'd get together with Max, remember? Listen, Vanny, I just went to sleep a few hours ago. Can I call you later?" He hadn't liked the idea of Max arriving home late at night alone, so after taking her to get her car, he'd followed her home and walked her to her door. She'd still been embarrassed by their putting on the brakes, but it only endeared her to him even more. She was more real than any woman he'd ever met, and for a man who had been chased by gold-digging women forever, he loved how different Max was.

"A few hours ago? Should I assume you two hit it off? I saw you guys leave, looking at each other like you couldn't wait to eat each other alive."

"Nice talk from my baby sister," Treat said with a smile. He draped his arm over his eyes and sighed. "I gotta go, Vanny. Love you." As always, he waited for her to say goodbye. No matter what mood he was in, he never hung up on his siblings. His mother's death had been a painful lesson about not taking his loved ones for granted. He never knew just when he'd see or talk to them for the last time.

His bedroom door swung open and Rex stepped in. "Hey. You gonna get up and help Dad today or what?"

"What the...?" Had he made a promise he'd forgotten?

"Just sayin'." Rex left the door open, his obnoxious way of telling him, *If I'm not resting, neither are you.*

Treat pulled his exhausted body from bed and trudged into the bathroom. He leaned over the sink and took a good, hard look at himself in the mirror. His looks had served him well over the years, and he appreciated the genes he'd been blessed with. He also acknowledged the fact that he'd abused that gift for a very long time, enjoying the comfort of women's arms based on nothing more than physical attraction. But all that had changed when, after weeks of talking on the phone with Max while she was coordinating the wedding, wondering what the sweet, professional woman on the other end of the line looked like, he'd finally met her. He'd been an idiot to think he could ever forget her.

He turned on the shower, stripped down, and stepped under the warm spray, letting it rain down on his shoulders. He could still feel Max trembling in his arms, and he wondered what the jerk she'd gone out with had done to her to have such lingering effects. As he washed up, he had a fleeting thought about the look that had come between them in Nassau and wondered if that had added to her discomfort last night. Even though she'd said it didn't, he wanted to be sure. He wasn't a kid anymore. He knew better than to do things that might hurt a person's feelings. He was going to have to prove to her that his momentary digression was just that, and not who he was at his core.

Even though they'd reconnected and appeared to be on the same page and being with Max felt righter than anything ever had, he shouldn't have let things go so far last night. He always led with his mind, not his emotions. It figured that the one time he got it wrong was the one time that it mattered.

He dried himself off and looked down at his groin. *Troublemaker.*

From that moment forward, he was going to do everything he could to make Max realize she could trust him to keep her safe.

TREAT FOUND REX at the stables, looking over Hope, the horse his father had bought for his mother when she'd first found out she was sick.

"The prince wakes," Rex teased. He pushed his Stetson down low, accentuating the sharp angles of his jaw and Grecian nose.

"Good morning to you, too." Treat ran his hand along Hope's back. She *neigh*ed, nuzzling her nose into Rex's chest. Her red coat had faded in recent years, and patches of white had begun to sprout. "How is the old girl?"

"She's holding up okay," his father said.

Treat hadn't seen his father bending down by a bucket in

the stall.

"I'm keeping an eye on her. She's got plenty of good years left. I never like our animals to suffer, and Hope here..." His father didn't have to finish the sentence—*was your mother's.*

Treat and Rex exchanged a sorrowful glance.

"You've done well by her, Dad. Mom would be proud." Treat laid a hand on his father's shoulder.

"I know she is," his father said. His father swore he still felt their mother's presence around the ranch, and though Treat had never felt her—not for a lack of trying—he believed his father did.

He remembered sitting in his room as a child after she'd passed away, night after night, praying he'd feel whatever his father had felt, hoping against all hope and making promises with whatever almighty powers would listen. *I'll be good. I'll never fight with my brothers again. I'll help Dad more. I'll do whatever you want, just please, please let me feel Mom one more time.* His prayers had gone unanswered, and now, as he thought of how painful those early years without his mother had been— and how much he missed Max after just a few hours—he was beginning to better understand the depth of his father's devastation.

"Dad, would you mind telling me about when you and Mom met?" Treat watched his father's eyes light up, and he caught that light and held on to it.

"Here we go," Rex said. "I'm gonna take Johnny Boy out for a quick ride while you two relive the good old days." He headed for Johnny Boy's stall.

Rex always escaped when they talked about their mother. Selfishly, Treat was glad to have his father to himself. If anyone understood matters of the heart, it was his father. He never hid his feelings for his children, or his late wife, which kept their family close.

"Your mother was so beautiful, sitting on her daddy's fence watching the horses when my father and I drove up. I swear, Treat, when she turned and looked at me, something inside me fell into place. Even at fourteen, I knew she was the woman I was going to marry. I just didn't know how to convince her of it." He continued reliving the story that Treat would never tire of. His father liked to remind him that his mother had gotten all her mother's beauty and her father's stubbornness. Her mother was Brazilian, and her father, a Colorado rancher.

Treat had heard this story dozens of times, but not until now did he understand the depth of his father's feelings of something inside him falling into place. That's how he'd felt when he'd finally met Max.

"But her heart…" His father looked up and away, as though he could see his wife standing in the distance. "Her heart was as sensitive as a newborn bird. The wrong word, the wrong look, and that bullheadedness that had angered you a minute before would wash away as quick as rain. And just like that, you'd crush her spirit."

Just like Max. "What did you do when that happened?"

His father looked at him for a long moment before responding. "Son, I did everything I could, that's what I did. There was nothing I wouldn't have done for her. My ego did not exist when it came to your mother, and heaven knows she knew it, too." He laughed under his breath. "I swear that woman used it to her advantage."

Treat was too busy mulling over what his father said to respond.

His father stood and set a hand on Treat's shoulder. "You

want to talk about her?"

"Mom?"

He shook his head. "The woman who's got my son so tied up in knots that he's coming to his daddy for relationship advice."

"Dad," he scoffed.

"Don't deny it, son. I've been there. Ain't no use pretending that noose around your heart doesn't tighten every time you see whoever this woman is."

Family knows no boundaries was their family creed, and while it played into taking care of one another, it also meant they would push their noses into each other's business when they felt one of them was hurting. But Treat was already formulating his plan, and he didn't need his father's advice. Every time he thought of Max, he had that feeling—the same one his father described—and there was no way he was going to ignore it.

Chapter Eight

IT WASN'T UNTIL Max stopped to buy coffee on her way to the festival that she realized she'd left her purse in Treat's truck. After she'd gone back to her apartment, she'd tried to sleep, but every time she closed her eyes, she saw his eyes looking back at her with so much emotion that it sent her mind into a whirlwind of embarrassment interlaced with gratitude at his understanding. She'd tossed and turned all night.

When she got to the office, Max consumed enough caffeine to hold her through the morning. Now her stomach was growling as loud as could be as she and Chaz went over reports and plans for the day. The second day of the festival always ran smoother than the first. She was amazed at how much more responsibility the staff could handle after a single day of being thrown feetfirst into the fire, and she was thankful for the breathing space.

"Want to take a break for lunch?" Chaz asked.

"No. I'm fine." *All these figures are blurring together, and I see Treat on every page, but I'll get through it.* Stopping would only give her more time to think about how she'd ended their romantic evening. What must Treat think of her after she'd first turned him down in Nassau and then stopped them last night?

What do I think of myself?

She didn't have an easy answer, but one thing was for sure. She was pissed at herself. It had been years since that awful night, and she was still letting it haunt her. Her stomach gurgled loudly, as if it agreed.

Chaz closed the ledger and stood. "Nonsense. We've been at it all morning, and your stomach is growling. Come on. We'll go to Kale's and grab a bite."

"I don't have my purse."

"Seriously? That's the lamest excuse ever. My treat."

She wondered if it would be rude to ask him to refrain from using the word *treat*. She pushed herself to her feet with a sigh. "Okay, you win."

"What's up with you today?" Chaz asked. "I don't think I've ever seen you this tired."

I was this tired the two weeks after your wedding when I was too heartbroken to function, but you were on your honeymoon. "I didn't sleep very well last night."

"You must have had a good time at the party after all." Chaz held the door open for her.

She shrugged, avoiding real communication.

They were graced with another warm afternoon, and Max tried not to let the beauty of the day get lost in her lingering mortification. She'd never allowed herself to get carried away as she had with Treat last night, telling him she wanted to touch him and urging him on. But she'd *wanted* to make love to him, and those primal urges were so new, they felt unstoppable— until the worry overcame the desire and she had been powerless to continue.

At the restaurant, she picked at her salad while Chaz caught her up on all the new things the twins were doing. Her phone vibrated, and she pretended not to hear it, wishing she had forgotten her phone instead of her purse. She was too embarrassed to speak to Treat, and she knew he'd call.

"Aren't you going to check that?" Chaz asked.

"No."

"Okay, Max, spill it. You always check your phone. What is it that you're always saying?" He looked up, thinking.

"If someone takes the time to text or call, you better be kind enough to check it."

"Right," he said. "That's it. I seem to remember you drilling that into my head before I got married."

"Yeah, well, I didn't do a very good job, considering I had to remind you about what I'd said."

Chaz's phone vibrated. "It's probably an issue. Maybe our earpieces aren't working?" He checked his text.

She turned on her microphone and spoke to one of the staff members, then turned it off and said, "Radio's fine."

"This is from Kaylie, and I'm reading this word for word. 'Something must be wrong with Max. She's not answering my texts. Check on her for me?' So don't tell me I'm reading you wrong."

She was too exhausted to argue about whether her head was or wasn't on straight today. It wasn't. And as much as she wanted to blame someone other than herself, it wasn't Treat's fault he was too hot, too kind, and too delicious for her to resist. It was her own fault. Her inability to control her runaway hormones had left her shaking like a ridiculous, inexperienced *girl*.

Not touching a man for years will do that to a person.

Somewhere in the back of her mind she kept trying to blame Ryan, too. But Max wasn't used to excuses. She was a doer, a fixer, and even though it was true, blaming what happened all those years ago felt like a crutch, and she was determined to get over it on her own. Especially now that she and Treat had a clean slate.

If only I could figure out how to get past this hurdle.

"I think I'll go back to the office. I'm really tired. Thanks for lunch, and please tell Kaylie I'm fine."

"Okay," he said hesitantly. "Is there anything I can do to help? Because I'm still not buying the tired thing."

Not unless you know how I can ever look Treat in the eye again without being completely and utterly embarrassed. "Sure. Can you please have them wrap my salad? Maybe I'll eat it for dinner." *Alone, while I figure myself out.*

Much later that afternoon, she was still unsure of how to face Treat. She thought up all sorts of ways, none of which made sense, like pretending she hadn't urged him on and then gotten so nervous he had to stop. She was responding to a text from Kaylie when her earpiece buzzed.

"Yes?"

"Max, I've got a guy down here, says he's looking for you."

She checked her watch. "Patron, delivery, or sponsor?"

"Hold on."

She heard a muffled conversation.

"He says none of the above."

Max's heart leapt. *Treat.* "Um, is he really tall?" She held her breath. *Please say no. No, please say yes. Or don't say anything. Just let him go away until I can figure out how to handle this.*

"Freakishly."

She closed her eyes, smiling. She loved how *freakishly* tall he was, how his hands covered the breadth of her thighs, and how his weight had felt perfect when he was kissing her. Her nerves pulsed with the memory of his touch.

"Max?"

She touched the earpiece, still not ready to face him. "Yeah, I'm here, but I'm really busy." Then she remembered her purse. *For heaven's sake.* She needed her purse. "Hey, does he have my purse with him?" she asked.

"No. His hands are empty."

Confused, she said, "Okay, please tell him I'm sorry but I can't see him right now, but that I'd definitely like to connect again another time." *When I'm not as nervous as a jackrabbit.* She clicked off the earpiece and read Kaylie's texts again.

How was hottie?

She debated asking Kaylie how to handle her situation, but she didn't want a crutch, and Kaylie would be just that. Instead she texted, *He's more incredible than I ever imagined.*

THE AFTERNOON DRAGGED into evening, with each issue taking twice as long as the last. By dinnertime, Max was starving, but she couldn't even eat her salad from lunch. As they neared closing time, she guzzled more coffee and decided to duck into a theater. Maybe she could close her eyes for a few minutes and no one would notice. The minute her butt hit the only available seat in the theater, her earpiece buzzed, and she hauled herself back out into the cool evening air.

"Yes?"

"Max? Delivery for you."

"I'm not expecting any deliveries. Who's the vendor?" she asked as she moved out of the way of the crowds.

"Forget it, Max. I'll have someone run it up to the office."

"Thanks."

Chaz was texting when Max entered the office. She relaxed into the couch and closed her eyes. Chaz's phone buzzed three times in quick succession.

"Text fight?" she asked.

"No." He responded to the texts, and his phone continued to buzz again.

She lifted her head and opened her eyes. "Anything I can do?"

He finally put the phone down on his desk and looked at her. "We're slow tonight. Why don't you take an hour off? Get off the grounds and do something non-work-related."

She snapped to attention. "What?"

"You heard me. Take a break."

Adrenaline drove her to the edge of his desk. "What's going on? I've never left a festival early, and you know we're anything but slow tonight." Max rubbed her temples.

"You're exhausted," he said.

"So? I can still do my job. Look, I'm sorry if I overstepped my boundaries by being so worn out. I take full responsibility, but there's no reason to make me leave early."

When he didn't respond, she said, "I love my job, Chaz. Have I done something wrong?"

"Relax," he said with a pinched face, sending another quick text. "No. Even when you're tired, you do twice the work of anyone else."

Max felt a wave of relief. "Then what is it? Why do you need to get rid of me?"

There was a knock at the door, and Max answered it.

Mark, one of the temporary festival staffers, came through the door carrying an enormous white box and set it on the table.

"This just arrived," he said on his way back out the door.

"Were you expecting something?" Chaz asked.

Max shook her head and lifted the lid, revealing a decadent chocolate cake with lavender-frosting roses in the center. The smell of rich chocolate sent her ravenous stomach into a flurry.

Chaz peered over her shoulder. "Sponsor?"

"Probably." She dipped her finger into the deep chocolate frosting and licked it off. "Holy cow, that's delicious. I love our sponsors." She removed the card that was taped to the inside of the box and read it aloud. "Max, I never want to forget last night. Dive right in…" She snapped the card shut as a flush heated her cheeks. *The lavender roses. He remembered my favorite color, too?*

"O-*kay*, then," Chaz said with an arch of his brow. "Someone either did something very wrong or very right, and I think now I understand why you're so tired today."

"It was something very right," she said a little dreamily, then quickly added, "But not what you think." She couldn't believe Treat had taken her comment to heart. The man had a memory like a vault. *And a heart sweeter than this decadent dessert.* She was elated. *Giddy.* She closed the top of the box, wishing she hadn't sent him away earlier. "I could never eat all of this. Why don't you take some home to Kaylie and the kids?"

"Max." Chaz shook his head. "I think whoever sent this probably meant for you to have it. That's not a cheap cake."

"No, it's not. It's indulgent and delicious, and exactly what I need." *Like him.*

Chapter Nine

TREAT WASN'T SURPRISED when Max refused to see him. She was a prideful woman, and he knew how hard it was for her to face him even on the ride back to her car last night, but he wasn't going to be dissuaded that easily. Embarrassing moments happened, and he wanted to be by her side for each and every flushed-cheek second, until the only thing that made her tremble was pure, unbridled passion.

He hoped the cake might ease her nerves and bring that wall she'd erected down just enough for her to realize that not making love last night was no big deal. After talking with his father, Treat was even more convinced that what he felt for Max was the real thing.

Now it was after eleven at night, and he stood at the far end of the festival parking lot, waiting under the cover of night for Max to walk through the back gates. It had been hard not calling her, but he wanted to look into her eyes, to see what she was feeling when they finally talked. His pulse raced when he saw Chaz and Max walking beneath the glow of the lighted gate. She looked gorgeous in jeans and a sweater, carrying the enormous box he'd sent. Chaz headed to his car as Max put the box on her passenger seat. Treat had the urge to run and swoop her into his arms, but he knew his sensitive bird needed careful hands.

He approached slowly as Max settled into the driver's seat, and before she closed her door, he said, "Max," startling her into a scream.

"Sorry. It's me," he said quickly.

Her hand flew to her chest as Chaz ran over.

Treat held his hands up. "Chaz, it's me, Treat. I didn't mean to startle her."

"Treat? Hey, man. Sorry I couldn't get her down here earlier. I tried."

He watched understanding dawn on Max's face, causing her cheeks to flame. He'd texted Chaz earlier asking if he could spare Max for an hour. But he hadn't anticipated a scene, and the last thing he'd wanted was to cause her more embarrassment.

"*That's* why you tried to get me to leave early?" Max asked.

Chaz shrugged. "Hey, Kaylie threatened to kill me if I didn't try."

She glared at Treat, but just as quickly as a scowl formed, her lips curved, wiping it away. "I can't believe you did that."

"What can I say? I was just following the bread crumbs." He smiled at her confusion. Savannah was right after all.

Chaz turned his back and leaned closer to Treat. "The cake? Impressive and pretty friggin' romantic. You realize you're setting the bar pretty high for us normal guys, right?"

"When it comes to Max, nothing is romantic enough."

"Nice," Chaz said with an approving smile. Then he headed back to his car.

"You scared the daylights out of me," Max said as she closed her car door.

"I'm sorry. I wasn't thinking. I wanted to see you earlier, but realized that was a mistake, too. I guess I'm full of them."

Her long lashes fluttered a little shyly. "No, you're not. I'm sorry for sending you away. I was too embarrassed to face you."

He stepped closer, needing to be near her, and handed her the purse she'd left in his car. "I think the best way for you to overcome embarrassment is for me to become a permanent fixture in your life." That earned another sexy smile. "How was your day?"

"My day was spent trying to figure out how not to be embarrassed around you, while handling a hundred issues. The cake is amazingly delicious, and it's exactly what I needed. Thank you."

He gazed into her eyes and said, "I hope one of your solutions was *not* to forget us."

She shook her head. "I don't think forgetting us is even a possibility."

"What do you say we take a walk? I'll keep my hands to myself and won't let us get caught up in any hanky-panky."

"Hanky-panky?" She laughed. "I haven't heard that since I was twelve."

"Maybe you're hanging out with the wrong crowd." He reached for her hand, then quickly withdrew it. "I said I'd keep my hands to myself, and I already made a liar out of myself."

"Maybe you were on the right track of how to overcome my embarrassment." She reached for his hand and lifted his arm, snuggling in beneath it, settling all the upended pieces of him into place again.

SOMEWHERE BETWEEN THE chocolate cake and seeing Treat, Max had convinced herself that there was only one way to move past last night, and that was to face it head-on. Snuggling up to Treat had done the trick, but as they walked along the street toward town, the cool air carried his masculine scent, and all she could think about was kissing him again.

Oh, for Pete's sake.

She needed to distract herself so she didn't make a fool out of herself again. "Was Savannah upset that you left last night?"

"No, but now that you mention it, she's probably upset with me right now. She called this morning, and I forgot to call her back. Do you mind if I just send her a quick text?"

Rather than finding fault that he hadn't called her back, she admired his dedication to his family. "No. Go ahead."

As he texted Savannah, his lips rose to a smile.

When she'd met Treat at the resort, he'd been professional and proper to everyone in the room. With the exception of the one misunderstanding between them, he was always a gentleman. And when he'd greeted Max, he'd kissed the back of her hand, as if she were someone special. She sensed he treated his family the same way.

"You really love your family, don't you?"

"Sure. Don't you?" he asked as he put his phone in his pocket.

"Yes, but I don't have any siblings. I think those relationships are different from parental relationships."

"I can't imagine life without them. My mom died when I was eleven, after being sick for years, and afterward I tried to step into her shoes and take care of my four brothers and Savannah, but I never really pulled it off."

She imagined him as a little boy, crushed by the death of his mother and trying to be strong for his siblings, and her heart opened even more. "I'm sorry about your mother. That must have been awful."

"It was very difficult, but I have great memories of her, and I think about her often."

"What was she like?"

He tightened his hold on her shoulder as the lights of the town came into view. "She was always there, smiling, hugging us. She loved the outdoors. My father would tell you she was stubborn, and I'm sure she was, but she had this spark of life about her...until she no longer did."

She leaned against him, her heart aching for him. "She sounds wonderful. I wish I could have known her."

"I think she would have adored you." He got a faraway look in his eyes and said, "This is a little embarrassing to admit, but when she first got sick, my father bought her a horse, Hope. And now he believes he can communicate with my mother through the horse. Like she's still around."

The hairs on the back of Max's neck prickled. "I'd really like to meet Hope."

"You would?"

"Yes, very much. After my grandmother died, I felt her around for a long time. I think there's some truth about the people we love never really leaving us. Not that I ever communicated with her after we lost her or anything. I was never that lucky, I guess. But I wouldn't disregard what your father feels. Do you feel anything when you're around Hope?"

"I don't know how to answer that, because I want so badly to feel something. Sometimes I think I do, or I see a look in Hope's eyes that makes me wonder, but that's probably the hopeful eleven-year-old in me coming out."

"Or maybe it's the hopeful man trying to have faith in something other than the tangible."

Treat pressed his lips to the side of her head as they crossed a street. He didn't say anything, but she felt a wave of appreciation rolling off him.

"You're lucky that you have so many siblings," she said. "You said you helped each other through your loss?"

"Sure, as much as we could. I'm the oldest, and I've always tried to protect them. But I couldn't be Mom." He shook his head. "I couldn't even come close. It wasn't that I wanted to replace her. I just wanted to make it hurt less for them."

"I'm sure they appreciated all that you were able to do," she offered.

"You know, that's just it. After years of hoping and praying that she'd be okay, I was so broken by her death that I really didn't *do* much. I listened when they cried, told them everything would be okay. But when it was time to go away to college, I was kind of relieved to get out from under all that guilt."

His emotions were so raw, as if he'd experienced leaving his family just yesterday instead of years earlier. Max wished they were sitting by a fireplace, or on a bench, somewhere she could crawl into his lap and comfort him.

He looked down at her, and she was drawn to the sincerity in his eyes. "I wish I'd known you then. To help you through."

His lips curved up and he said, "How old are you, Max?"

"Twenty-eight and a half."

He laughed. "Well, let's see. You would have been *two*. I'm not sure you could have done much, but I appreciate the sentiment."

She buried her face in his side and said, "Still."

He tipped her face up and kissed her tenderly. Then he brushed his lips over her cheek and whispered, "Still," and pressed another warm kiss to her lips. A minute later he said, "Everyone expected me to help my father run the ranch, and as much as I wanted to help him, it would mean reliving those memories, and that was too much for me."

"I'm sure your family understands," she said.

"I've never told them. It's not something I'm proud of."

There it was again, another crushing blow to her heart. How many men would admit to things they find as faults within themselves, much less something so intimate? Everything he said proved what she'd already known. Treat Braden was one of a kind.

"I've never told anyone that before."

"Thank you for sharing it with me."

"I want to share things with you, Max," he said as they came to Main Street.

Sparkling lights shone through large storefront windows, and the sound of music filtered out of restaurant doors. Max soaked in the romantic feel of the evening, wanting to share her secrets with him, too, to tell him the *rest* of the story about Ryan. But even the thought of bringing such ugliness into their relationship made her feel sick. She wasn't ready for that. Would she ever be? At least she could share the secrets that she was sure wouldn't send her spiraling into darkness.

"I wish I had a brother to listen when I was younger. I would have done anything to have someone to confide in," she admitted. "I still wish I did."

He gathered her in his arms and gazed into her eyes. "Hopefully one day you'll feel like you can confide in me."

Oh, how she wanted to. Max's stomach growled, and they

both smiled.

"Want to grab a bite?" he asked. "I haven't eaten all day, and you're obviously hungry."

"Yes, I'd like that. I'm sure existing solely on chocolate cake isn't the best idea."

A few minutes later they were sitting in the back of a quiet Italian restaurant. Max scanned the menu, knowing that although she was hungry, she wouldn't be able to eat a whole meal while butterflies were tap-dancing in her stomach.

"It's late. Would you like to share a dish instead of getting two whole meals?"

She looked up at him incredulously. The one time she'd suggested sharing a meal with Ryan, he'd looked at her like she was crazy. She'd never asked another man to share. Chalk that up to just one more thing to like about Treat.

"I'm sorry. Are you not a sharer? I forget that some people don't like to eat off other people's plates."

"No. I love to share. Why don't you choose, though. I'm no good at making food decisions."

"Most women don't like men to order for them, either. Seems like we're a good match."

His smile held so much contentedness that Max almost reached for his hand. But after what happened last night, she wasn't taking any chances. *First I'll reach for your hand, then your shirt, your pants…*

She felt her cheeks flush and tried to stifle the smile tugging at her lips as Treat reached over and placed his hand over hers, taking the worry off her plate.

Chapter Ten

AFTER SHARING A bottle of wine and a delicious shrimp and pasta dinner, Max and Treat walked back to the festival grounds. The parking lot was empty except for their cars, amplifying the end of their evening. The last thing Treat wanted to do was leave Max for another day. These stolen hours were nowhere near enough. He wanted to spend days and nights getting to know everything about her. When he drew her into his arms and gazed into her eyes, enjoying the way her breathing went shallow, he knew she was right there with him.

"What are you thinking right now?" he asked.

She'd been careful with what she said and how she said it over dinner, probably because she was afraid of stepping over the line they had last night. But he couldn't ignore the flicker of heat in her eyes, or the way she pressed her body against his on the walk home. He was learning more about Max from the things she didn't say than the things she did.

"That I'm not ready for the night to end," she said softly.

He'd bided his time as long as he was able, but he couldn't wait another second, and he lowered his lips to hers, drinking in her unique essence coalescing with the wine they'd shared. When she melted against him, he threaded his fingers into her hair, angling her face so he could take the kiss deeper. She moaned into their kiss, and his body flamed. His hands ached to touch her, but he reluctantly held back, taking her in a series of tender kisses instead.

She was hardly breathing as he brushed his lips over hers and said, "Then let's not end it just yet."

Her fingers curled into his shirt and her lips curved up as she glanced toward her car. "I do have dessert."

"I want you for dessert, but I'll settle for more time with you."

Her eyes widened, and she trapped her lower lip between her teeth.

"We'll go slow, Max. I'm not going to hurt you, and I sure as heck don't want to scare you."

"You don't scare me, and I believe with my whole heart that you won't hurt me."

After several more steamy kisses, Treat followed Max to her apartment. He parked beside her car and came around to help her out.

"I can't believe I'm taking you into a one-bedroom apartment."

"What do you mean? What's wrong with that?" He grabbed the cake box and put his arm around Max as they crossed the parking lot.

"You own gorgeous resorts. I wish I could magically create a glamorous house for me to call my own, but…"

He stopped at the entrance to the building and swept her into his arm, balancing the cake box against his side. "You need to get over whatever is going on in that pretty head of yours."

"My apartment is small," she said apologetically.

He kissed the corner of her mouth. "I love small."

"It's not glamorous. It's…utilitarian."

He held her tighter. "I'm all about efficiency."

"There's nothing special about it."

She swallowed hard as he set the box down and gathered her in his arms. Her breath was sweet and warm as he tilted her chin up so she had no choice but to look at him and said, "It's yours. That makes it special."

He covered her lips with his, and her keys dropped to the concrete. They both smiled into the kiss.

"I think we'd better get inside before you try to take advantage of me," Treat teased.

They went up to her apartment, and he was aware of her watching him as he took in the secrets of her private world. Max's home was exactly as he'd envisioned, meticulously tidy and beautifully put together, yet understated. The beige couch and overstuffed chair spoke of comfort and stability, just like Max. His gaze skimmed over the bar separating the cozy kitchen from the rest of the living space.

"It's small, I know," she said, "but—"

"It's perfect," he assured her, and it was. Just like her. "As much as I appreciate the finer things in life, I don't get off on them the way other wealthy people do. My bungalow in Wellfleet is a testament to that. It isn't much bigger than this. So, let's both relax, Max. I'm with you, and if you lived in a tent it wouldn't change the way I feel about you. I'm just a regular guy," he said as they went into the kitchen and he set the cake on the counter.

Max took two plates from a cabinet. "If you call guys who look like Greek gods, smell like hot summer nights, and whose eyes scream of sinful promises *regular*, then yeah, you're just a regular guy." She leaned against the counter looking painfully alluring, and slightly amused. "I've had exactly two males in my apartment before, and I'm pretty sure the Cub Scout selling popcorn with his mother didn't count."

"Please don't tell me about the other guy," he said under his breath. He opened the box and found a plastic fork standing upright in a half-eaten layer of cake. "My, my, my. What have we got here? You might think you don't know what to do with a man like me in your apartment—and I assure you, I'm much more of a man than whoever the other guy was—but you sure know what to do with a chocolate cake."

"Hey, don't judge." She laughed and carried the cake to the table. "A girl has to have her priorities straight. And the other guy was just a date. I knew exactly what to do with him, and I did it. I said goodbye at the door. But then you came into my life. You were just this deep voice over the phone, the owner of the resort where I was planning my boss's wedding. You were a mystery, and after we spoke a few more times, you became a fantasy." Her expression turned serious, and she said, "And then you walked into the room and my heart nearly stopped. For the first time in my life—in my *life*, Treat—I couldn't think straight."

"I remember every second of the day we met," he said as he closed the distance between them. "My first thought was, *Where have you been hiding?*"

She blushed, and he ran his fingers down her cheek.

"It's the truth, Max. You were looking at me in the same way you have been since we came together again, like you wanted me but you were unsure. And from that very first second, when your cheeks flushed and you opened your mouth to speak but no words came, I was hooked. Danica had to introduce you, and I thought you were the sweetest, sexiest woman I'd ever met." He took her hand in his and brushed his thumb over the back of it. "I remember how soft your skin was when I kissed your hand and how you looked shocked, as if no one had ever done that before."

"No one had," she confessed.

"That's a shame, because a woman like you deserves to be treated like a lady." He placed his hands on her hips and said, "A lady *and* a lover."

She inhaled a shaky breath.

"I made one mistake with you, Max, and I'll spend the rest of our time making it up to you. I don't want to make you nervous, but I don't want you to think that you can't be the woman you are beneath the proper professional when we're alone. I got a taste of the passionate woman you are, and one day I hope you'll feel comfortable enough to let those feelings come out without embarrassment, without worry of judgment or fear of the unknown."

"I want that, too," she said just above a whisper.

"I don't want only a sexual relationship with you, Max. I hope you know that. I adore who you are, and have since the first time we spoke on the phone. You were confident and smart, and it was clear that your primary concern was that your friends' weddings came off as perfectly as they'd hoped. That spoke to me because friends and family come before anything else in my life. It didn't hurt that you had the sexiest voice I'd ever heard in my life. Even without seeing you, I knew you were special."

She lowered her eyes, and he lifted her chin again, falling heart first into her. "When we finally met, when you didn't respond to me immediately, you then stood taller, pushed your glasses to the bridge of your nose, and told me you had jet lag."

He lowered his face closer to hers and whispered, "I wanted to take you back to my room, tuck you into my bed, and let you rest just so I could have all of your energy when I wore you out later that night."

"I knew you were special, too. But why didn't you push me to come back to your room later that night? When I said I wasn't ready?"

"I didn't want to coerce you into my bed. I would never do that to anyone, especially you. I thought we'd have the rest of that weekend together, and eventually, when you were ready, we'd come together naturally."

A rush of air left her lungs. "And then we had the misunderstanding."

"It made us stronger," he said, and touched his lips to hers.

"I felt the same way, Treat. That's why, for the first time in forever, I didn't want our night to end, and I didn't want to say good night at the door."

"Because we're meant to be together, Max."

EVERY PART OF Max wanted to drag him into the bedroom and love him until the sun came up. She was nervous, and he'd feel her trepidation no matter how much she tried to hide it, but how could she get over her fears unless she faced them? She slid her arms around his neck and went up on her toes, but all she could reach was his chin, so she pressed a kiss there.

The second her lips touched his skin, he shifted, capturing the kiss and taking it deeper for a long, heated moment, leaving her breathless.

"Max." Her name came out strained. "You do remember

why I sent you this cake, don't you? I can't have you freak out on me again. It makes me feel guilty."

She buried her face in his chest, her heart beating wildly. "I didn't *freak out*. I just got nervous, and I would have gone through with it if you hadn't stopped us."

"We moved too fast for my girl, and I will never, *ever* ignore your well-being." He kissed her lips. "We're going to be very careful about not going too fast tonight."

"Why do you have to be such a gentleman?" Would this be easier if he were pushy? One look in his caring eyes and she knew the answer. *I wouldn't be with you if you were.*

"Because it's how I was raised, and I care about you too much to let you rush into us. Waiting a day, a week, a month won't make or break us, Max."

"It might break me," she mumbled, earning a devilish grin.

"If you still feel this way tomorrow, maybe we'll revisit those sinful promises you mentioned seeing in my eyes."

He held her so close, it was impossible not to notice his arousal. Her pulse spiked as they stared hungrily into each other's eyes. She swallowed hard. *Hard. Oh gosh, don't think about that.* After going years without intimacy, then finding a man she adored, not thinking about him in that way was pure torture.

It was *impossible*.

His eyes turned dark as night, and she wondered if he could read her mind.

"Cake!" She reached for the fork, stabbed a hunk of the decadent dessert, and shoved it into her mouth. Treat's deep laughter eased the pulsing knot that had formed inside her. She shoveled another forkful into her mouth.

"Does that work?" he asked.

She piled more cake on the fork and fed it to him.

"Mm. That is good. But um…" He glanced down at his groin. "Apparently it's not a remedy."

"Trust me, this *will* work. I've relied on chocolate cake many times in my life." She fed him another bite. "Of course, I've never tried it with the object of my desire standing a few inches away."

A rumbling, growling noise climbed up his throat, and it was the sexiest thing she'd ever heard. He took the fork from her hand, shoveled cake onto it, and fed it to her. Crumbs tumbled down her chin, and he kissed them away.

"There's not enough cake on the planet," he said, and pressed his lips to hers. Sweetness exploded into their kiss.

Sometime later, after too much cake and not nearly enough kisses, they made their way to the door to say good night.

"I haven't *ever* had this much fun," Treat said.

Her heart was so full, she couldn't stop grinning. "Me either."

"I should go. What time do you work tomorrow?"

"Seven thirty until we're done for the day. You know how that goes. I should be home by ten."

He gathered her in his arms and gave her another heavenly kiss. "That's a long day. I wish you had the day off so we could spend it together."

"I only work crazy hours during the festival, but I wish I had a day off to spend with you, too." A week. A *month*. "But you're supposed to be visiting with your family, not spending all your time with me anyway."

"Josh and Savannah left for New York an hour ago, and Hugh and Dane took off late last night. I have plenty of time during the day with Rex and my father."

"They came all that way just for a short visit?"

"Family's important to all of us. We make it happen when we can. Now, let's talk about us. I'll pick you up here tomorrow evening."

"Are you asking me on a real date?" she teased.

His lips lifted in a wicked grin and he crushed her against him. "Not asking. You don't have a choice. Tomorrow evening is *mine*."

His mouth came coaxingly down over her smiling lips. When he intensified the kiss, she was thankful he was holding her up, because every second of their kisses dragged her further under his spell.

"Tomorrow," he said, and held her hand as he walked out the door.

His fingers slipped along the length of hers, and when they parted, she mourned their connection.

"Good night." He took a few steps toward the stairs and turned back. "One more kiss."

Elation filled her as his lips met hers. She had never craved kissing anyone, and every single one of Treat's kisses left her breathless.

When their lips parted, she whispered, "Night," missing him already as he headed for the steps again.

He glanced back.

"One more?" she asked hopefully, and then she was in his arms, pushing her hands into his hair, wanting so much more.

When they reluctantly separated, he said, "If I don't leave now, I won't leave at all." He touched his lips to her cheek, her chin, and then he cradled her face in his hands and said, "See you in my dreams, sweetness."

She watched him descend the stairs, listened until his footsteps were no longer discernible, and then she went inside and leaned her back against the door. She closed her eyes, reveling in his scent lingering on her clothing and skin. She pressed her hands to her thundering heart, completely and utterly drenched in happiness, and when she opened her eyes, she saw his image everywhere—there in her private world—and she hoped it never changed.

Chapter Eleven

THE NEXT MORNING Max was still high on Treat as she flew out her apartment door at seven—and ran smack into her new boyfriend's hard chest with an *oomph*.

"Whoa." Treat raised his arms, flashing his knee-weakening smile. "Sorry, sweetness. I thought I'd catch you before you left." He carried a to-go cup in each hand, along with a white bag from the bakery down the street.

"Sorry! I'm not used to big, burly guys standing in the hall-way."

He leaned down for a kiss, and she wound her arms around his neck, her lips lingering on his.

"I think I could get used to this." She ran her finger down the trail of buttons on his shirt. "You look quite handsome today."

"I have a hot breakfast date with a sexy festival organizer." He kissed her again and handed her a cup. "A little bird told me you loved French vanilla lattes."

"Which bird would that be?"

"Chaz. I called to see if you'd gone in early. I wanted to surprise you."

"Sneaky. I like that. You're very good at surprises, by the

way." She took a sip and closed her eyes, savoring the taste. "Mm-mm. Delicious." When she opened them, Treat's hungry gaze bored into her.

"The way you just looked?" He made a greedy, utterly *male* sound. "*That* was delicious."

She giggled and hugged him.

"Better be careful pressing your gorgeous body against me." He gave her a seductive look. "I've got several weeks of fantasizing about you built up inside me."

"Sorry," she whispered as she stepped back. She wrinkled her nose and said, "Not really."

He hauled her against him and said, "Me either," before taking her in a penetrating kiss that she felt all the way to her toes.

"I'm not going to be able to walk down the stairs if you keep kissing me like that."

He chuckled. "I know you're in a hurry, but I couldn't wait another minute to see you. Overnight was far too long."

She sighed, wishing she had more time.

"I'll walk you to your car." On the way down, he handed her the bakery bag. "I wasn't sure what you liked, so I brought you a few choices."

She peered into the bag, surveying the muffins and crois-sants. "These look amazing. Do you want some?"

"Yes." He winked and said, "But not what's in that bag."

"Oh boy," she said breathily. "I'm supposed to work all day with *that* look in my head?" She reached into the bag as her feet hit the pavement. "Hm. I notice there's nothing chocolate in here."

"I might have stacked the deck in my favor." He set his coffee on the roof of her car and took her keys to unlock her door.

"Ah, no substitutes for the real thing, huh?" Tingles of anticipation climbed up her chest. She'd dreamed about him all night. Dark, erotic dreams about his hands and mouth all over her and hers all over him. The kind of dreams that, if she were awake, would have made her entire body blush. She'd woken up hot and bothered, and now, as she thought about them again, she felt the tightening of arousal low in her belly.

"Look under the napkins."

She reached into the bag, and beneath the pastries and napkins she found a chocolate croissant. She held it up for him to take a bite. "A hidden crutch?"

"I'll never pressure you *or* leave you hanging. But where you're concerned, I can't help dreaming big."

TREAT PACED BY the windows in his father's home office later that afternoon while on a conference call, discussing the possible acquisition of a resort in Brewster, Massachusetts, that he'd had his eye on for several years. The Ocean Edge Resort and Golf Club was the largest luxury resort on the Cape and had been owned by the same family for more than twenty-five years. It was only a short drive from Treat's property in Wellfleet. He'd tried to acquire the resort on multiple occasions, but the family was hell bent on keeping it in their hands. Treat had it on good authority that the family would be shifting their focus to international properties in the next twelve months, making it the perfect time for him to get a foot in the door before they had a chance to go public. He'd spent the day completely immersed in logistics, legalities, and finances as he considered both the Ocean Edge Resort and the Thailand resort.

After dinner, he helped his father and Rex with the evening ranch chores, finding that he enjoyed getting his hands dirty again, but the evening still ticked by too slowly. It took all his willpower not to drive over to the fairgrounds just so he could see Max sooner.

Once his father turned in for the night and Rex took off for who knew where, Treat finally headed over to Max's apartment. She answered the door looking radiant. Her hair framed her beautiful face in lustrous waves. She wore a pair of dark jeans tucked into knee-high leather boots and a soft gray sweater. A long silver necklace with a heart charm hung between her breasts. On anyone else the simple outfit might look just that— *simple*. But Max had a gentle and overwhelming beauty. She could be wrapped in a burlap bag and make it look exquisite. Her smile climbed up her delicate features, bringing stars to her eyes as Treat reached for her hand, drawing her into his arms, and she went up on her toes, her smile widening as their mouths came together wordlessly, passionately.

Desperately.

When they parted, her cheeks were brighter, her lips glistening pink. He'd never seen Max wear lipstick, and he was glad. Not only did she have the most perfect lips, but it meant he could kiss her all he wanted. The longing in her eyes brought his mouth to hers again. His hands traveled up her back and into her hair. He loved her hair. It wasn't full of sticky product or overly fluffed. Her silky locks were as natural as she was, and in a world where women vamped themselves up like hurricanes, she was a summer breeze, and he wanted to disappear into her.

"Hi," she said breathlessly.

"Hello, beautiful." He took her hand and said, "I missed you today."

"I missed you, too. I'm not used to missing anyone."

"I'm taking that as a compliment."

Max grabbed her purse and they went down to his car. "Where are we going?"

"You'll see."

He held her hand on the drive to his father's house, and when he pulled into the circular driveway, he realized it had been a long time since he'd felt compelled to share the most private parts of himself with anyone. He parked and noticed Max squinting into the darkness in the direction of the house.

"Whose house is this?" Max asked.

"My father's." Her fingers tightened around his, and he said, "We're not going in. My father is sleeping." He kissed the back of her hand, and then he came around to help her out. "I thought I'd take you to meet Hope."

"Your father won't mind?" she asked as she stepped from the truck, looking a little nervous.

"Not at all. He'll like that Hope gets extra love tonight." He found Max's careful nature incredibly alluring. Probably because he was a careful man when it came to matters of the heart. He draped an arm over her shoulder and led her across the lawn toward the barn.

"It's gorgeous here. I can't imagine what it must have been like growing up with all this land."

"All this land means lots of chores every morning and night," he said as he pulled open the barn door and the scents of his youth surrounded them. "My father grew up helping breed Dutch Warmblood show jumpers, and he followed in his father's footsteps. When I was a kid, I would look out my bedroom window at the barn thinking about how my father's entire life had revolved around horses and barns. I love my family and I had a great childhood here, but ranch life wasn't what I wanted back then."

"Maybe that's because of losing your mom. You said you felt relief when you went away to college. Is it hard for you when you come home to visit?"

Hope craned her neck toward them, reaching for Treat as they came to her stall, her big brown eyes watching Max. "No, actually. Home is where I feel most centered. This is Hope, the horse my father gave my mother when she found out she was sick."

"Hi, Hope," Max said as if she were greeting a relative of his. Hope gently moved her head in Max's direction, and Max reached up to pet her. "Horses are the most honest creatures, aren't they?"

"I've never thought about them that way, but yes, I suppose so."

"I had a friend in college who grew up on a farm, and she said horses didn't trick each other like people did. That always stuck with me."

"I have a feeling my brother Rex will like you. He's the biggest horse aficionado in the family. He takes after my father in that way."

Hope rubbed her muzzle against Max's neck, and Max put her hand on the horse's cheek, holding her there for a moment.

"Looks like Hope is all for Team Max." He leaned against the stall, warmed by Max's easy affection.

"For what it's worth, I'm for Team Treat and Max," she said with a sweet smile.

He loved that she could be as playful as a girl or as serious as the intelligent woman he knew her to be. "Me too, sweetness."

"If Rex inherited your father's love of horses, in what way do you take after him?"

Treat crossed his legs at the ankle, thinking about the question. If he believed his father's thoughts about Hope, he'd say the tender look in Hope's eyes as they shifted to him were those of his mother, awaiting his answer. But he had enough emotions flowing through him when he was with Max. He didn't need to add to them.

"The easy answer is that we look alike, but I assume you want a real answer."

She moved in front of him. "It's been my experience that *real* is always better than *easy*."

He reached for her hand and planted his legs in a wide stance, guiding her between them.

"Don't think you'll distract me from answering with your wicked kisses." She slid her fingers into his belt hoops.

"Distract you?" He pulled her closer and kissed her neck. "Would I do that?"

She framed his face in her hands and said, "In a hot second. And it would work, so I'm holding your face right here where I can keep tabs on your mouth. No kisses until you answer."

He chuckled. "You drive a hard bargain, Max Armstrong. I like that about you."

Hope *neigh*ed, her big head bobbing up and down.

"Apparently, so does Hope. Okay, let's see. How am I like my father? You're asking how I'm like the man who I'm not sure anyone could live up to. I've admired him my whole life. He's the strongest man I know emotionally, and when it comes to standing by his beliefs. He's a shrewd businessman, a ruthless negotiator, and a kind and generous human being. I always thought if I could be half the man he is, I'd consider myself lucky."

"I'd say you surpassed your goal."

"Why, thank you, sweetheart. But we have our differences. He does business with country charm, while I lost that touch years ago. I'd like to think he taught me how to maintain focus on the human aspects of business deals while not losing my edge. But my father has his downfalls, too. If you cross our family, he doesn't let that go, as is evident by his long-term feud with his childhood best friend, Earl Johnson. But that's a story for another day, and thankfully, I didn't inherit that grudge-holding ability. If I had, Dane and I still wouldn't be on speaking terms."

Max studied his face for a long moment, her brow knitted, as if she was considering what he'd said. "I'm glad you didn't."

"Forgiveness is crucial for your spirit, don't you think? I'm thankful you don't hold grudges, or we wouldn't be here right now."

She lowered her gaze to his chest, her smile fading just enough for him to notice. He found her doing that a lot when she was thinking about things, looking anywhere but into his eyes. This time he didn't lift her chin, curious to see if she trusted him enough to share whatever it was she was mulling over.

She moved beside him against the stall, fidgeting with the hem of her sweater, and a pained expression settled over her face. "I'm not so sure I don't hold grudges."

His gut seized. He thought they'd moved beyond what happened in Nassau. "What are you saying?"

"That there's something I haven't told you, and I want to be completely honest with you. We got so close in Nassau, and even after just a few dates I think we both know that whatever this is between us, it's bigger than both of us. I want to keep seeing you, and…I want to see *more* of you. A *lot* more."

Her innuendo hit him right in the heart. "I want that, too."

"Then you need to know why I got so nervous the other night. I should have told you then, but I couldn't. I was too embarrassed. And the truth is, I was also scared about how strongly I feel for you."

"Max, it's overwhelming for me, too."

She breathed a sigh of relief. "I'm so glad I didn't misread that." She looked around the barn and said, "Can we sit here? Is that okay?"

"Would you rather go for a walk?"

She shook her head. "No. I feel safe here."

She glanced up at Hope, and Treat swore Hope's big brown eyes were saying, *Sit down. Hold her. She needs you.* They settled onto the floor, their backs against the rough wood, and Treat pulled her against his side, wanting her to feel safe. He watched her struggling to climb out from the shadow of whatever was haunting her, and he ached to fix whatever it was.

Max inhaled a shaky breath and stared at her hands in her lap as she spoke. "When I was a senior in college, I dated this guy. Ryan. He was smart and funny, the kind of guy everyone loves. Things were fine for a long time, and we eventually moved in together. But as we got closer to graduation, he changed. I've never understood what caused him to change, but he did. He became verbally abusive and withdrawn."

Treat's protective juices were flowing, and he did his best to rein them in. "Go on," he said. *If he hurt you, I'll kill him.*

"It became a way of life on and off for several weeks. I'm not proud of the fact that I took it. In all honesty, I was weak." She met his gaze. "You look like you're ready to explode. Maybe I shouldn't say anything else."

"No. Continue, please." The thought of someone being abusive to Max pushed every button in his body. The anger coursing through him was stronger than any fury he'd ever felt, but for her sake, he fought to tether the rage. Max needed him to hear this. She trusted him, and going off about the guy would only scare her.

"My parents are great," she said softly. "But my mother and I have never really talked about relationships. We lost my grandmother about ten years ago, but before she passed away, she told me that the secret to a lasting relationship was to always speak my mind. I should have listened, but I think watching my parents for so long had already convinced me that I shouldn't complain or try to change things."

Her brow furrowed, and Treat wondered if she was thinking about her grandmother, or like him, was thinking about how not speaking her mind was the wrong tactic to take in any aspect of life.

"But now," she said, "I wonder if my grandmother told me that *because* of my parents' relationship. My mother is very submissive. Not that my father is abusive or anything like that. He's a good, quiet, kind man. But my mom has never really spoken her mind about anything as far back as I can remember."

Treat pulled her closer, wanting to protect her from the past he couldn't control. He thought about Savannah. If any man had ever mistreated her, Treat and his brothers would have broken down the door and wrung his neck. Max didn't have anyone to protect her.

"Anyway, he'd grabbed my arm and—Treat, you're holding

me too tight."

He unclenched his jaw and eased his grip. "I'm sorry, Max. I don't want to scare you, but I'd like to kill this lowlife."

"There's more, but I'll stop—"

"No, please don't. I'm not going to track him down like an animal and hurt him. But I'd be lying if I told you I wasn't mad enough to *want* to do those things."

She climbed onto his lap, sitting sideways, and put an arm around his neck. Their closeness brought his anger down a notch. *She's here. She's safe.*

"This next part is worse," she said. "You're not going to like it."

"Is that why you're on my lap? To keep me from getting up, tracking him down, and beating the tar out of him?"

She didn't manage a smile, though she tried. "No. It's because I need to be here while I tell you."

"Baby, you're safe with me. I'll never hurt you again, and I'll sure as heck never let anyone else hurt you."

"I know. That's why I want you to hear this sooner rather than later." She took a deep breath and blew it out slowly. "What led up to him grabbing me was that he asked me to try a sex toy with him."

She looked away, and Treat's heart tore.

"It's okay, sweetness. I'm not going to judge you."

"I was young," she said in a shaky voice, "and I had the guy everyone wanted, so I thought…" She shrugged. "It can't be that bad. Okay, I'll try."

He didn't want to hear what that lowlife had done to her, but he wanted Max to heal from all the hurts that plagued her, so he clenched his jaw and gave her his full attention.

She closed her eyes and spoke in a flat, even tone. "We were in the bedroom, and he had undressed me, but he still had his pants on."

Treat felt her trembling. "I'm here, and I'm not going anywhere. You don't have to continue if you don't want to, Max."

"I want to." She opened her eyes and looked into his. "He used *it*, and at first it wasn't bad. He was being gentle. And then I don't know what happened. His eyes changed, almost like he became a different person."

A tear slipped down her cheek, shredding his heart to pieces. He wiped her tears with the pad of his thumb, struggling to keep his anger in check.

Max continued speaking, this time with an icy tone. "He was suddenly shoving it into me so hard and saying horrible, nasty things. Cursing at me, calling me names, and somehow...*somehow* I was able to crawl away from him and grab my clothes. I ran for the door, and that's when he grabbed my arm." Tears streamed down her cheeks.

"Shh. It's okay," he said, holding her tighter. "You don't have to go any further. I get it, sweetheart." He rubbed her back, silently vowing to track the guy down and rip him to shreds.

"I want you to know everything." She wiped her eyes. "He drank a lot of beer and passed out in the bedroom. I remember crying so hard, and later that night, my mom called. I didn't even have to say anything. I *couldn't* say anything. She must have known from my sobs that something horrific had happened. That was the one and only time she ever gave me relationship advice, and it changed my life. She said, 'Get out.'"

Thank goodness. "So you left?"

She swiped at her tears, but they continued to fall. "I did. I packed my car and drove all the way to Colorado and I never looked back. But, honestly, I think I still hold a grudge against him for the fear and insecurities he sparked in me."

"That's understandable," he reassured her. "He should be punished for what he did. Did you report him to the police?"

"No, and, Treat, please don't. I didn't tell you so you could take vengeance for me. I told you because I want to try to move past this with you. I can't do that if you get tied up in some sort of vengeful mission."

His entire body pulsed with rage, but more important than the urge to hammer the life out of the guy was the desire—the visceral *need*—to help Max heal. He pulled her close again, speaking through gritted teeth, and said, "I won't, but that doesn't mean I don't want to with every fiber of my being."

He held her while she cried, remembering the way Max had reached for him the first night they were together. He now understood how much courage it must have taken for her to even try to open up to him in such an intimate way. It was easy to see how the look he'd given her in Nassau would translate in her mind as a precursor to hidden aggression, and that clarity nearly shattered him.

Chapter Twelve

ON THE DRIVE back to her apartment, Max gazed out the window into the darkness, clutching Treat's hand and feeling like a great weight had been lifted from her shoulders. She wasn't rid of her ghosts, because she had no doubt that she still harbored a grudge, but at least now Treat knew the truth. Even though it was late and they were both tired, they'd gotten so close she didn't want their night to end. She wanted to be in his safe, loving arms.

When they arrived at her apartment she could see by the set of his jaw and the fierceness of his eyes that he was still stewing over her confession.

As he unlocked her apartment door, she grasped for something to break the tension and said, "Thank you for sharing Hope with me." He nodded absently, and she knew he was still mired in darkness. "I shouldn't have told you what happened. I'm sorry."

He pulled her into his arms, embracing her so tightly it was hard to breathe. "That's not it, baby. I just want to be with you. I don't want to leave you tonight."

"Then don't."

Hope and worry brimmed in his eyes just like the nervousness whipping around inside her, but she had to follow her heart.

She took his hand and led him inside, walking toward the bedroom. "Stay with me."

He drew her into his arms again. His lips were warm and loving on hers, and she drank in the sweetness of his kiss.

"I didn't say that so we could fool around," he said tenderly. "I just want to be with you, to hold you and know that you're okay after reliving those memories. I can wait as long as you need to before doing anything more than kissing you."

"I know, but maybe I can't," she said honestly. "I trust you, Treat. That's why I felt safe telling you my secret."

"You can always trust me, baby."

He cupped her cheek, and she leaned into his palm, reveling in his touch. She knew he could feel her trembling, but she didn't want him to hold back.

"I'm nervous," she admitted. "But please don't back off. Just be patient with me. I've only been with two other men. The man I just told you about and one other during my senior year of high school. I thought I loved him and that we'd be together forever, but you know how that goes. What do you know at eighteen? We went to separate colleges, he cheated on me, which broke my heart, and I got the inevitable Dear Jane letter a month later."

"I wish I'd known you then. I'd have stayed with you forever."

The honesty in his eyes made her heart beat even faster. "No, you wouldn't have. As I told you, I was weak. Not the strong, self-sufficient person I am now."

"You weren't weak, baby. You were inexperienced and thrust into a situation you didn't expect. But you got out of it and made an incredible life for yourself. You took care of *you*, Max, and that makes you supremely strong. But no matter what you might have been like back then, I know I would have been attracted to you. It's your very essence that draws me in, your strength and your softness. If we were together back then, I would have *wanted* to hear your thoughts and dreams, your insights and inspirations, and of course your fears and worries, so I could help alleviate them. I would have listened to your criticisms of me and tried to better myself to become the man you needed me to be. That's how we grow as people and in relationships. We would have helped each other become the best we could be, and now we've got a chance to do just that."

"Oh, Treat." Max tried to speak past the emotions clogging her throat. "Now I wish we would have known each other back then."

He brushed his lips over hers and said, "I didn't think I'd ever feel as strongly about anyone as I do about my own family, but the magnitude of what I feel for you puts those feelings to shame. Can you feel it, the energy between us?"

"Yes. I knew it in Nassau. All the defenses I'd worked so hard to erect came crumbling down, and I felt that softer side of me that I had hidden away reemerging. I *wanted* you to take care of me—and that, more than anything, scared me." She'd never met anyone so loving and patient or so strong and sure of himself. "It was overwhelming, which was why I didn't spend that first night with you when you invited me back to your room. I mean, how could I feel so much after a few romantic hours?"

"I don't have the answers, but I felt the exact same way. I wanted to be with you, to take care of you, yes, but also to *experience* you. To talk and spend time together, get to know you, and learn about what makes you tick. That's why I was such a jerk when I saw you with Justin. I thought after our night together that connection was mutual. I made a stupid assumption about the two of you, and it threw me right back to the situation with Mary Jane and my brother Dane."

"We've both been betrayed," she said.

"And now we'll help each other heal."

She clung to his arms as he held her and exposed the very heart of her. "I might get scared."

"I'll make you feel safe."

"I'm not easy, Treat. My defenses go up when my feathers are ruffled, I'm stubborn, and I can be savagely strong when I need to be, but like earlier today, sometimes it's easier to hide than to face the truth."

"I admire your strength and your stubbornness, and as you've seen, when you hide, I'll come find you."

Her heart opened further with each of his responses. "I need to know that if that happens, if I get scared and my walls go up, you'll be patient with me and help me through it. Don't let me turn my back on us out of fear of my past."

"I'll love you through anything, Max."

Love? Her heart soared. He gazed into her eyes with so many emotions in his it made her even dizzier than his promise.

"I will love you through the good and the bad." He kissed her softly. "The fights and the..." His gaze darted to her bed, then back to her, soft and alluring, making her heart sprint in her chest. "The frisky nights." He took her in a passionate, bone-melting kiss. "I want you to be strong and tell me I'm full of crap. I want you to call me on anything I do that's hurtful or uncalled for. Max, I was brought up by a man's man who was also the most gentlemanly person I know. I don't want to be any less than he is, and you deserve everything I have to give."

"Love me, Treat. Love me with your whole heart."

She went up on her toes, and he met her halfway in a kiss full of promises, of hopes and dreams, and of soothing, unconditional love.

He ran the back of his hand down her cheek. "I want every piece of you, but after all we've gone through, are you sure? Do you want to sleep on it and see if you still feel the same tomorrow?"

"No," she said, and began unbuttoning his shirt. "I want you to love me into tomorrow."

Moonlight basked them in a romantic glow as he carefully undressed her, pressing tender kisses to each body part as it was revealed. She was shaking by the time her panties slid to the floor, but it wasn't from fear or old ghosts pushing their way in. She was adrift in a sea of emotions as he touched and loved her. Lost in his exquisite beauty as he stripped off his own clothes and came down over her. She expected his strength to overpower her, his muscles to squeeze her too tight. Instead, his grasp was gentle, his weight safe and enticing, and when he cradled her in his loving arms and their bodies became one, her nerves fell away.

"I'm going to love you far longer than tomorrow, Max. I'm going to love you forever."

Chapter Thirteen

TREAT LIVED UP to his promises, loving Max well past tomorrow. A week and a half later they were still falling into each other's arms at night, and Max woke up every morning in a bubble of surreal happiness. Now that the festival was over and Max was working normal hours, they had more time together. Tonight they were meandering through the quaint village of Allure, where ornate iron fences and old-fashioned streetlights lined narrow brick-paved roads and brick and stone town houses served as storefronts and restaurants.

"A shop made just for you," Treat said as they entered Divine Intervention, a chocolate shop.

Bells chimed above the door and a woman's voice sailed through from a room in the back of the store. "Be right out! Please don't rob me. My hands are a mess and I just cleaned the front door. I'd hate to get it dirty again."

"So much for those plans," Treat replied loudly.

"I appreciate y'all holding off," the woman called out. "At least until I get my hands washed."

Treat and Max looked around the shop. Shelves of cute wooden blocks with sayings about chocolate on them were interspersed with bags of candies and other goodies. On the wall behind the display cases hung red sweatshirts with DIVINE INTERVENTION printed in brown swirly letters.

Treat put a hand on Max's back and said, "Tell me the truth. Why did you choose to come to Colorado and start your life here? Was it because of this store?"

"Believe it or not, I've never been in this store."

"Unbelievable," he teased, and pressed his lips to hers. "Why, then?"

"I had interned for a festival throughout college, and I always wanted to attend Chaz's festival, but I was in school and I didn't have a lot of money." Max peered into the display cases at a variety of chocolate cakes and candies. "I had corresponded with Chaz a few times and he'd left an open door for me to apply for a position."

She glanced up and caught Treat watching her intently. That was just one of the things she adored about him. He didn't give lip service. *Although he is very talented at servicing me with those lips.* When he asked a question, he was sincerely interested in hearing her answers.

"I had always admired pictures of the Village, and I had read all about the town keeping holiday lights up in the trees and the shops year-round. It seemed like such a peaceful place, where ugliness couldn't survive. I know that sounds silly, but when I got into my car that night, I drove straight here. I never contemplated going anywhere else. Not even back home."

Treat stepped closer, drawing her into his arms, which had become her favorite place. "You said you believe fate brought you here. I was never a big believer in fate, because of losing my mother. But you've changed that, Max. You've changed everything."

Before she could respond, a pretty blonde breezed into the

room from the back of the store carrying a tray of chocolate. Despite the cold weather, she wore cutoffs, a shirt that had SURRENDER TO DIVINE INTERVENTION printed across the chest, and a pair of knee-high fuzzy black boots. Her hair was pinned up in a messy bun, and she had the biggest blue eyes Max had ever seen.

"Hello there, *lovers!*" Her impossibly wide smile grew even bigger. "Carly Dylan at your service." She opened the back of a display and slid the tray in. "Sweet of you not to rob me," she said as she rose again, her gaze moving between them. "Then again, by the way this man's looking at you, honey, I doubt he'd put those big ol' hands anywhere else!"

"You've got that right," Treat said, and pressed his lips to Max's. "My girlfriend has a thing for chocolate. What do you recommend?"

"Your girlfriend has a thing for crazy-tall men. Wow, they don't make them like you in Pleasant Hill, that's for sure. You are one big, handsome man. I recommend chocolate syrup poured on you from head to toe."

"Excuse me," Max said with a laugh. "He's a big, handsome, *taken* man."

Carly waved her hand dismissively. "Honey, I have no interest in stealing anyone's man, but look at his hold on you. He's not going anywhere. Besides, I gave my heart away in seventh grade. Ain't no man gonna claim it but one, and he's too busy to realize what he's missin'."

"Pleasant Hill, Maryland?" Treat asked.

Carly busied herself straightening up the counter. "The one and only."

"I've got relatives there," Treat said. "It's a nice small town."

"A nice town, great people, and one fewer brokenhearted

girl." Carly set her hands on her hips and said, "I wish I could bottle up the energy thrumming off you two and put it into chocolate. I'd make a fortune with that love potion. So, tell me. What's your secret?"

Treat set his loving eyes on Max and said, "First you need to have an incredible evening together followed by a big misunderstanding. Then, just when you're trying to forget each other, if you're lucky, fate will step in."

Oh, this man!

"Well, y'all are inspiration, and I've got just the thing for you. Why don't you two check out the shop while I put it together."

Treat took Max's hand and they looked over the goodies. A few minutes later Carly handed Treat a bag. When he reached for his wallet, she said, "Don't even think about it. You can name one of your children after me and give them a fabulous life."

"We're not even engaged," Max said, and shot a look at Treat, who was grinning like a lovesick fool. Her heart tumbled inside her chest.

"Thank you," Treat said with a nod. "We'll do that."

As they headed outside, they peered into the bag and found a big jar of chocolate syrup, several chocolate hearts, and a handwritten note that said, *You two make me want to head back to Pleasant Hill and find the piece of myself I left there. Thanks! Carly Dylan.*

THEY HAD DINNER at a café and enjoyed a few chocolates for dessert as they walked through the town square. A crowd had gathered by the outdoor pavilion, where a group of young guys were playing guitars and singing. Treat swept Max into his arms and began dancing.

Max's gaze skittered around them, and he knew she was embarrassed.

"I don't care that no one else is dancing," he said. "I want you in my arms." He'd received a message during dinner about negotiations for the Ocean Edge property, and he'd been trying to find the right time to share the news of his impending trip with Max.

She smiled up at him, falling into sync as they danced. "And I want to be in them."

"How about being in my arms in Wellfleet?"

"As in, *Massachusetts*?" Her eyes widened.

"I have to go to the Cape for a few days to handle negotiations for a property I'm interested in acquiring. I'd like you to come with me."

"Oh! That sounds amazing. But won't you have to work?" she asked, her embarrassment forgotten.

"Yes, but my team has been preparing for this and negotiations should only take a few hours. We can enjoy a few days at my bungalow and make up for the time we lost in Nassau."

"When are you going?"

They continued dancing even after the song ended. "Sometime tomorrow. I'm waiting for confirmation."

"Tomorrow? I'd love to go, but I can't just take off on a Thursday and leave Chaz hanging. As much as I'd like to go, I'm afraid I can't do that to him, no matter how wonderful it sounds."

"Then come up Friday night and spend the weekend with me," he suggested. "I'll be done working by then, and we can just enjoy our time together. I'll make all the arrangements and have a car pick you up at your place after work."

Her eyes brightened. "Really? That sounds wonderful."

"Almost as wonderful as you."

She laughed. "That might be the corniest line I've ever heard, but coming out of your mouth it sounded…"

"Corny," they said in unison.

"I'll give you corny." Treat captured her mouth in a plundering kiss. He wanted to give Max everything, to make all her dreams come true, and he couldn't wait to share his favorite place on earth with her.

Chapter Fourteen

CHAZ WAS ALREADY at the office when Max arrived Thursday morning. He looked up from the spreadsheets he was studying, hints of fatigue shining in the dark circles beneath his eyes. "Hard night?"

"I could say the same to you." Max sat across from him at the table and began sifting through the reports. "Perfect night," she said without looking up, although it would have been more perfect if Treat had stayed overnight. But he'd left to prepare for his trip. She knew it was silly to miss someone so much after only a handful of hours, but she couldn't deny the ache inside her.

"Good to hear." They worked in silence for a few minutes, and then Chaz said, "You're not usually this quiet. You sure everything's okay?"

"Yup. I'm just concentrating." *Trying to figure out how to do forty-eight hours' worth of work in three or four hours.* She was excited about the prospect of going away with Treat, and on the way to work she'd toyed with the idea of trying to leave with him today. Though she had no idea what time he was actually leaving.

They worked through reports, discussing next year's festival strategies, and prioritizing sponsors. Afterward, Max got started on her calls, but for the first time since she'd begun working for Chaz, her heart wasn't in it. She forced herself to focus and made it through only a few before she caught Chaz watching her with an odd expression.

"What?" she asked.

"You tell me. What's going on? Did Treat do something? Because if he did, I'll take care of it."

Max laughed. "You really are like the big brother I never had. As much as I appreciate your offer, he did nothing other than ask me to go away with him. I'm sorry if I'm a little sidetracked. You know I love my work, but I…" *Love Treat more.*

The realization momentarily stunned her into silence.

Chaz set the papers down. "Are you okay?"

"Mm-hm," she said distractedly.

"You look like you're trying to figure out how to tell me something but are not sure if you should. You haven't looked like this since the day Treat first showed up. It's nice to see that you're as normal as the rest of us."

"Is that supposed to be a compliment?" she asked.

"Yeah, actually, it is. You're always so on top of things. It's nice to know you have a less perfect side to you."

She arched a brow. "That doesn't sound complimentary. I'm a really good work wife. Just ask your…*wife* wife."

"I don't have to. I know how great a work wife you are. Are you going to share the reason behind your being *off*, or do I have to guess?"

"I'm thinking." She looked down at her papers, and after a couple minutes of feeling the weight of his stare, she said, "Stop it."

"What?"

"Looking at me like a big brother who refuses to leave me alone until I give you all the juicy details."

Chaz laughed. "Is that what I look like?"

She glanced up and said, "It's either that, or I've grown a third eye in the middle of my head."

"Let's go with the juicy details thing."

She didn't want to talk about Treat asking her to go away with him, because the more she thought about it, the more she wanted to leave.

"Let's go with the third eye thing." She buried her nose back in the spreadsheets.

"Max."

"Chaz," she said without raising her eyes.

"You're talking in circles. Just tell me this. Are you going to fall in love, get married, and move away to a tropical island?"

Max sat back and pushed her glasses up on her nose. "Is that what the stare is for? You're wondering who will do your sponsor coordination if I'm whisked away under the guise of love?"

"Embarrassingly, no, because I know that no matter where you live, I can convince you to still do the coordination and show up for the festival. I just want to know if I'm going to lose my work wife and, more importantly, my friend."

Max looked back down at the spreadsheets, thinking about how much that meant to her. "You could never lose me, Chaz. But no one is running off and getting married."

A few minutes later, she couldn't hold back and said, "But I want to run off. Treat invited me to Wellfleet with him, but I know we have all this work to do and he's leaving today, so I told him—"

Chaz pushed to his feet and grabbed her purse. He pulled her to her feet, shoved her bag into her hands, and pointed to the door. "Go. *Now*. You work your butt off for me. A few days isn't going to make or break these deals."

"But this is our busy—"

He pushed her out the door and said, "Max, I love you like my own family, which is why I want you to be happy. Now get the hell out of here and don't come back until next week. Got it?"

She threw her arms around his neck and hugged him. "Thank you! I'm sorry! I'll make up the time, but thank you!"

In the car, she tried to call Treat, but her call went to voicemail. Too excited to wait, she headed out of Allure and toward his father's ranch.

SHOWING UP AT Treat's father's house had seemed like such a good idea when she'd first thought of it, but the sight of the sprawling brick home and several expensive cars around an enormous circular driveway had her second-guessing her plan. She parked behind a black Mercedes SLS and looked down at her clothes. *Sneakers?* What was she thinking? She should have gone home to change her clothes first, or just waited for Treat to call her back.

She nearly jumped out of her skin when someone banged on her window and was relieved, and confused, to see Savannah's smiling face. She'd thought Treat had told her Savannah had gone back to New York.

"Max! Hi!" Savannah said as Max stepped from her car.

"Hi, Savannah. How are you?"

Three of the most gorgeous men she'd ever seen were heading in her direction, each one more striking than the next. Behind them followed an older version of Treat, who she assumed was his father. She felt like she'd walked into a modeling agency or *GQ* headquarters. She caught a glimpse of her reflection in the car window and quickly took her hair out of her ponytail and shook it free. Then she scanned the grounds for Treat. Her gaze fell on the barn, and her heart squeezed with the memory of the night she'd opened up completely to him.

"What are you doing here?" Savannah asked. Before Max could answer, Savannah said to the others, "This is Max. *Treat's* Max."

One of the men stepped forward and said, "Hi. I'm Dane."

Dane? The one who slept with Treat's girlfriend? Max already didn't care for him, though he had a kind face and an easy nature.

"We're Treat's brothers," Dane said, pointing to each of the others. "This is Rex and Hugh. Too bad Josh isn't here. You could have met the whole crew."

Each of the men stepped forward and shook her hand with a ready smile that lit up their handsome faces. She'd thought Treat was big, but Rex was enormous, rivaling a professional bodybuilder. He wore a dark cowboy hat, and his thick black hair brushed his collar. He had guarded eyes and an edge about him that the others didn't seem to. Hugh reminded her of Patrick Dempsey, with his cocky smile and amused eyes. Even with their good looks and fine physiques, none of them struck the same fluttery chord in her heart as Treat had. Where was he?

"I'm sorry," Max said. "I didn't realize everyone was in town."

"We just got in today," Hugh said. "I'm between races and

Dane missed me."

Dane scoffed.

"It's just coincidental," Savannah explained. "I'm getting together with my cousins from Trusty this weekend, and Dane had a glitch in his schedule."

The older man stepped forward and said, "Max, it's a pleasure to meet you, darlin'. I'm Hal, Treat's father. Welcome to the Braden ranch." He drew her into a warm embrace.

"Oh, um…" She put her arms around him, feeling awkward and strangely comforted at the same time.

"We were just going to barbecue and have an early lunch. I hope you'll join us," Hal said as he put his arm around Max, guiding her toward the backyard before she could say a word. She didn't miss the coy smiles and nods from the others as she was shuttled away.

"Thank you, sir. I actually—"

"*Hal.* There are no *sirs* on the Braden ranch unless you're here to piss one of us off." Hal smiled and continued walking toward the backyard, as if Max were an invited guest.

"Thank you. Hal, I actually came to see Treat. Is he here?" She caught Dane sneaking glances in her direction as he and Hugh made their way to the barbecue pit.

"Treat was called away," Hal said.

"Called away?" she asked, wondering if he'd left for the Cape already or was simply attending to something else. "Do you know when he'll be back?"

Hal was already on his way to Rex's side. He slung an arm around his son's shoulder in an easy, comfortable fashion and said something Max couldn't hear. Savannah came out of the house carrying a plate and took Max's hand, dragging her to the table, while chatting about the after-party. Hugh headed back inside and reappeared a minute later with a beer in his hand.

"Did you get one for our guest?" Savannah asked with a nip of irritation.

"No, really—" Max interrupted, but Hugh was already on his way back inside.

He came back with an ice-cold beer. "Here you are, Max."

"Thank you, but I really shouldn't stay," she said.

"Nonsense. You don't have to eat if you're not hungry," Hal said just as her stomach growled. "But then again…"

Why do I keep forgetting to eat?

The family moved so quickly that Max was a little over-whelmed, which seemed to happen a lot around the Braden men. She should be helping, organizing, doing something other than standing around with her jaw hanging open. Instead she was letting them guide her from one place to the next. She was itching to get out of there in case Treat had already gone to the Cape, but before she had a chance to make her feet and mind work in unison, she had a plate full of food in front of her and was laughing at a joke Dane had made.

"How did you and Treat meet?" Hugh asked.

"I can answer that," Dane said.

Savannah nudged him. "Let her speak."

Hugh reached across the table in front of Max for the ketchup, and Savannah narrowed her eyes at him. After a moment of confusion, Hugh took the hint and said, "Excuse me," as he withdrew his arm from in front of Max.

"That's okay," Max said, noting how Savannah had jumped in just as a mother might have. It struck her how different each of Treat's brothers were. Treat had impeccable manners, and he'd never sneak glances at anyone—at least she couldn't imagine him doing so. When they'd met, he'd kept a steady gaze locked on her, like he had nothing to hide, and that openness hadn't changed.

"How do you know Treat?" Hugh asked again.

She'd been surveying them so intently, she'd forgotten he'd asked. "Oh, sorry. We met at a friend's wedding."

"Cousin Blake's wedding. Remember? You were all too busy to attend." Dane glared at Hugh.

"What? I had an award ceremony." Hugh's eyebrows drew together, as if he didn't understand what the issue was.

"Don't you always?" Dane said. He was as quippy as Hugh was clueless to what Max was sure his siblings saw as his self-centeredness.

"Oh, please. You ran off to some shark-infested area and missed it, too," Rex said, and shoved a hunk of steak into his mouth.

"At least I made an appearance first, which is more than I can say for any of you," Dane said with a smirk.

Max enjoyed their banter, so different from her own family's silent meals. She couldn't help but wonder what it must be like to have that many siblings—that many people who would be there for her.

"We were supporting Hugh," Savannah explained.

"Right, for his five minutes of fame that he gets every couple of months. How long has it been since you've seen Blake?" Dane asked.

"For your information, I spoke to Blake and Danica and they completely understood. Forgiveness is a beautiful thing," Savannah said with a pointed expression. "Of all people, Dane, I'd think you'd understand that. It's not like they'll never talk to us again, or hold a grudge."

Silence settled around them, and Max swore tension rose

like a fog as each of Treat's siblings visibly made a concerted effort not to look at Hal, except Rex, who was glowering at him. It was then she remembered what Treat had said about his father holding a grudge. She pushed the food around on her plate with her fork, trying not to look like she wanted to flee. Her mind traveled back to her conversation with Treat about what had happened to her with Ryan, and the pain that accompanied those thoughts returned. Was forgiveness a beautiful thing? She wasn't sure she could ever forgive Ryan for what he'd done to her. She'd run away and had never given him a chance to apologize. Not that she wanted an apology.

He doesn't deserve the right to clear his mind.

But do I?

"You know, Blake spent a lot of time with us when we were younger, and you get married only once," Dane said, bringing Max's mind back to the moment.

She had a feeling he was trying to ease the mounting tension.

"As far as I can tell, none of my brothers are walking down the aisle anytime soon," Savannah said as she buttered a piece of bread.

"Max, have you ever been married?" Hugh asked.

She was about to take a drink and stopped midair.

"Hugh." All it took was one word and a harsh glare from Hal for everyone at the table to understand that that line of questioning was off-limits—including Max.

The talk quickly turned to the lighter topics. They asked Max about her job and raved about the festival. Other than the one blip about forgiveness, the meal was comfortable and, Max had to admit, aside from the time she spent with Treat, it was more fun than anything she'd done in a very long time. She tried to picture what it might be like to be there with Treat. How much ribbing would he dole out? What kind of teasing would they thrust upon him? How would he act around her? Would he be openly affectionate, as he usually was with her, or would he be more reserved around his family?

She needed to find him before she got sucked into hours of entertainment watching his siblings taunt each other. "Thank you for the lovely meal, but I'm afraid I really need to go."

The entire family walked her to her car. *Do they do everything together?*

"Do you know if Treat has left town yet, or was he called away locally?" Max asked.

"Yes, darlin'," Hal answered. "He was planning on leaving later, but he received a call this morning and ran out in a hurry."

"Okay. Thank you again for the meal." Max reached for her car door as Hal reached for her, drawing her into his arms again and holding her longer than most friends might. He held her like a father might hold his daughter. Sad about missing Treat, Max struggled to suppress the emotions bubbling up inside her over his warm and welcoming family.

"This was fun," Savannah said. "You should come by with Treat sometime. He'll be upset that he missed you."

In the next breath she was being crushed in Savannah's embrace. After being passed from brother to brother for goodbye hugs, Max finally climbed into her car and drove away. When she was out of eyeshot, she pulled over to the side of the road to check her messages. Her heart leapt at the sound of Treat's voice. *Hi, sweetness. I had to head out earlier than planned and was slammed with calls from the second I left. I'm stuck in meetings all day, but will try to call you tonight. Can't wait to see you tomorrow night.*

With a smile on her face, she made a split-second decision to surprise him. She left a quick message—*Can't wait to see you, too! Good luck with your meetings*—and called the travel agent she used for the festival. When it came to travel, Selena Shirlington could make miracles happen, which was exactly what Max needed.

Chapter Fifteen

TREAT DROVE DOWN the narrow road leading to his bungalow overlooking the bay early Thursday evening. He'd forgotten the Oyster Festival was this weekend, which meant driving anywhere on the Cape took hours rather than minutes. He rounded the last bend carefully, avoiding the enormous rosebush that he continually forgot to ask the gardener to trim back. *Knock Out roses. Max's favorite flowers.* He'd listened to Max's voicemail message twice after his last meeting, missing her so much he debated flying home tonight, but he was excited to show her around Wellfleet over the weekend. He'd called her back, but the call had gone to voicemail and he'd had to leave a message.

The bungalow came into view and he parked on the seashell driveway. He hadn't had time to drop off his bags before his first meeting, though he'd called Smitty, the caretaker who watched over the house. Smitty had known Treat's mother, and he'd always had an affinity for Treat. He knew the bungalow would be stocked with enough groceries for the weekend, there would be wood by the fireplace, the windows would be open to air the place out, and the beds would have freshly washed linens.

Inhaling the salty sea air, he retrieved his bags and headed up the front steps. The Cape had a rejuvenating effect on him, like coming up for air after being underwater, and tonight was no different. The only thing that would make it better was if Max were with him to share in what had been one of his mother's favorite places. They'd rented this bungalow on several occasions when he was young, before his mother had become too sick to travel. As soon as it had gone on the market, Treat had purchased it.

He climbed the front steps, taking in the weathered cedar shingles. He could almost hear his mother's voice. *Oh, Treaty, look! The shingles have weathered. Don't you just love the graying and the texture of them?* She'd loved anything where each of the pieces that held it together were different from the rest.

Inside, he set his luggage by the door and dropped his keys in the pottery bowl on the kitchen table. The curtains whipped around the open casement windows. He stood in the breeze and stared out over the bay. Goose bumps formed on his arms, and he found the thick, gray cable-knit sweater his mother had knitted for his father lying on the arm of the sofa table. *Good old Smitty.* He slipped it on, and a strange feeling came over him, as if he were not alone. He looked around the cozy space, and if he didn't know better, he'd have thought his mother were right there with him, pleased that he was wearing that sweater. A strand of guilt tugged at his heart for dismissing his father's beliefs so easily.

He wondered what Max was up to and hoped she was out for a girls' night with Kaylie and their friends.

A knock sounded at the door, and he went to answer it, wondering if Smitty was checking on him. His childhood friend, Charley "Chuck" Holtz, stood before him.

More gray than brown up top and more belly than muscle

in the middle, Chuck beamed with the same vibrancy he'd always possessed. "TB!"

"Chuck, how are you?" Treat waved him in, and they greeted each other with a manly hug.

"Smitty told me he opened the old place up for you. I was on my way into town and figured I'd stop by. Haven't seen you in a while. What brings you out?" Chuck had a thick New England accent.

"Just closing negotiations on some property." He and Max had reason to celebrate this weekend. After hours of negotiations, the owners of the Ocean Edge Resort had agreed to his terms. He wanted to tell Max before he shared the news with anyone else.

"Must be nice. Man, I'd kill to get my hands on more property up here, but it's too pricey for my blood. I'm meeting Bonnie at the Pearl for dinner. Why don't you join us? You won't get reservations anywhere else this weekend, and eating alone is no fun. We'll surprise her. She tells everyone she knows about you. You know how that goes. Around here you're a big deal, a big fish in a small pond." He winked.

The last thing Treat wanted to deal with was to be shown off like a trophy, but he adored Bonnie, and he knew she was just proud of his accomplishments. "Why not."

"Great. Let's go." Chuck headed for the door.

"Now?" Treat looked down at his suit. He desperately needed a shower. He touched his chin. *And a shave.*

"You're right. Go get out of that monkey suit and put on some comfy clothes."

"All right, then. Just give me a few minutes to wash up and change." He picked up his bags and said, "I'll meet you there."

"Nah, I'll wait."

On the way upstairs, Treat said, "Make yourself at home." He heard the refrigerator open and the clink of beer bottles. *Good old Smitty.*

"I already am," Chuck called up.

MAX STARED AT her phone, wishing it had a direct line to Treat. She'd Googled his name, hoping to find the street where his house was located so she could surprise him, but of course he was too private to have that information listed. His phone number was restricted, for heaven's sake. Where the heck was fate when she needed it? At least she'd gotten a direct flight to Boston, and the rental car agent had been efficient. She followed the GPS toward Wellfleet. It was a straight shot up the Mid-Cape Highway, which ended at a rotary in Orleans. With less than twelve miles to go, she'd be in Wellfleet in no time.

Traffic moved at a snail's pace around the rotary, and when she pulled onto the main road, it came to a grinding halt.

Twenty minutes later, she was still stuck in traffic. She'd entered Eastham, a quaint little town with cottages and a few shops off the main drag. Treat had said it was the off season, but as she inched down the narrow highway, she noticed that each of the cottage rental communities had No Vacancy signs out front. She was in desperate need of a bathroom, and she had absolutely no idea where Treat's house was. Finally, after sitting in traffic for what felt like forever, she pulled into the parking lot of a Four Points Sheraton.

The expansive lobby was packed with people milling around the registration desk. She squeezed between a large man and a petite blonde and spotted a sign for the restroom. After using the facilities, she tried to make her way through the lobby again, but there were even more people blocking her path now.

"Excuse me," she said to a middle-aged man.

"Sorry, hon. We're waiting for the rest of our club members to arrive. You can squeeze right between those two women."

Max looked at the two plump women who were deep in conversation and standing so close together that there was no way she'd get through. She looked back at the gentleman who had suggested it, and he held up his index finger.

"Harriet, Kelly, please let this young woman through," he said in a friendly tone.

The women parted, never pausing their conversation, and Max slipped by, then wove around two children and another couple and finally reached the desk.

"Excuse me. Is there a back road into Wellfleet?" Max asked the white-haired woman behind the desk. "The main road is really backed up."

She looked at Max as though she'd lost her mind. "Honey, you aren't gonna find a clear road anywhere this weekend. This is Oyster Fest weekend. We've got more people in the area this weekend than we do space. It'll be like this through Sunday."

A heavyset woman squeezed in beside Max and asked about transportation to the festival. A man nudged his way in front of Max, and she stepped back, wondering what in the world she was going to do until she heard from Treat. She grabbed a flyer about the festival and a Cape Cod map from a table in the lobby, then went out to her car and stared at the bumper-to-bumper traffic.

"Not exactly the romantic surprise I had in mind," she mumbled, vowing not to let this bring her mood down. She'd find Treat one way or another.

She climbed into her car and studied the map on the festival flyer, then flipped it over and scanned the event information. It was obvious that she would never get her car anywhere near the festival, but according to the flyer, she was only a few miles from White Crest Beach, where she could catch a shuttle to the festival. She might as well make the most of waiting for Treat's call, and enjoy the scenery.

When she finally made it to the beach, she wondered what kind of a fool set out across the country to a place she'd never been without a plan.

The same kind that left in the middle of the night and drove to Colorado without a plan.

She debated leaving another message for Treat saying she was there, but she wanted to hear the excitement in his voice when she told him. Besides, she knew her man. He'd call as soon as he was able. As she got out of the car she told herself this was just a little delay to what would be a fantastic weekend. Fate had brought them together before; it would happen again.

Twenty minutes later she climbed out of the shuttle in front of the Wellfleet Town Center. The narrow streets and sidewalks were crowded with people moving between stores and vendors. Without even realizing what she was doing, she began studying every dark head of hair that rose above the crowd, despite knowing he was working.

Large white tents lined the parking lot across the street. Max's eyes lit up at the mass of people packed in as tight as a school of fish, leaving barely enough room to step between. She moved with the crowd across the street and into the first tent, where handmade baskets and driftwood painted with beach scenes, boats, and gulls lined long tables.

Max went from one tent to the next, tasting oysters made

fifty different ways, while local artisans smiled and chatted about their crafts and the festival, and soon looking for Treat fell by the wayside.

"Shuck this!" a man yelled, handing Max an oyster shell.

"Thank you, but I've eaten so many that I think I might explode."

He leaned over the table and said, "That's what your husband is counting on." A wink and a nod later, Max finally got the joke—and it brought her mind right back to Treat.

She already felt like one big, uncontrollable hormone when she was with him. She needed help like she needed a hole in her head. She grinned at the thought as she moved to the next tent.

Time passed swiftly and, as the sun began to set, Max made her way back toward the shuttle bus. She took a window seat, and an elderly man with a shock of white hair sat beside her. She smiled and then faced the window, not in the mood to talk. As the rest of the passengers boarded the shuttle, the disappointment of not hearing from Treat settled in, putting her hopeful energy through a sharp reality check. What if Treat had to work late into the evening? What if he didn't call? She pressed her hands to her chest, trying to quell the doubt blooming there. She glanced behind her at another stream of people getting off a shuttle bus and began to shake from the cold, her confidence about finding Treat coming down a notch.

"Are you okay?" the man beside her asked in a sympathetic voice.

Max nodded. "Mm-hm."

"Are you sure? Because you look a might bit upset."

"I am a little upset," she admitted.

"I thought you might be. You're too pretty of a gal to let anything make you so upset. Wanna talk about it?"

Max smiled. "No, thank you. It's a little embarrassing."

The old man scratched his head. "All righty, then. Did you enjoy the festival?"

"Yes. It was nice," she answered as the shuttle ambled along the busy road.

"Are you from around here?" he asked. "Wait. Don't answer that. Just say this for me. Park the car in the Harvard yard and party hearty." Every "ar" came out as "ah."

Max laughed. "I know this one." She feigned a New England accent. "Pahk the cah in the Hahvahd yahd and pahty hahty."

"So, you *are* from around here," he teased.

"Colorado, actually. Well, that's where I live now. I'm originally from Virginia."

"Either way, you're a long way from home. I've lived here all my life."

He told her the history of the festival and about how it had changed through the years, but Max was too lost in her own thoughts to retain any of the details. She listened instead to the calming cadence of his voice. By the time the shuttle stopped at White Crest Beach she felt less anxious, and she thanked him for making her feel better.

"If you just got in today, you probably don't have any dinner plans," he said. "You're welcome to have dinner with me and the missus, if you'd like. I'm sure Vicky would enjoy having company, and I promise, no oysters."

Max thought about her options. She didn't know how long it would be before she heard from Treat, and she was a little hungry and cold.

"There she is now," he said as a woman pulled up in an old pickup truck.

"Chris, are you bothering that young lady?" the woman asked. She wore her long gray hair pulled back in a ponytail much like Max's, and her wide smile brightened her friendly blue eyes.

"No. He's been really sweet," Max said.

"She just got into town today, and I was inviting her to have dinner with us," he answered.

"Why, sure! I have plenty of salmon and chicken, corn on the cob, and I know we have enough Jell-O for dessert," the woman said. "By the way, I'm Vicky Smith, Chris's better half. His manners could use a good overhaul."

"I don't know," Max said. The responsible side of her wondered if she was getting herself into an unsafe situation. They seemed nice enough, but...

A car pulled up with another older couple in it, and the driver rolled down his window. "Hey, Vicky. Y'all coming to the bonfire tonight?"

"Oh yeah, we'll be there," Vicky answered. "Hey, Marge." She waved to a woman walking by. "You coming to the bonfire?"

"I'll be there!" the woman answered, and continued on her way toward another couple.

Max watched the interactions, and unless she had entered some alternate Stephen King universe where the entire town was involved in hacking up tourists, why shouldn't she go spend some time with them? After all, she could answer Treat's call at their house just as easily as she could sitting on the dune in the cold.

MAX HAD BEEN hungrier than she'd thought she was, and the meal was delicious. She helped Vicky with the dishes while Chris gathered blankets and chairs for the bonfire she'd heard them talking about earlier. She was glad she'd accepted their generous invitation. But now that the conversation had stalled, thoughts of Treat came rushing back, and she wondered how much longer it would be until she heard from him. It was already dark out.

"Did you come out just for the festival this weekend?" Vicky asked as she handed a plate to Max for her to dry. She reminded Max of her own grandmother. She had the same generous spirit and made the same type of quippy remarks to Chris as her grandmother used to make to her grandfather.

"No." *I came searching for my boyfriend.*

"Work?" Vicky pressed.

"No, not work." Max dried another dish and placed it on the counter.

"Love?"

Yes was on the tip of Max's tongue, but she didn't say it. She didn't want to get into a big conversation about Treat. She was already nervous about finding him at all tonight.

"No wonder you seem sidetracked." Vicky set down the dish she was scrubbing. "I'm gonna tell you what my mama told me many years ago. She said, 'Men are like weeds. Some will strangle you until you can't breathe, and some will strangle you once, see you can't breathe, and till your soil for the rest of their lives to make sure you're never strangled again.' Then she would wink at me and say, 'If he strangles you again, get your caboose right back here. If he tills your soil, make me some grandbabies.' And that was that. I've never looked back. You just need to find your tiller, Max."

"I think I already found him. I just have to find him *here*. We keep missing each other's calls."

"Gotta love technology," Vicky said. "It's not like the old days when you dated the boy down the street from the time you were thirteen until you married him at eighteen."

"Is she telling stories again?" Chris came into the kitchen with his coat on.

Max loved these two already. "I like Vicky's stories."

"See that, Chris? Not everyone has heard my stories as many times as you. Are we ready? Truck packed?" Vicky asked, drying her hands on a dish towel.

"All set." Chris waved toward the door. "Let's go."

"Max, did you bring a coat? It gets cold, even with the bonfire. Chris, grab one of my coats for her."

"Um…? I thought you were taking me back to my car."

"To your car?" Vicky asked. "Oh goodness, Max. You can't wait around for a man all your life. Come for a little while. Meet our friends."

Max pulled out her phone one more time, and the voicemail message light was on. "That's weird. I didn't hear my phone ring, but there's a message."

"Sometimes that happens around here," Vicky said. "I think it's the Lord's way of telling us to put the darn things down every once in a while. Unplug. Relax."

Max excused herself and walked into the dining room to listen to the message. *Hi, sweetness.* She melted a little inside at the sound of Treat's voice. *I thought I'd try to catch you again. I tried to text, but it wouldn't go through. I'm heading out with some old friends for a little while. I'll try you again when I get back. I love you, Max, and I can't wait to see you.*

She couldn't suppress her elation as she joined Vicky and

Chris on their way out to the truck.

Vicky took one look at Max and grinned. "Looks like some-one got her call."

Max knew her answer was in her mile-wide smile.

"So?" Vicky raised her brows. "Are you coming with us for a little while? Or heading out for a romantic rendezvous?"

"I'd love to come with you for a bit if you don't mind. My *tiller* is out with friends." Max followed them to the truck, her belief in fate reinstated once again.

Chapter Sixteen

THE WIND PICKED up, turning Treat's thick hair into a mass of waves. He'd gone home to grab a sweater, and now he stood at the top of the dune looking down at the beach and counting the bonfires, realizing he had no way of knowing which one was Chuck and Bonnie's. There were enormous groups of people around each fire pit, and for a minute Treat considered going back to the bungalow. Maybe Chuck and Bonnie wouldn't even notice his absence.

All he really wanted was to talk with Max, but Chuck and Bonnie had been good friends to him for more years than he cared to remember. He kicked off his loafers and descended the steep sandy ramp to the beach below. The deep, cold sand covered his bare feet with each step. He took a moment to listen to the waves breaking against the shore, and his thoughts traveled to the night in Nassau with Max. They'd come so far. The moon hovered over the water like a beacon in the clear dark sky. Laughter filtered up from his right, where children were tossing a ball and diving into the sand to retrieve it.

The feel of the sea air on his cheeks had always been one of his favorite sensations. It reminded him of playing along the water's edge when he was younger, while his mother and father watched from nearby. He bent down and rolled up the legs of his gray linen pants. From his crouched position, he watched a group of teenagers drawing pictures in the air with sparklers, just as he and his siblings had done. He remembered his mother's laughter as she teased him, chasing squeals from his lungs as she'd swoop him from the sand and tickle his belly years before she'd been too weak to even lift her own chin. He didn't allow himself to visit those memories too often. But now, while he was missing Max, he reveled in the warmth of them.

"Go ahead. I'll catch up!" Treat heard someone yell. He blinked away the memories and headed down the beach toward the first bonfire. *Might as well get this over with.*

A few minutes later he heard his name from behind.

He turned, expecting to see Chuck. Smitty stood a few feet away, carrying an armful of blankets. Treat walked back through the dense sand and took the blankets from Smitty's arms.

He embraced his old friend. "I didn't know you'd be here."

"Oh, you know Vicky. Any excuse for a party." Smitty's white hair looked almost gray in the moonlight. "Are you with our bonfire tonight?"

"I don't know. I'm looking for Chuck and Bonnie Holtz."

Smitty shook his head. "They're not with our group." He scanned the people closest to them. "Isn't that them right there?" He pointed to a couple roasting marshmallows around the nearest bonfire.

"Your eyes are better than mine. I think you might be right."

"Treat!"

Treat groaned at the sight of Amanda, the daughter of Bonnie's friend, who had been at dinner with them. He'd made it clear that he was not on the market, but she was like a gnat, refusing to be deterred.

"Looks like you have a lady friend waiting for you. Here. Give me the blankets and go join your party." Smitty reached for the blankets.

"That's okay. I'll bring them to your bonfire." *Anything to avoid Amanda.*

Smitty yanked the blankets from his arms, eyeing the woman who was heading their way with a determined look on her face. "That one's not taking no for an answer. We're the last bonfire down on the left. Stop by later, and bring your friend if you'd like."

"She's not my friend!" Treat called after him.

Half an hour later, Treat could no longer stomach Amanda, even to spend time with his friends. She was clingy and vile, offering to do all sorts of dirty things to him and refusing to accept his gentlemanly denials. She was so persistent that he half expected to hear, *All that for a cool five hundred dollars.* He was on the verge of telling her flat-out, *I will not ever sleep with you.* He'd never had to go that far before. Then again, he'd never been so in love with one woman that he'd turn down another.

"I'll tell you what," Amanda said as she pawed at his arm. "If you'll take a walk with me—one walk." She leaned closer and whispered, "I promise you, I'll rock your world. I'll be *your* treat."

Treat gritted his teeth against his anger. He could have a string of nameless, faceless women if he wanted them. But now he knew what it was like to feel more than lust, to look into someone's eyes and want much more than sexual gratification— a lifetime of smiles and handholding, breakfasts, and yes, saucy, sumptuous, scorching-hot nights of lovemaking. Enough was enough.

"Excuse me," he said for the hundredth time, and walked away from Amanda, making a beeline for Chuck. *Why did he have to be such a gentleman?* He smiled to himself with the thought. It was the same question Max had asked.

"Chuck, I had a great time, but I really have to run. Bonnie, you know I think the world of you, but you should think twice before inviting Amanda out again. She's a bit aggressive."

Bonnie flushed. "I'm sorry. I had no idea you were taken until you told us over dinner, and by then it was too late to uninvite her."

"It's okay, though I'm surprised you'd think I'd be interested in someone like her."

"I guess I thought that a guy like you was used to women throwing themselves at him," Bonnie explained.

"Yes, but have you ever seen me take any of them up on their offers? For that matter, have you ever seen me with a woman since you've known me?"

"Well, no," she admitted.

He put his hand on her shoulder and kissed her cheek. "Then please don't underestimate me." He patted Chuck on the arm. "Thanks, buddy. We'll catch up soon."

Treat headed down the beach toward Smitty's bonfire to say a quick hello and get back to his bungalow to call Max.

MAX PULLED THE top layer of a roasted marshmallow off and put it in her mouth, then licked the sticky goodness from her fingers. It had been ages since she'd roasted marshmallows, and she was having a wonderful time talking with Vicky and her friends. She'd had a few cups of wine and she was feeling good. This was just what she needed. A little time to destress and pull herself together after her long trip.

As much as she loved the mountains of Colorado, there was something about being by the water that made her feel good all over. A young family was walking down the beach, two children running ahead with their toes in the water, while the parents walked arm in arm. She allowed herself a momentary fantasy of having a future, and a family, with Treat. She was getting miles ahead of herself, but she couldn't escape the hope in her heart.

Smitty nudged Vicky's arm and said, "I forgot to tell you who I ran into."

"God himself?" Vicky teased.

"Sort of. Treat Braden."

Max choked on her marshmallow.

Vicky patted her on the back. "Get her a drink! Quick, Chris."

Chris handed her a bottle of wine, which Max chugged, and when she stopped choking, she drank some more to calm her nerves, until she'd downed nearly half the bottle. Her heart was racing as she tried to figure out how to surprise him. Should she run down the beach and into his arms? Or be coy about it and sneak up, as he had to her in the parking lot after work? She remembered Kaylie's advice and decided calm, cool, and collected was probably the most seductive way to make her entrance. *This is going to be the best surprise ever!*

"A little thirsty, Max?" Vicky said with a curious smile.

"Sorry. Thank you. Did you say 'Treat Braden'?" she asked.

"Yes. You know him?" Chris asked.

Her pulse spiked. "Yes, I know him very well." *I'm in love with him.* Max looked down the beach, but it was too dark to make out anything more than basic figures. "Tall guy, hand-some as the day is long?" *Long as the day is handsome!*

"He's got a place here in Wellfleet. I've known his family for years." Chris laughed. "He still calls me Smitty, like his pop does. It was a nickname I had as a younger man."

"A much younger man," Vicky teased. "If I'm reading that spark in your eyes correctly, I'd think that Treat might be the reason you're here."

Max grinned and pushed to her feet, swaying a little from the wine. "You'd be reading me perfectly. I think I'll just go to the bathroom and freshen up before I go looking for him. It's in the parking lot, right?"

"I'll go with you." Vicky popped up from her chair.

"No. I can manage. Thank you, though." She started for the dunes. She climbed the sandy ramp to the parking lot and found the small cinder-block bathroom. Inside, she flicked on the light and stood in front of the mirror, staring at her glassy eyes. Her cheeks were pink from the alcohol, but she didn't care. She was beyond happy. Her surprise was going to work out after all.

She fluffed her hair, turned her face one way, then the oth-er, narrowed her eyes, and then opened them wide again. She'd never considered herself to be someone special, but Treat thought she was, and that made her believe she just might be. She washed her hands, excited to surprise him, and headed out to find her man.

She scanned the beach, spotting his height first, and her hand flew to her heart. *Look at him.* He took her breath away. She started down the ramp, her gaze trained on Treat as he strode down the beach. A blonde ran after him calling his name, and Max's stomach pitched. She stilled as Treat stopped in his tracks and the blonde touched his arm.

"Hey. Don't touch him," Max said aloud, though too quietly for anyone else to hear, and started down the steep incline.

She spotted Vicky approaching Treat as the blonde moved in front of him and tugged him down by his shirt. It was such a possessive move, Max stumbled and fell to her butt on the hard sand at the same moment the blonde pressed her lips to Treat's cheek.

Treat turned in Max's direction, and for a beat she couldn't breathe. She could only see Treat's silhouette, but she swore the air between them electrified. What was going on? Who was that witch? *No, no, no, no, no!* This could not be happening. Not with Treat.

Chapter Seventeen

"MAX!" VICKY YELLED, running to help her to her feet.

Max was too stunned to move, watching as Treat grabbed the blonde by her shoulders and said something Max couldn't hear, but his body language told her all she needed to know as he hulked over her, moving rigidly, not languid and loving the way he was with Max. He released the woman's arms and strode directly toward the ramp, falling into step beside Vicky.

"Way to go, Treat. That woman's got a fairly loose reputation," Vicky said.

"She deserves it." Treat's gaze locked on Max. Grief and confusion riddled his handsome face as she pushed to her feet and he rushed to her side. "Max...? What are you doing here? That wasn't what it looked like. I can explain."

"Like it wasn't what I thought when you saw me with Justin?" she asked, brushing sand from her butt.

"Yes!" Treat insisted. "Exactly like that."

"One minute you're professing your love to me and the next you're making out with a strange blonde," she said teasingly. The glint of relief in his eyes told her he knew she wasn't angry, but still she couldn't stop herself from saying, "No wonder this is your favorite place. You probably have a woman at every port."

"Max?" Vicky said. "Honey, I've known Treat since he was a boy. We see him when he's in town. We know his whole family, and he isn't who you think he is."

"See? Even she knows what you're like," Max teased.

"No, Max. He's not the person *you* think he is. It's none of my business, and I'll leave you two alone to hash this out in a second, but first…" She turned to Treat. "She's the sweetest, kindest woman I have met in a long time."

"I know," Treat said as he slid an arm around her waist.

"Max," Vicky continued, "Treat has women after him all the time. Of course he does. Just look at him."

"He's a hot one," Max said.

"It's a wonder he can go anywhere looking like that. But he's a gentleman. He doesn't have a girl in this port. I've never seen him bring a woman here, or even date a woman here, and he's no spring chicken."

Max giggled. Treat scowled.

"That's a lot of years without a steady woman on his arm." Vicky took Max's hand and said, "Max, he's your tiller." She nodded. "Trust me."

Vicky kissed his cheek, and then said in a hushed tone, "Hurt her and I'll kill you. I want a front seat at the wedding."

"Thank you for everything, Vicky." Max hugged her. "I know all those things you said about Treat. This was what I call Treat's Justin-by-the-elevator moment."

"I don't even want to know what that means, honey, but by the look in your eyes, I'd say it's a good thing."

When Vicky walked away, Treat cocked a brow and said, "There's only you, Max."

"I know. I'm tipsy, but not too drunk to see the truth." The truth wasn't what Max expected. She'd assumed the worst not because of Treat, but because of those ghosts rattling the chains in her closet.

"What are you doing here, baby?"

"I wanted to surprise you, but I kind of suck at surprises. I had no idea where you lived or anything."

"Efficient Max didn't have a plan? A map of every house on the Cape?"

"It's not funny!" she snapped.

"No, it's not. Some might say it's fate. You know what this means, don't you?" he asked as he gathered her in his arms. "You were thinking with your heart."

"That seems to be the only part of me that works when I'm thinking about you."

"Well, then." He scooped her into his arms, making her laugh with elation as he carried her up the ramp and said, "I plan to inspect every one of your parts to see if that's true."

Chapter Eighteen

TREAT CARRIED MAX into his bungalow and laid her on the couch, despite her protests. He slipped off her shoes and covered her with the softest blanket Max had ever felt, and then he went to work making a fire.

"I am not an invalid, you know," she said, though she was tired. Treat had retrieved her bags from her car, and refused to let her worry about anything—including her car, which he promised would be fine in the parking lot at the beach.

"You've had a long day and a little wine, and I have been *starved* for you since I left you last night." He blew her a kiss and said, "Rest up so I can wear you out later."

She liked the idea of that. As she watched him make the fire, she wondered how hearts were so resilient. Her love for him was so big she felt like she was drowning in it. But she knew that wasn't what was suffocating her. It was the ghosts of her past creeping into the future she wanted. Putting unnecessary cracks in the foundation she and Treat were creating. How could she ever completely trust again without understanding what she'd done, or hadn't done, to cause the pain of her past?

She looked around the cozy room, which was not much bigger than her apartment but much nicer, with a stone fireplace that went up two stories and a cathedral ceiling. Besides the couch, the room boasted only a coffee table and bookshelves to match, both intricately carved from wood and painted white. She was glad to see the bookshelves not only full of books, but also decorated with knickknacks and candles, much like her own. There were family pictures, too, and that made her ache a little for thinking for even a second that a man who was so loyal and had been so honest would have intentionally hurt her. That wasn't in Treat's nature. She believed that all the way to her core, and for the first time ever, she thought about tracking down Ryan and trying to gain closure.

But she didn't want to think about that ugliness now. She didn't want Ryan to have the power to ruin anything else with Treat, or anything in her life in general, so she focused on her surroundings again. There was a staircase between the kitchen and the living room, and she assumed it led to the bedroom. She closed her eyes, and her mind traveled to that bedroom and the closeness she knew would come. She felt the couch dip beside her and opened her eyes, finding Treat gazing lovingly down at her.

"Are you warm enough?"

"Mm-hm."

He caressed her cheek and said, "I'm going to run a bath for you."

Just the thought of being submerged beneath warm water eased her tension, but hearing the love in Treat's voice comforted her even more.

"Thank you," she said. "But you don't have to spoil me so much. I should be spoiling you."

He pressed his lips to hers in a long, scintillating kiss. "Don't ever worry that I'd choose someone else over you. I promised I'd never hurt you, and you can count on that promise."

"It wasn't really you I doubted. I knew in my heart you would never hurt me, but there was this instant fear that trampled through me. I realized pretty quickly that it was my inability to trust my own instincts, and I know that comes from my past. But I'm trying to figure out how to get those ghosts to stay in the past."

His expression grew serious. "We'll figure this out, babe. There's nothing we can't figure out together."

He went upstairs, returning a few minutes later. He scooped her into his arms again, and although it went against every fiber of her being to be carried, she cuddled against him, allowing herself to enjoy his pampering.

The smell of warm vanilla filled the spacious candle-lit bathroom. Treat set her down on the ceramic floor, and she longed to be back in his arms. The idea of taking a warm bath seemed wonderfully decadent. When she looked in the mirror, Treat's intimate gaze sent a sobering dose of reality through her, and she vowed that come hell or high water, she would find a way to put her past behind them.

She took a step toward him, and he slipped her sweatshirt from her shoulders and laid it neatly on the counter next to a basket of soaps and lotions. She lifted her arms as he took off her shirt and bra.

"You're even more beautiful in the candlelight," he said.

She unbuttoned his shirt and said, "So are you."

They stripped off the rest of their clothes, and Max had to close her eyes against the primal urges spreading through her like wildfire. When he took off her glasses, she opened her eyes, meeting his steady gaze.

"Sweetness," he whispered in a voice full of lust as he drew her naked body against his and kissed her deeply.

He guided her to the tub and helped her in before he stepped in behind her and settled her back against his chest. She closed her eyes as he washed her arms with a warm, soapy cloth and gathered her hair, placing it over one shoulder. He bathed her shoulder and neck so tenderly, she melted against him. He washed each of her fingers, her palms, her wrists.

"Relax," he whispered as she leaned forward, hoping to turn and wash him, but he gently brought her back to his chest again. "Let me love you."

He washed along the bend of her hip and slowly down to the crest of both knees, and then he bathed her lower belly, caressing her rib cage, hips, and inner thighs. Max closed her eyes. His body held her as a willing captive, creating a loving cocoon that made her feel small and feminine—and very desirous.

He wrapped his arms around her middle, touching his cheek to hers. His breath warmed her damp shoulders, and Max wanted to stay right there, with his heart beating against her back, forever.

NOTHING IN HIS life had ever given Treat the ceaseless feeling of happiness as taking care of Max had for the last hour. He felt her tension releasing in every breath she took, in the weight of her against him. Everything about her was sublime, and as much as his body cried out for more, sex wasn't what he craved. Knowing she trusted him and felt safe was paramount. If they did nothing else tonight, he would be sated.

The bubbles dissipated and the water cooled. Max snuggled closer, borrowing his warmth.

"Let me dry you off, sweetness."

She moved as if she were half asleep, her slender arms reaching for him as she stood. Treat helped her step from the tub and wrapped her in a thick towel, then used another to gently dry her off, wiping water from her neck and shoulders, remembering the way his heart ached the first time he'd set eyes on her and how the unfamiliar emotion had rattled him. Now he understood the emotion and had no fears, but he knew Max did, and he had to find a way to help ease them.

As he was wiping the water from her body, he knew just what to do. He would protect Max's heart with simple acts of kindness and love, until that was all she knew. He was surprised when Max reached for his neck, wanting him to carry her to the bedroom. He knew the first time he'd carried her from the car that she might fight him. She was strong and self-sufficient, and she was proud of that. The woman he was carrying to his bed never failed to astonish him—even the way she'd gone from intensely sexual to full-on fear on the hill in Colorado had showed her strength. Most women would have continued making out and rationalized it in their minds just to complete the act. In his experience, most women feared losing the men in their lives. As Max had told him, it was clear that she didn't fear that as much as not being able to trust her own instincts.

He drew back the covers with one hand and laid her on the clean sheets, then grabbed one of his T-shirts from his dresser. He carefully helped her put on the shirt. It fell almost to her knees. She looked adorable *and* sexy.

Treat pulled on a pair of boxer briefs, then retrieved the candles from the bathroom and placed them on the slate in front of the fireplace. He lay beside Max, leaning on one elbow. "Feel better?"

"Much. I didn't think I'd had that much wine, but I am definitely still a little tipsy." She wiggled closer and pressed her lips to his.

"That's okay. I'm not. I won't let you take advantage of me." He rubbed his fingers lightly down her back, and she closed her eyes.

"Mmm. That feels good. I want to stay right here. Forever."

Forever was just what he wanted. She was so sleepy and relaxed, he kissed her softly and said, "Sounds perfect to me. Why don't you get some rest, babe."

"Resting isn't what I had in mind."

She yawned, and he knew she was exhausted.

"Part of loving someone means letting their body do whatever it needs to do, and your body obviously needs to rest."

She kissed his chest and gazed up at him. "But my heart needs *you*."

"Then you shall have me, baby." He pressed his lips to hers, shifting and aligning their bodies, cradling her beneath him, and said, "All of me."

Chapter Nineteen

MAX AWOKE TO the smell of coffee and Treat, only she was alone in the bedroom. She went into the bathroom and was surprised to find her toiletries laid out in a basket beside the sink. Her shampoo and conditioner were already in the shower. She loved his propensity for organization, which was so much like her own. After brushing her teeth, she headed downstairs in search of him.

As she stepped onto the first floor, a floral scent surrounded her. She spotted an enormous antique metal bucket overflowing with Knock Out roses. *Oh, Treat.* She found him in the kitchen, showered, dressed, and strikingly handsome in his jeans and T-shirt. Two more vases of roses sat on the counter and in the center of the table, which was set for two, with warm croissants, fresh fruit, and hard-boiled eggs. Max's hand covered her heart.

"You are the most thoughtful man on earth."

"Good morning, beautiful. I had to take care of some business this morning, so I got up early." His gaze traveled slowly down her body from head to toe, heating her up from the inside out.

"You didn't have to do all this," Max said as Treat handed

her a delicious-smelling cup of coffee.

"It wasn't much, and I figured you'd be hungry. Vicky called. She said that she wanted to make sure you were okay, but I think she really wanted to make sure we'd made up."

"Did you tell her we weren't really fighting?" She set the coffee on the counter and wrapped her arms around him.

He kissed her and said, "I told her we had a horrible fight but the makeup sex was incredible."

"At least you were half honest. These roses are *gorgeous*."

"They line the driveway. Fate?" he asked with a shrug.

"Fate indeed." She gazed out the windows at the gorgeous view of the bay. The sky was a clear powdery blue, mirroring her feelings, like the fog that had hung over her and Treat had evaporated and all that was left was the beauty between them. But she knew the skeletons of her past had only gone back into hiding and feared the time they might poke their evil heads out again.

Treat took her hand in his, and she pushed those thoughts away, focusing on the incredible man who was as real and present as he was good.

"Thanks for all of this, and for bringing my things inside," she said.

He placed her hand on his hip and stepped closer, drawing her against him so their thighs brushed and her breasts pressed against his torso. "I put your clothes in the dresser drawers."

"Treat, it's not like I'm moving in."

"Not yet, anyway. See? That's why I didn't want to get too close last night. Women are fickle," he teased, and began kissing her neck.

"I'm not fickle." She clung to his waist, breathing harder with each slick of his tongue. "I've never stopped wanting you."

"Good, because you're stuck with me."

"I like being stuck with you," she said flirtatiously. "But I forgot to ask how your business deal went."

"It was a great success. Soon I'll be the proud owner of the Ocean Edge Resort and Golf Club. And you, my beautiful girlfriend, will have to help me celebrate."

"Treat, that's wonderful!" She threw her arms around his neck and kissed him.

"I want to show you around today," he said between kisses.

"How can we go anywhere with the crowds?"

He took her in another sensual kiss, and suddenly those crowds didn't matter. His hands moved over her back, down her hips, and then snuck beneath her shirt, warming her bare skin.

"So it'll take a little longer to get where we need to go?" He brushed his lips over her cheek and whispered in her ear, "We have nothing but time. It's only ten thirty."

"Ten thirty! Why didn't you wake me up?" She buried her face in his chest. "I'm so embarrassed."

"You were tired. Besides, what did I tell you last night about loving someone?"

"That part of loving someone means letting their body do whatever it needs to do."

"And your body needed sleep." He took her chin between his finger and thumb, his hungry gaze awakening her desires. "Especially since I kept you up so late."

They'd both been insatiable last night, and as his heat consumed her, she wondered what it would be like to wake up beside him every morning and go to sleep in his arms every night, without breaks, without questions about whether they'd end up there. Vicky's words came tumbling back to her—*He's your tiller*—as his mouth moved to the nape of her neck.

Till me, baby. Till me good.

"Treat," she said breathlessly. "*You're* what my body needs."

"HOW CAN I miss you this much after only a few hours' sleep?" Treat practically growled.

He crushed his mouth to hers and Max pressed her whole body against him. Love and lust coalesced, and his deepest desires rushed forward. He struggled against the urge to lay her on the kitchen table and make love to her until she forgot her own name.

"I can't get enough of you," he said between hungry kisses.

Max pushed her hands beneath his shirt, sending a bolt of anticipation to his groin. She stood on her tiptoes as he slanted his lips over hers and lifted her into his arms. She wrapped her legs around his waist, her hair falling like a curtain around their faces. She smelled like sunshine and madness at once. And he was mad all right, crazy in love with her. Their kisses were rough and messy. He wanted to bury her doubt, to love that burn out of her body.

He set her bottom on the table and wedged his hips between her legs. "What have you done to me?"

"I don't know, but whatever it is, I want more of it." Her words came out in a rush as she pushed at his shirt, trying to get it off.

He wished they were upstairs, on the couch, anywhere more respectful, but he was too far gone, and in the next breath his body took over.

Chapter Twenty

AFTER PICKING UP her rental car and dropping it off at the bungalow, Max and Treat headed into town. They walked hand in hand through the shops she'd spotted yesterday. They picked out toys for Kaylie and Chaz's twins at a cool kids' store called Abiyoyo. Treat bought a scarf that he said set off Max's eyes. When they were waiting in line for the cashier, he squeezed her hand and told her that when they were old and gray he'd still remember the day they'd bought it. Max found hope in the things he did and said so naturally, things that confirmed that she could trust her instincts where Treat was concerned.

They walked around the corner and had lunch at a little restaurant called the Juice, where they shared a bowl of New England clam chowder and a sandwich. Treat rooted himself in her heart more with each passing hour. The simple act of sharing meals together felt exciting and like they'd been doing it forever at the same time. Treat didn't rush her through the meal, or make her feel hurried later, as they meandered with the crowds through an entire street of art galleries. He showed her pieces he loved and took interest in the ones she swooned over. He told her stories of the galleries he'd seen overseas and how he'd like to take her to see each and every one of them.

She wondered where he called home, and she knew his time in Colorado was only a reprieve. He had come to Colorado to see his family, and though he'd left to attend to business, where would he go once they were done here?

"If you're not too tired," he said as he tucked her against his side, "I'd love to go to Provincetown, grab some dinner, and maybe see a show? Or we could just go back to the bungalow and watch a movie and relax. Whatever you want."

That sounded wonderful, but she was already so vested in them, it suddenly seemed important to know what would happen after this trip. "Treat?"

"Uh-oh. What's that look?"

"I'm just curious. Where do you live?"

"You mean, like, where do I keep all my belongings?"

"Yes. Where do you call home?"

"It doesn't matter, because the moment you tell me it's okay, my home will be wherever you are." He kissed her, and the sheer delight of it brought her to her toes, and he kissed her longer.

When they finally pulled apart, "Wow," slipped from her lips. "I love to kiss you."

He put his hands on her waist, and she could see in his eyes that he was thinking the same thing she was—that he wanted to lift her so she could wrap her legs around him and they could kiss each other senseless.

Oh, wait. Maybe he isn't thinking that.

Why was he covering his mouth and looking away?

"Did I say something wrong?" Max asked tentatively.

He shook his head. "You just had my mind racing in ways that it shouldn't be." He looked down, and the problem was evident by the tent in his pants.

She tried unsuccessfully to stifle a laugh.

"You're laughing at this? This is not good, Max. I'm not a twentysomething kid. I'm a grown man. I should be able to kiss you without the world knowing that I can barely think past wanting to"—he lowered his voice to a whisper—"be inside of you."

Max grabbed her side and bent over in a fit of laughter.

"Oh, you think it's funny, do you?" He took her hand and walked behind two enormous hydrangea bushes, then kissed her until her legs turned to spaghetti and her laughter was replaced with wanton moans. They sank to the ground, where he deepened the kiss, his body crushing hers in all the right places. His hot mouth moved over her chin, her neck, and down the open V of her shirt.

"Treat," she pleaded.

She clutched his head, bringing his mouth back to hers. Every molecule in her body ached for him.

"Max," he whispered.

Her brain refused to work. She lay beside him panting, wanting, *craving* more of him as he slicked his tongue along the dip above her collarbone. Then he moved off her. *What're you doing? Where are you going?* She tried to blink through her lust-filled fog as he rose to his feet beside where she lay on the grass, and a cocky grin appeared on his face.

"Get over here," she managed, smacking the grass beside her.

Treat crossed his arms. "Two can play at this game."

Max groaned. "You are so unfair!"

He took her hand and pulled her to her feet so hard she collided with him. And then he kissed her again, probing her mouth with such delicate care that it made her want him even more. She moaned before she could quell the urge, and that was all he needed to pull away with a victorious smile.

"Provincetown?" he asked.

PROVINCETOWN WAS AN artsy community along a beautiful coastline, with eclectic shops and a multitude of street performers. They caught a comedy show, and Max doubled over with laughter in her chair, tears of joy streaming down her cheeks. Watching her laugh had become one of Treat's biggest delights, and he swore he'd do everything he could to keep her just as happy as she was right then.

After the show, they made their way out of the club, into the cool evening air, and wandered down Commercial Street, the main road through Provincetown.

"Treat!"

Treat saw his old friend Marcus heading their way. He was dressed in drag, complete with a wig, high heels, and heavy makeup.

"Hey, buddy. How's the hottest guy around?" Marcus asked, and kissed Treat on each cheek.

"Marcus, how are you?"

"*Maxine* tonight," she said with a wink and a toss of her long brown locks.

"You look beautiful, *Maxine*." Treat glanced at Max. "This is my girlfriend, Max."

Max extended a hand. "Nice to meet you."

"My man Treat does not do *girlfriends*. You must be someone *very* special if you're up here with him. Get in here and give Maxine some love." Maxine drew her into a warm embrace and said, "And I can see why. You are *gorgeous*. I absolutely love your red frames, and your name!"

"Thank you," Max said, touching her glasses.

"Everything going well?" Treat asked. "How's Howie?"

"Oh, sugar, he's just as painful as ever. The man has more mood swings than a pack of PMSing women. But you know I adore him."

Treat put his arm around Maxine and lowered his voice. "And his cancer?"

Maxine's excitement waned for a second, and then she righted her smile and said, "He's hanging in there. He really appreciates—*we* truly appreciate—you pulling those strings with the hospital." Her eyes welled with tears, and she wiped them away and fanned the air. "Whew. I can't go there right now, sugar. I have to perform tonight."

Treat hugged her again, longer this time, as his father had embraced Max. "I'm here, okay? If you need me, call me anytime. You know that. Give Howie my love, please."

"Will do, Treat." Maxine leaned in closer to Max and said, "The man is a saint."

Treat could feel a million unasked questions from Max as they continued walking along the sidewalk, passing a street performer who looked as though he'd been dunked in thick gold paint, standing still as a statue while tourists threw money into a hat at his feet and took pictures standing beside him. Treat waited for her to ask about Howie and Marcus, and when she didn't, he fed her unspoken curiosity.

"Howie lost his health insurance a while ago," he said as they walked into Shop Therapy, a small retail store that specialized in retro clothing. "I made a deal with the hospital and medical providers here so when he needed care, they'd bill me directly."

"That's so generous of you. Who is Marcus…*Maxine*? I mean, how do you know him, *her*?"

"He's a friend. I've gotten to know many of the year-round residents over the years."

"So many people would have trouble embracing a man in drag, and you had no hesitation."

"You didn't seem to have trouble," he said with a question in his eyes.

"No, but some guys are weird about that stuff. I don't know. I guess I'm wrong."

"I'm not most guys."

"You can say that again. I actually fell for you a little harder when I saw you hug him," she admitted.

"I'll have to remember that," he teased. They walked toward the back of the shop, and Treat said, "You know, dressing in drag isn't who he is. It's what he does for a living."

"Oh. No, I didn't know. I assumed that drag was a way of life."

"No, at least not for him," he said as they looked through a rack of shirts. "He's a fantastic performer. If you'd like, I'll take you to a show sometime."

She slipped into the space between the clothing rack and his body. "I would really like that. Love is beautiful, and it should be praised, not picked apart. I'm glad we share the same view where that's concerned."

"The more I learn about you, the more I love you." *Love* slipped so easily from his lips. He liked the way it felt. He lowered his lips to hers, intending a chaste kiss, but once he tasted her, he didn't want to stop there. Max leaned into him, putting pressure on all his greediest places. He reluctantly pulled away, knowing if he didn't, he'd be walking around aroused all night.

Max laced her fingers with his and flashed a rascally smile. "Paybacks are so fun."

He groaned.

She looked at the staircase where a sign with colorful arrows pointed up and asked, "What's up there?"

He guided her away from the steps, which led to an adult toy shop. "Nothing, babe. Let's go get some gelato."

They walked to the Purple Feather Café for gelato and then headed to the beach to eat it. It was chilly, but they cuddled and fed each other tastes.

"What was upstairs in that shop?" Max asked as she held up a spoonful of tiramisu gelato for him to eat.

"It was an adult toy shop," he said uneasily.

"Oh." She gazed out at the water. "Do you like to use *those*?"

"No, Max." He set his gelato down and pulled her onto his lap. She smiled, but it was the shy smile that told him she had many more questions in that brilliant mind of hers. "I don't need toys, or anything besides you. But if you ever want to explore, we can do it together."

"It's a little embarrassing to talk about this," she whispered.

"Then we won't," he reassured her.

"No, it's embarrassing but it's good. I like knowing that I don't have to hide my past with you. That you accept me with my insecurities and they don't make you run away."

"Baby, nothing will make me run from you." That earned a bigger smile. "You can count on me, Max. Always."

"What if I never want to explore?" she asked carefully.

"Then we won't. I want to help you heal."

"You've already helped. Just being able to accept and trust you in my life is a healing step for me." Her expression turned serious. "But what if you want to explore one day? I don't want to hold you back."

"Max, I'm thirty-seven. I've explored. I've sowed my wild oats. Any further exploration will be because we want to do it together. You can trust me when I tell you that beyond sharing you, there's nothing sexual I wouldn't do for you or with you if you wanted me to. On that same note, though, all I need is right here on my lap. When we're close, it's not about toys or pushing limits; it's about intimacy."

She lowered her face toward his, and her glasses slid down her nose. Treat righted them for her, and she said, just above a whisper, "But guys need excitement."

"My excitement is drawn from the pleasure I bring you, not whether you're willing to get off on sex toys."

"Will it be enough? In the long run?"

"Max, *you're* enough. You'll always be enough. I'm not your ex, and I've never been someone who needed to dominate a woman. That's not me, and honestly, most of the guys I know aren't like that either. Real men don't dominate. They cherish, they love, they pleasure, but it's mutual, not an ego trip."

"I hope you're right, because I want to believe you."

He sealed his promise with a kiss. "It's cold out here. Let's go home."

Max had asked him about his home, and as they walked back to the car, he knew his answer had been completely honest. His home would be anywhere Max was.

Chapter Twenty-One

LATER THAT EVENING, Max sat with her legs stretched across Treat's lap in front of a roaring fire as he massaged her feet, pressing his thumbs deeply into the arch of her foot.

"You can't even begin to understand how good that feels." She closed her eyes, enjoying his touch.

"Oh, I think I can."

She opened her eyes. "Yeah?"

"It's touch, and touch is good," he said in a husky voice.

Why does your voice turn my entire body on? She pulled her feet from his lap and sat up, tucking them beneath her.

"Let me do you," she said.

"Why, Max, what kind of man do you think I am?"

She playfully swatted his chest. "Not like that. Let me rub you and make you feel good."

He wiggled his eyebrows. "You naughty girl."

"Seriously, let me give you a massage."

"If you insist." He kissed her, then pushed to his feet and went to a closet by the stairs. He withdrew a comforter, then spread it out on the floor in front of the fireplace. When he pulled his shirt over his head, her breath rushed from her lungs. She'd seen his perfectly sculpted physique enough times that she

shouldn't still react to it like that, but her love for him continued to grow, and she had a feeling her reactions to him would,
too. Her grandmother once told her that she would know she
was in love because she'd be able to imagine loving the person
no matter what they looked like. As Treat stripped off his pants,
she imagined him gray and potbellied, and her heart still adored
him. She took that further, imagining an even harder thing to
think about. What if he was hurt in an accident? If he lost a
limb or was disfigured? As he lowered himself to the blanket
wearing only his boxer briefs, she knew her love for him was
soul deep, and nothing could change that.

He patted the space beside him. "Sit with me."

"This might be more dangerous than I had anticipated." She
was only half teasing. Did he really expect her to touch him
without wanting to devour him?

He opened his hand, revealing a small bottle of oil.

"You just happen to keep this in the secret closet with the
blanket? How much do you pay your friends to say that you
don't bring women up here?"

He tickled her ribs, causing her to squeal. "I don't lie,
sweetness."

"I was kidding!"

"Good, because I want to be sure you know you can trust
me on every level. I've never had anyone but Savannah here
with me, and I slept on the couch, which is why the blanket is
down here. She left the oil here."

Kneeling by his side, she couldn't help teasing him. "I'm
supposed to buy the old *only my sister* routine?"

In the next second, Treat was on his feet and heading for
the kitchen, where he retrieved his phone. He pushed a button
and, a few seconds later, said, "Hey, Vanny. Hold on a sec."

Max jumped up. "Oh my gosh. No! You *know* I was kidding!" Mortified didn't begin to describe the embarrassment she felt.

He lowered his voice and said, "I'll never have anything to hide from you, and I want you to know it and believe it."

"I *know* I can. I was teasing!" she said in a loud whisper.

He put Savannah on speakerphone and said, "Vanny, say hi to Max. I've got you on speakerphone."

"Hey, girl! I had no idea you were going to the Cape!"

Max was surprised by Savannah's enthusiasm. "I wanted to surprise Treat."

"Aw, that's so romantic," Savannah said happily.

"Hey, Vanny, I found your Apricot Kernel Oil." Treat grinned, twisting the bottle between his index finger and thumb.

Max covered her face. *This cannot really be happening.*

"Oh, good. It's great for aromatherapy. You guys should use it. It's awesome, and it won't leave your skin oily."

"Thanks, Savannah." Treat blew a kiss to Max and said, "I'm sure we'll put it to good use." He took Max's hand, leading her back to the blanket, and lowered himself to the floor with another victorious smile.

"Was that all you needed?" Savannah asked. "I gotta run. I'm with Connor."

"I just wanted you to know I had it." Treat ended the call as Max tried to dodge the mortification bullet. He set his phone aside and said, "You can ask me anything, Max. I'll always give you an honest answer, and I'll never blame you for not believing me, because I know people lie and you've been hurt."

"I was *honestly* only teasing you. You didn't have to call her."

"I knew you were teasing, but I also know you've been cheated on and lied to. I'm not taking any chances." He kissed her tenderly. Then he flipped onto his stomach and stretched out. "Now that that's out of the way, I believe you wanted to *do* me?"

"You believe that, do you?" She dripped oil onto his back and began kneading it into his muscles.

"How do you know I didn't have this preplanned with Savannah?"

Max's hands stopped moving as she considered his tease. She cracked a smile and said, "Because she'd never go along with it. She likes me."

"How about because I like you, and I'd never go along with it?"

Swoon! She bent down and kissed his cheek. "That works, too."

Max used both hands, massaging along either side of his spine, working the tension outward, urged on by his appreciative moans. Treat's eyes were closed, and a small smile lifted his lips. She loved knowing she was bringing him pleasure as she followed the lines of his body, kneading in a slow and steady rhythm over the curve of his biceps and across his shoulders. She slid her hands over the crest of his lats and slid her fingers forward, pushing deeper along his pecs.

The scent of apricot hung in the air. Massaging his slick, hot skin felt erotic, and his sexy noises of appreciation heightened her arousal.

She moved lower, oiling up his hamstrings and kneading the tension there.

"Your touch is magical," he said in a guttural voice.

"Mm-hmm." She tried to ignore the pulsing sensation

thrumming through her as he spread his legs wider. She moved between them so she could work each leg with both hands.

She pushed at the cotton at the top of his hamstrings, sliding her fingers beneath, taunting them both. Every press of her fingers into his flesh brought another wave of desire, until she was desperate for more. He lifted his hips, shifting his weight, and she knew he was aroused, too.

She silently removed her clothes. The fire warmed her skin as she lay down beside him, her body grazing his slippery flesh.

"Sweetness," he whispered as he turned to face her.

"Shh. Lie on your back." She trailed kisses over his neck and shoulder, along his cheek, and pressed a kiss at the soft spot just beneath his ear.

He groaned, and the sound rumbled through her. She moved lower and began massaging his legs again, using both hands to knead the tension from his calves, ankles, and eventually, his feet, which were just as gorgeous as the rest of him.

He reached for her, but she was enjoying giving him pleasure, making him want her the way she wanted him.

"Uh-uh," she whispered, peeling his hands away. "Let me touch you."

He made a guttural sound of frustration, and she stretched out beside him, tracing the lines of his abs with her finger and pressing kisses to his pecs. Treat's hungry groan mixed with her quiet moan as she kissed his lower lip. This time when he reached for her, she didn't stop him, enjoying his raw, needful kisses, the scratch of his whiskers, and the press of his hard body against hers as he pulled her against him.

"You're driving me crazy."

"All touch is good, remember?" she teased.

The need in his eyes was tangible as he took her cheeks between his hands and kissed her urgently, then eased to a softer, decadent kiss that made her writhe with desire.

"Max, I couldn't love you more."

"That's a shame. I was sort of counting on you loving me more each day."

Chapter Twenty-Two

THE NEXT MORNING Treat was talking on the phone on the back deck when Max came downstairs. She sat beside the open window with a mug of coffee, watching him pace as the tide rolled out. After they'd made love this morning, they'd showered together, which Max decided was the perfect way to greet the day. She loved his little bungalow, and she knew it had less to do with the time she spent there and everything to do with whom she spent it with.

Treat lowered his big body to a chair, and his voice sailed in through the open window. "I know I said I was sending an offer, but it's off. I can't move forward with it right now."

She didn't mean to eavesdrop, but the frustration in his voice was alarming. She wondered what he wasn't moving forward with, and she realized the response he'd given her about where he lived hadn't really answered her question. Did he have a place that he called home, or did he literally travel *all* the time? It sure seemed that way to her.

He pushed to his feet, sending his chair skidding across the deck. "Cut it off. I'm done. No more acquisitions."

Max froze, now intent on listening to every word.

"I've got enough money to last me two lifetimes. I don't

care. I'm done with it," he said, pacing angrily. "It's one property. Yes, I know it's only three months, but I can't spare the time right now." He paused, obviously listening to whoever was on the phone.

Max hoped she hadn't had anything to do with his spoiled plans.

"Understood," Treat continued. "I know it's Thailand. Yes, I know what this will mean for my international business."

Thailand? He'd been working on that deal when she first met him in Nassau. He'd canceled his flight there to officiate the wedding. Her stomach sank.

He ran his hand through his hair, staring out over the bay. "I'm changing things, beginning right now. I've got someone important in my life. No more constant traveling. No more foreign acquisitions that consume all of my attention."

As much as Max knew she should be flattered by what she was hearing, she was too conflicted to enjoy it. There was no forgetting the look in Treat's eyes when he told her how his work provided the biggest thrill he'd ever known. She braced herself as he came inside.

"Hey, sweetness. Sorry about that." He kissed her cheek, refilled his coffee cup, and sat at the table as though the tense phone conversation had never happened.

"Everything okay?"

"Fine, why?"

"Nothing. I just thought…Never mind." More worries burrowed into her. She'd been eavesdropping. She couldn't come out and ask about what she'd overheard.

He reached for her hand, and Max said, "If you have to do something for work, I totally understand. Don't let me hold you up. I can catch an earlier flight."

"There's nothing I have to do."

Max swore there was a hint of discomfort in his response, and she worried that even if it started as a hint, it could grow to something much bigger. She knew couples who gave up too much for their relationship could end up resenting each other. In the back of her mind, she'd always wondered if that had been the thing that had changed Ryan. Since he'd studied hotel management and could likely find a job anywhere, he'd agreed to move to wherever she found a job. He'd been prepared to relinquish any goals he'd been reaching for in his career in order for Max to follow her dreams. *And then he ended up hating me for it.*

She decided not to ruin their day with her worries and tabled her thoughts as much as she could. By midafternoon temperatures had risen, and they took a walk along the beach.

"I've never been a beach walker until that night in Nassau." Treat lifted their interlaced fingers and kissed her hand.

She loved knowing that. "I guess we've got a world of firsts between us, then, because I've never been a masseuse or had anyone give me a foot massage."

"Really? You've never had a foot massage? Well, sweetness, I'll be sure to take care of that from now on."

The tide was beginning to come in. They went down to the jetty and walked the length of it as the bay rose along the edge of the enormous rocks. Treat looked out over the water with his brows drawn together. Max had been watching his face go from placid to contemplative throughout the morning. She was dying to ask about Thailand, but she knew that if she brought it up, he'd tell her he would change his life for her without ever looking back. The thought of him giving up the aspects of his career that brought him such joy scared her. She couldn't shake the prickly reminder that being the impetus for such a major change was not a good thing. An intelligent, successful, overachiever like Treat would eventually get bored and blame her for everything he never had a chance to accomplish.

The thought weighed heavily on Max's mind all afternoon. They ate dinner at the Bookstore Restaurant by the harbor, and despite the cozy atmosphere and the beautiful evening, Max was too sidetracked to eat.

"Are you all right?" Treat asked.

"Just tired." She feigned a smile.

"That would be my fault for keeping you up so late the last two nights. I'll let you sleep tonight."

She reached for his hand, intending to ask him about the call, but before she could say a word, he said, "Max, I thought we should talk about what we want to do after this weekend is up."

She swallowed against the dull pain in the pit of her stomach. Now was her chance to let him off the hook, give him an easy out to say he needed to spend a few weeks away. She clenched her napkin in her fists beneath the table and said, "I'll be swamped at work, and I'm sure you will be, too."

"Never too swamped to spend time with you."

She loved him so much, but was this a fantasy? Could he really be happy giving up a piece of himself? Maybe she could go with him? Follow his career wherever it took them? Chaz had already said she could telecommute. But would she be happy traveling all over the world? Treat had built an empire, and she knew he needed the excitement of chasing down resorts and handling tough negotiations. He was a mover and a shaker, while she was a homebody. A *broken* homebody. She never knew when the issues from her past would pop up again, and though she knew for certain Treat would help her through them, part of her wondered if that was fair to him.

"Max? What am I feeling here?"

"Aren't guys supposed to hate talking about their feelings?" she asked.

"Not your guy," he said as he paid the bill.

They drove back to the bungalow and sat together under thick blankets on the back deck, watching the night sky bloom above the bay. Max wished she could freeze the evening right then and never have to make another decision.

"Are you ready to talk to me yet?" Treat asked.

Max's head rested against his chest, and she desperately wanted to tell him no, she didn't want to talk about it at all. They'd go back to their normal lives and either it would work out between them or it wouldn't. She wanted to tell him to go through with the acquisition of the Thailand property and not to put his life on hold for her—but she wanted to hold on to him for dear life and never let him go just as much. She'd once worried about trust, but lack of trust would have been easier to deal with than what was looming over her like a waiting storm. Being the reason he gave up what he loved versus holding on to him forever was a tug-of-war that had no winner.

He pulled her closer, and she closed her eyes, allowing herself once again to play with thoughts of spending every night with him, or being there for him when he returned from work. She realized she didn't even have a handle on what it was that he really did beyond buying resorts.

"Tell me something about what you do. I know you own resorts, but what does that really mean?"

"I don't want to bore you," he answered. "It sounds more glamorous than it is."

She sat up. "I would really like to understand it."

That flicker of excitement she'd seen back at her apartment appeared in his eyes again. "Well, I don't have a set schedule of things that I do on any given day. I have staff that take care of the resorts, and I have managers who oversee the staff, so I spend most of my time working on what comes next."

"What comes next?"

"New acquisitions, mergers, researching areas and distributors, running business valuations. I plan, scheme, analyze, and strategize." He leaned forward with a burst of enthusiasm. "I've been doing this for twelve years and I swear it never gets old. There's always something new to think about—and then there are renovations, grand openings, social events. I have to keep a pretty heavy social calendar to maintain professional relationships. It's a crazy, fantastic life. It's been a dream, really, a very good dream."

He looked at Max and must have read the worry in her eyes, because when he sat back, the excitement dissipated. "It's been fun, and I'm set for life now. I don't need to keep doing more. This is what I did before I found you, Max." His voice turned serious. "You have to remember, I was filling my days with work and my nights with whatever I could that held no chance for permanence. I was running from having a future outside of work, Max, not living the most fulfilling life I could."

He put his hand on her leg and squeezed it gently. "What I do is thrilling, and yes, I love it, but now that I'm ready to *really* live my life, now that I have you by my side, I want *more*. I want a house, permanence, and maybe even children one day. I want the dream that I've spent so many years running from."

Max didn't hear anything after *It's a crazy, fantastic life. It's been a dream, really, a very good dream.* She knew better than to take an aggressive, successful man and steal him out of his element for good. That would be like caging a bear. Eventually the bear would recognize the bars for what they were and tear them down—even if it meant hurting the person who had been nurturing him, tending to his needs, loving him for years.

Chapter Twenty-Three

THE FROWN MAX was trying so hard to hide cut right through Treat. He knew his enthusiasm for his work was intimidating, but he'd promised to always be honest. He wanted to take her in his arms and promise her the world that he knew he could give her, but something told him that she also saw his own turmoil. He had no concerns about Max, but Thailand was riding his nerves. He'd worked hard for that acquisition, and truth be told, he would give up everything to be with Max, but one last foray into negotiations would be a sweet send-off. It was the three months of international travel that caused him concern. There was no way he could expect Max to pick up her life and go with him. It was an unfair request.

"I've been clear about what I want," he said, holding her gaze. "What do you want, Max?"

She shrugged, tugging at his heartstrings.

"Max?" If she didn't want all those things, then what were they doing together? Why had they revealed their souls to each other?

She looked up at him, and he asked her again, "What is it that you want with me, babe? Where do you envision this going?"

Max pulled away. "I guess maybe we're moving a little fast."

Her words sent a swift kick to his gut. "A little *fast*? I thought you felt the same connection that I did. I thought you wanted this just as much as I do."

"I do, but—"

"But? Max, we can move slower. I never meant to push you."

"I'm sorry, but I overheard you on the phone talking about your Thailand deal. What if you give that up and then you resent me? Or if I *never* come to grips with my past? If I don't, that could suck for you."

His chest constricted. She worried so much about him. "First, I'll never resent you. I understand your concern, but, Max, there are plenty of properties I can acquire that don't require that type of travel. And as far as your past goes, I'm here no matter what. My only concern is that you don't drive yourself crazy with worry because of what you've been through. You never had closure. I don't want you facing that guy again, but maybe talking with a therapist would help."

She nodded, tears in her eyes, and rested her head on his chest. "Maybe," she said just above a whisper. "I don't want you to give up what you love for me, especially when I still have so much to work through."

"We'll work through it together."

MAX WAS EMOTIONALLY exhausted. She wanted nothing more than to close her eyes and erase the anxious evening that had found them. She was relieved when Treat took her hand and led her upstairs. They took a warm bath together and lay talking into the wee hours. Long after Treat fell asleep, Max's heart still wouldn't settle. Every time she closed her eyes she saw his gorgeous dark eyes dancing with excitement as he told her how much he loved his work. She'd also felt his genuine honesty when he'd talked about wanting to live a fuller life. Who was she to question what he really wanted?

As she lay in the confines of his loving arms, staring at a streak of moonlight streaming through the curtains, a sudden and jarring thought occurred to her. What was she *really* afraid of? She trusted Treat with her whole heart. If he told her something, she knew it was true. She thought about what he'd said about closure and wondered if he knew her better than she knew herself.

Was she really trying to save him from a lifetime of resentment, or was she running from happiness because she didn't trust that Ryan hadn't ruined her for life? She'd missed the signs back in college. The way he'd suddenly started drinking more, going out to bars, becoming mean, and lost interest in talking with her. She'd never miss those signs again, but she didn't want to *recognize* them in Treat years from now and know she was the cause. She had no doubt that Treat knew himself well enough to make the right decision for both of them. But did she know herself well enough to do the same?

Too restless to lie still, she stepped quietly from the bed and went to the window, gazing out at the reflection of the moon rippling on the water. She needed a guidebook to navigate her past and create a future, or a mother who could tell her the *right* way to handle this. Since she didn't have either, she had to make a decision.

With her heart in her throat, she grabbed her phone and went downstairs.

She was shaking as she sank to the couch and pulled up Facebook. She loathed social media for anything other than promoting the festival. The idea of posting updates about what she did all day seemed an enormous waste of time, right up there with tweeting and getting manicures. Well, maybe a manicure now and then would be nice. With a deep breath, she typed *Ryan Cobain, Texas A&M* into the search bar. Within seconds several Ryan Cobains appeared. Her ex-boyfriend's photo stared back at her, and her heart nearly stopped. She hadn't set eyes on him in years, and she hadn't prepared herself for the stab of hurt slicing through her. His thick brown hair was cut shorter now, and his face had thinned. If she didn't know him, she'd think he was a handsome, happy man. But she did know him. She looked into his green eyes and saw the same fiery mess of a man she'd seen the day she left.

She told herself to put her phone down and go back to bed, to disappear into the safety of Treat's arms. But Ryan would always be lurking in the shadows. With a shaky hand, she clicked on the message icon. She was pretty sure there was no way he would respond, but she had to try to slay the demons that were poisoning her like a disease.

She stared at the message box with absolutely no idea what to type. *Hey, this is Max. Remember me? The girl you mistreated?* She closed her eyes, and it was Treat's voice whispering through her mind, telling her he'd be there no matter what and that they'd heal together, that gave her strength. She struggled for what seemed like hours but in reality was probably only fifteen minutes before finally typing, *Hi.* That was all she could do. She hit return and then stared at the screen like it might come alive. Her body was poised to flee, or fight, which was silly since it was only a message.

"That was stupid," she said to the empty room, and padded into the kitchen. She set her phone on the counter while she poured herself some juice.

A few minutes later her phone chimed, and Max's pulse sprinted. Holding her breath, she reached for the phone, then stopped. *I don't want to do this. Yes, I do.* She closed her eyes, gathering courage like a cloak, and finally picked up the phone. With her jaw clenched so tight she worried she might crack a tooth, she read his message.

Hey, Max. How are you?

She bit her lower lip and typed, *Fine.* Since when had she become a liar? She was so far from *fine* right then, she could barely think.

His response was instant. *Glad to hear it.*

She stared at the screen, trying to figure out what she wanted to achieve. She never did things without a plan in place, and suddenly she was adrift in a sea of worries. Why had she reached out? What did she really want? Closure? To see if she was strong enough to actually face him? To see if he regretted how he'd treated her?

All of the above?

She typed, *Where are you living?* Again, his response came quickly. *Yakima, Washington. You?*

Max's hands stopped cold. She didn't want him to know where she lived, but somewhere in the back of her mind, she was already forming a plan.

She typed, *I'm in your area tomorrow for work. I'd like to come by and talk.*

He answered quickly. *Working all day.*

Where? She stared at the screen after sending the message and then read his response twice—*Crowne Inn, off Central*

Ave—before making her decision and typing, *Can I stop by?*

She held her breath as his response rolled in.

I never thought you'd speak to me again. Yes, I'd like that. I have things to tell you.

She had things to tell him, too, though she had no idea if they'd come out in tears or rage, and she didn't care. She needed to do this, if for no other reason than to get the hatred she'd been harboring out at the *right* person. Her efficient, organized mind was already racing through the travel and work arrangements she'd need to make. She hated the idea of leaving Treat to deal with this, but she knew if they had any chance at a future, it was necessary.

She responded with, *Okay. 7:00 p.m.?*

Once he agreed, she went to work making travel arrangements before she could chicken out. She'd left Ryan once, and she'd carried the nightmare of him with her like a silent predator.

After tomorrow she hoped to never feel like his prey again.

Chapter Twenty-Four

TREAT'S ARM FELL on an empty sheet. He opened his eyes and found Max curled up in the chair by the window. "Hey, babe. You okay?"

"Yeah," she said softly as she came to him and sat on the bed. "I need to talk to you."

"I'm all ears."

She pressed a kiss to his bare chest and said, "Well, not *all* ears."

He put his arm around her, pulling her down for a kiss. "What's going on? You seem tense."

"I am. I have to leave."

"Leave?" He sat up, feeling gutted. "Why? What's going on?"

"Nothing bad. I promise."

The uncertainty in her beautiful eyes worried him. "Then why are you leaving?"

She drew in a deep breath and blew it out slowly. "When we were in Nassau, I knew right away how much we felt for each other. And when we reunited in Colorado, my feelings for you became crystal clear. Being here these past few days has only solidified that in my heart and in my mind."

"Then why are you leaving? Is it because of the Thailand deal?"

"Not really, but in a sense, yes. I've been where we are now, where one person has to give up something big to make the relationship work. And I know that the love that drives people together can turn to resentment. Once the honeymoon stage wears off and real life comes in with deadlines, pressures, and late nights and all you want is to be left alone, you can't help but lose the feelings that drove you together. And then resentment creeps in."

He took her hand in his and said, "Max, that's not true. I don't know who you're using as your basis for that knowledge, but if it's your ex, then please, throw that out altogether. That's not going to happen with us." He gripped her hand tighter, unwilling to let her break their connection.

"Maybe you're right, but we need to think about a way around that, and while we're thinking about it, I need to finally get closure with my past. I don't want to bring my ghosts into our relationship, no matter how willing you are to let me. I love you for that, but it's time for me to grow up and finally face the man who hurt me. That's the only way I'll ever put what happened behind me."

"What are you saying, exactly? Where are you going?"

"To see Ryan. To unbury my ghosts and finally set them free. I spoke to Chaz and told him I needed a few more days off."

The thought of Max facing that deviant brought Treat to his feet. "I'm going with you." He strode toward the shower, rage and concern warring inside him.

"Treat, *stop*."

"You're not doing this alone, Max."

"You told me you liked that I was supremely strong," she said as she closed the distance between them. "That if we were together back then, you'd want to hear what I had to say. I love you for wanting to go with me, but this is *my* past, *my* hurt, and letting you deal with it would make me as weak as I felt when it happened. I'm finally taking my grandmother's advice and speaking my mind. I have to do this, and I have to do it alone."

"You're asking me to let you walk into the hands of a deviant. The hands of a man who hurt you so badly that it still haunts you."

She wrapped her arms around his middle, gazing up with trusting, determined eyes. "I am, because if we are going to have any chance at a normal future, I need to do this. The same way you need to not give up the things that make you happy. You deserve a woman who is whole in every way. Let me try to become that woman."

He embraced her too tightly, gritting his teeth against all his basal instincts. "I want to go with you. I'll wait in the car, whatever, just let me be there."

She shook her head, and it was that fierce determination that made him cave. "I will never go through with it if you're with me. It's too easy to let you take care of me in that way. Please grant me the space to do it."

He ground his teeth together. "For the record, I hate this idea, no matter how proud of you I am for taking this step. I'm driving you to the airport, and I want to know this guy's name, where you're meeting him, and when."

"I already wrote down everything. It's on the counter. I knew you'd want it, and don't worry. I'm meeting him in a public place, where he works." A small smile lifted her lips, and she said, "I'd really like it if you would drive me to the airport, but what about my car?"

"Smitty will take care of returning it."

"Okay, but we need to hurry. I don't want to miss my flight."

AFTER DROPPING MAX at her gate for her flight, Treat's protective urges surged even stronger than they had all morning. He had his bags packed and in the trunk, but Max had remained adamant about doing this herself. He strode toward the ticket counter, hoping she'd forgive him for showing up anyway.

His phone rang, and he pulled it from his pocket without looking at the number.

"Max?"

"Uh, no. It's me."

"Sorry, Savannah." Treat's mind was reeling. He had to get a ticket.

"I thought Max was with you."

He tamped down the urge to snap at her. "She was. What do you need?"

"It's Dad. He's sick, and I'm really worried about him."

"I just saw him. He was strong as an ox." He decided to hell with the ticket for a later flight. He'd charter a plane and beat Max there, so he could be waiting when she arrived.

"Treat, are you listening to me?"

The edge in Savannah's voice pulled him back to the call. "Yes, sorry."

"You have to come home. Dad's having bouts of dizziness and chest pains, and I'm scared."

His gut wrenched at the position he was in, but Max had made her choice, and his father may not have one. "Get him to the hospital. I'm on my way."

Cursing under his breath, he called and left Max a message telling her he was heading home, and then he called his buddy Brett Bad, owner of Elite Security, and arranged for an investigation into the man who had hurt Max, as well as a private, plain-clothed security professional to watch over her in his absence. She might get pissed at that, but he wasn't taking any chances with her safety.

Chapter Twenty-Five

THINGS BECAME CRYSTAL clear to Treat as he sat by his father's bedside in the hospital. It was time for him to come home and put down roots, and he wanted to do that with Max. He had built his empire based on his keen negotiating skills and his belief in personally being involved with every transaction. He'd entrenched himself so deeply that when it came to acquisitions, partnered with his legal and financial advisers, there was never a need to look outside of his own abilities. Now he was seeing another side to what he'd always done. He'd been hiding—from the guilt of leaving his family, from commitment, and from love. For the first time in his life, he cared about someone enough to want to stop hiding.

He took his father's hand in his own, hoping it wasn't too late for him to make up for all the years they'd missed.

"Do you want to go to Dad's and put your stuff away? Relax for a little while?" Savannah asked.

"I'm not leaving," Treat insisted. "But you can. I'll be here when he wakes up."

"I'm not ready to leave. Rex is coming back after he takes care of the evening chores. I'm sure it'll be fine if you want to take shifts."

"Savannah, I'm not going anywhere." He didn't mean to sound gruff, but seeing his father in the hospital bed brought painful memories of his mother's last months. She'd been in and out of the hospital too many times to count, and though his father was much bigger, the hospital had the same effect on both of them, making them look diminished and weak beneath the sterile sheets.

"Okay. Dane finally got my messages. He's in Australia and he's taking the next flight home."

"Did you reach Hugh?"

"He's on his way, and before you can ask, Josh is on his way, too. He had to move his schedule around before he could leave," she said. She moved to the seat closer to Treat. "Do you want to talk?"

"No. I want the doctors to finish the frigging tests and tell us what's wrong with him."

Their father stirred.

"Dad?" Treat rose to his feet as Hal blinked the sleep from his eyes.

"Treat? What are you doing here?" He looked around the room, confused. "What the…?" He looked down at his gown. "Aw, come on." He frowned at Savannah.

Treat breathed a sigh of relief to see their father hadn't lost his spunk. That had to be a good sign.

"You weren't able to breathe, Dad. What did you want me to do, let you die right there in front of me?" Savannah asked.

"Wait." It suddenly struck Treat that Savannah was supposed to have been back home in New York when this happened. "Why were you at Dad's? I thought you went back to the city."

His father's low, rumbly voice answered him. "Turns out

Connor Dean's more than a client, and your sister here seems to have had a falling out with the man who isn't good enough for her family to meet but is apparently good enough for her to jet all over the world with."

Treat lifted his brows in Savannah's direction.

Savannah half shrugged, then turned away—her familiar *I can't talk about it right now* mannerism.

As much as Treat wanted to find out what was going on with his sister, he couldn't focus on her love life right then. Not while Max was across the country preparing to face down her nemesis and his father was lying in a hospital bed. "Dad, you should probably settle down. They're running all sorts of tests to see what happened, but they think it might have been your heart."

"*Pfft.*" Hal waved a hand as if that were absurd. "I saw your mother again, that's all. Your sister overreacted."

Savannah and Treat exchanged a worried look. Treat thought back to when he'd first arrived at the bungalow. He'd sworn his mother was nearby, and even now he wondered if she had been.

Their father pushed the button on his bed, raising it so he could sit up properly. "Don't think I didn't see that look, you two."

"Dad," Savannah began. "We're just worried about you."

"Well, how about you worry about yourself. And *you*." He pointed at Treat. "Your mother is worried sick about you. What the hell are you doing about that sweet girl, Max? I met her, you know. We all did. Reminds me of your mother. She's a darlin' thing, and I bet she's got a stubborn side, too."

Treat smiled to himself, thinking about their morning. "Yes, she does."

Luckily, before they went any further down the *your mother* road, the doctor came into the room. Dr. Mason Carpenter had been their father's physician for as long as Treat could remember. When he retired two years earlier, his son and partner in the medical practice, Ben, had taken over. Ben and Treat had grown up together, and Treat not only trusted his medical judgment, but he had always found Ben to be a loyal friend. He shook Ben's hand.

"Treat, good to see you," Ben said, his eyes shifting to Savannah.

Ben had harbored a crush on Savannah when they were younger. Treat remembered the summer after Savannah had completed ninth grade and he and Ben had been home from college. Savannah had realized that her body was no longer that of a young girl and had flaunted it as such, much to Treat's dismay. Ben hadn't been able to take his eyes off her then, and from the looks of him now, those feelings hadn't changed.

"Savannah, you're still here," Ben said with surprise. "Nice to see you heeded my suggestion to go home and relax for a while."

"Yes, and I'm not leaving anytime soon." She crossed her arms and narrowed her eyes at him.

"Benjamin, when am I getting out of this place?" their father asked.

Ben smiled and said, "Well, Mr. Braden, I have to ask you a few questions. What were you doing when your symptoms began? Savannah wasn't sure. Were you doing anything strenuous?"

"I told you. He was in the barn when I found him—"

"The last time I looked, honey, I was Mr. Braden," their father said. "Now, he might have been talking to Treat, I suppose, but Ben here has been to medical school, and I can't imagine by the way he looks at you that he would mistake you for a *mister*."

Ben blushed.

Savannah stewed.

Treat laughed under his breath. *Yup, Dad. You're just fine.*

"To answer your question, I was in the barn with Hope," their father answered. "And, Ben, call me Hal, please. How many years have I been telling you that?"

"And were you brushing her? Mucking out the stall?" Ben asked. "What exactly were you doing?"

Treat had to smile at the way Ben ignored his father's request. Ben had told his father at least a dozen times that he had too much respect for him to call him by his first name, and his father still hadn't stopped grumbling about it.

Hal set his mouth in a serious line and crossed his arms. Treat watched his father's biceps bounce to the same rhythm of his clenching jaw, reminding him so much of Rex, it was uncanny. Sitting up straighter, with annoyance stewing just under his skin, his father no longer looked small or sickly in the hospital gown. He looked like he was ready to haul his butt out of bed and get back to work.

There's the dad I know and love. Treat looked up at the ceiling and mouthed, *Thank you.*

"Mr. Braden?" Ben urged.

Hal grumbled under his breath, then said, "Oh, all right. But I don't want to hear any crap about this, you hear me, Benjamin?"

"Yes, sir. No crap," Ben said with a nod.

Ben had seen Hal through every mood on the spectrum. He and his parents had enjoyed many barbecues at the ranch with his family.

"I was talking to Adriana." Hal scanned his children's faces first, then his doctor's.

Treat knew his father saw exactly what he did on Savannah and Ben's faces—pity. He used to have to work hard to keep that same look from his own, but after the Cape, he was no longer certain of anything where his mother was concerned.

"Don't look at me like that. It doesn't matter what you think of it. Adriana was there, and she was watching over Hope the same way I was." He shifted his eyes to Treat and pointed a finger. "She's worried that you're going to get so lost in your own little world of resorts and whatever else eats up your time, you'll forget about the thing that matters most." He patted his heart.

Ben drew his eyebrows together, and Treat held his hands palms up, as if to say, *That's Dad for you.* But Treat couldn't lie to himself. His father's words spoke directly to his thoughts where Max was concerned.

"Mr. Braden, I don't doubt that you believe you saw your wife," Ben said carefully, "or that you have ongoing conversations with her."

"Oh, for crying out loud, Ben," Savannah said with a sigh.

Treat touched her arm and shook his head. She sat down and crossed her legs, bouncing her foot up and down.

"Hear me out, please, Savannah." Ben continued. "Your father had all the symptoms of a heart attack, but I believe he actually suffered from broken heart syndrome."

"Okay, you know what?" Savannah rose to her feet and headed for the door. "I can't listen to this nonsense anymore. Treat, get me when…just get me after, okay?"

"I'm sorry, Ben," Treat said. "She's apparently had a rough

time lately. Please continue."

"Broken heart syndrome can mirror all the symptoms of a heart attack, from difficulty breathing and chest pain to low blood pressure and even weakening of the heart muscle."

"That sounds like a heart attack. What's the difference?" Treat placed his hand over his father's.

"Well, BHS is also called stress cardiomyopathy, because it's caused by severe stress, usually emotional—intense fear, anger, surprise. There are two major differences between a heart attack and BHS. The first is that most heart attacks occur due to blockages and blood clots forming in the coronary arteries. If those clots cut off the blood supply to the heart for a long enough time, the heart muscle cells can die, leaving the patient with permanent and irreversible damage. But with BHS, patients have fairly normal coronary arteries, like your father does, without the presence of severe blockage or clots."

No blockage. No clots. Good arteries. Treat squeezed his father's hand.

"The second difference," Ben explained, "is that with stress cardiomyopathy, the heart cells are stunned by the adrenaline and other stress hormones, but not killed as they are with a heart attack. And as I'm certain we'll find with your father, that stunned effect gets better very quickly, often within just a few short days. So even if a patient suffers heart muscle weakness at the time of the event, the heart completely recovers within just a few weeks, and in most cases, there's no permanent damage."

"And that's what you expect with Dad?" *That's it. I'm definitely spending more time at home.*

"Yes, exactly. From what we've seen with BHS, there's no pattern of recurrence. It can happen, but we've never observed it."

"So, you're saying I was too emotional and had a fake heart attack that weakened the heart muscle, but it'll repair itself and I'll be fine?" Hal asked.

"Yes, sir. The damage to your heart muscles was minimal, so you should make a full recovery."

"Well, then, I can go home and run my ranch." Hal started to get out of bed.

Ben put a hand on Hal's arm. "Not so fast. We gave you some medication to lighten the load on your heart while you recover. I want to monitor you for the next few hours, but then you should be good to go. I'll go over the protocol with you before you're released."

"So he should be okay?" Treat asked.

"Yes." Ben looked at Hal and said, "But, Mr. Braden, you cannot go back to working the ranch right away, as I know you'd like to. You should recover in a few weeks. But during that time, I don't want you to do any strenuous work. Treat, can I count on you to ensure that he complies?" Ben ignored Hal's groan and his harsh stare.

"Of course," Treat answered.

"He's got his own life to lead, Benjamin. What kind of garbage is that?" Hal lowered his voice and mumbled, "I don't need a babysitter."

"Of course you don't. I'm sure you'll go home and do exactly what I advise, because you were always so compliant with my father." Ben coughed and said, "Broken arm," at the same time.

Treat cracked a smile at his friend's levity and his father's simmering anger. Years earlier, his father had suffered a fractured arm, and instead of listening to Ben's father's medical advice, he was back on his favorite horse later that afternoon— and in the doctor's office two hours later, after the fracture had morphed into a full break and he'd needed a cast.

"Ben, thank you. I appreciate you taking such good care of him." Treat shook Ben's hand.

"Do you want me to send Savannah in if I see her?" Ben asked.

"No need," Savannah said as she walked in with her cell phone in her hand and suspicious red rings around the edges of her eyes. "I heard all of it."

Treat knew she'd been crying, though if that was due to their father or Connor, he couldn't be sure. He put his hand protectively on the small of her back.

"I'm sorry if I upset you, Savannah," Ben said.

She nodded, then took her father's hand. "So, basically, Dad needs to stop talking to Mom and stop worrying about us?"

Ben smiled. "Well, given that I don't think your father will ever stop doing either one of those things, no. For now we'll go with something a little easier, like maybe talking out some of his frustrations instead of holding them in."

"I'm not talking to a therapist, if that's what you're saying, Benjamin. Your father would never ask me to do that," Hal said.

"Dad, you'll do whatever he tells you to do," Savannah said.

"Don't worry. I would never think of advising such a thing. My father schooled me well in the way of the Bradens. What I recommend is that when you are worried—or your wife is worried"—he ignored Savannah's eye roll—"about something like your children, talk to them about it. Don't keep it inside. And if there are troubles with the ranch, talk it through with Rex."

"Or me," Treat added.

"Did I hear my name?" Rex came through the door. His

eyes locked on his father's, then slowly met Treat's. "Talk what through with me?"

"I was telling your father that he needed to stop holding things in, and if he has issues with the ranch, to talk them through with you...or Treat, I suppose," Ben said.

"Treat's never here," Savannah argued.

"Of course." Rex kept his eyes locked on his father. "You can count on me, and Savannah's right. Treat's never here."

Treat met Rex's cold gaze and said, "I will be from now on."

Chapter Twenty-Six

MAX SPENT THE long flight praying that she could carry out her plan, then second- and third-guessing it altogether. Several times she'd been ready to nix the whole thing, and by the time she arrived in Washington she was a nervous wreck. After listening to Treat's message, she felt sick to her stomach. It was bad enough that his father was ill, but that she wasn't there with him because of Ryan made her feel a hundred times worse. In his message, Treat had asked her again not to see Ryan alone, but now it was more important than ever that she finally lay her past to rest so she could focus on their future. Despite the ache in her heart, she had to believe she was doing the right thing.

She checked into a hotel near the airport and riffled through her clothes, looking for just the right thing to wear. Something that said, *I'm strong and capable. You didn't break me.*

Hopefully not forever, at least.

After shuffling through her clothes, trying on a few outfits, and shedding tears, Max knew what she had to wear. She went to the front pocket of her suitcase, where she'd stuffed Treat's T-shirt that she'd slept in. She inhaled the scent of the man she loved and then pulled it on. Tucking it in was interesting, to say the least, since it hung almost to her knees. She finally gave up and gathered the long shirt in her hands, tying the bottom into a knot at her waist. She threw a sweatshirt on over it and put on her most comfortable jeans, then stared at the two pairs of shoes she'd brought to the Cape.

Sneakers. In case I freak out and have to bolt.

THE CROWNE INN was built on the flattest piece of ground Max had ever seen. It stood alone among parking lots and grassy lawn. There was no place to hide. She drove slowly past the hotel, scoping out the place where she would finally confront her demons. The building looked like any other hotel, a few stories high, big windows, mostly curtained, and a circular drive that led to a covered entrance.

As fear bloomed inside her, settling in her gut like lead, she tried to remember why she'd thought going there made sense. She turned the car around, driving by the hotel in the other direction, contemplating getting back on the highway and returning home. She crossed in front of the hotel two more times, until she was sure the police would spot her and arrest her for stalking. *That would be just my luck.*

She surveyed the parking lot again, and a shiver ran down her back. The hotel was far off the beaten track. Anything could happen out here. Maybe that was Ryan's plan. Lure her to a remote location and do something horrible to her. He'd said he had something to talk to her about. Maybe that was a ruse. Wait—she'd contacted *him*. She was being stupid. They were in a public place. She'd be fine. She *hoped*.

She parked at the far end of the parking lot, giving herself plenty of time on the walk inside to change her mind and turn back. She held on to the hem of Treat's T-shirt, trying to remain courageous. When she reached the entrance, she stopped and breathed deeply. She paced the sidewalk, then unzipped her sweatshirt so she could see Treat's shirt beneath, pulling forward memories of the way he cared for her, the way he'd nurtured her strength and her heart. That's what she wanted, to be loved and to heal. She had to do this. To cleanse herself from the memories that stalked her like prey and pulled her back from every forward step she took.

Inhaling deeply, and feeling like she was living on deep breaths, she entered the hotel. A burly, dark-haired man glanced up from behind a newspaper in the lobby as Max walked past.

The perky woman behind the desk smiled and said, "Welcome to the Crowne Inn."

Her high-pitched enthusiasm cut right through Max's anxiety like a knife, causing her to freeze in the middle of the large, open lobby. *Walk. Leave. Do something!* Her mind warred with itself, confusing her legs into unmovable pillars. Was she insane? This was the worst idea ever!

She finally managed to turn around and headed for the doors. She was *not* staying here.

"Max?"

The hairs on the back of Max's neck stood on end at the sound of Ryan's voice. She was vaguely aware of the man who had been reading the newspaper rising to his feet. She clenched her fists against the fear crashing over her and reminded herself that she was *superbly strong*.

She forced herself to turn around, trying her best to feign a smile, but the way her teeth were grinding together, she knew she hadn't pulled it off.

She could hardly breathe as she looked at the man she'd

trusted and thought she'd loved. The man who had hurt her so badly, she'd fled like a thief in the night. He wore a dark blue suit with a gold badge over his breast pocket that read RYAN COBAIN, HOTEL MANAGER, and he was smiling as if he was truly glad to see her. That's not what he'd looked like at the end, in those weeks she'd spent stifled by his aggression.

He took a step forward, and again she had no control over her legs as they took a step back.

He stilled, his gaze turning apologetic. "Max?"

She willed herself to stand tall, and this time her body obeyed. She looked down at Treat's shirt, wishing she had dressed a little nicer. Ryan had an edge on her in his nice suit and on his turf. *Wait! What am I thinking? I am in control.* She willed herself to pull it together, straightening her spine as she drew her shoulders back. She felt the familiar strength she'd called upon so often with her career, the powerful energy that began in her gut and traveled into her limbs.

She took a step forward, then another. She could do this! She extended her hand. "Ryan," she said in a frosty tone she didn't recognize.

He took her hand and buried it within both of his. She steeled herself against the initial jolt of panic.

"So good to see you, Max. You look gorgeous, of course."

"Thank you."

He motioned toward a door beside the front desk. "We can talk in my office."

Public. Stay in sight of others. "You know, I'd really like a cup of coffee. Is there a restaurant on-site?"

"Sure."

She walked beside him down a wide hallway, stealing glances out of her peripheral vision. He didn't seem nervous, and he wasn't acting sketchy. In fact, he seemed like the old Ryan, the guy he'd been before he changed—comfortable, confident. He led her to a small, dimly lit restaurant, where they were seated at a table off to the side.

"I was surprised to hear from you," Ryan said. He called over the waitress and ordered a cup of coffee for Max and a glass of water for himself.

Max watched his mannerisms and found them to be reflective of the guy she'd met when they'd first begun dating. Gone were the jumpy eyes and fast, uncontrolled movements she remembered. It was a mask; she was sure of it. *A game he's just gotten better at.*

Ryan said something she didn't quite hear. She was too busy remembering how he'd changed over the duration of their relationship. She'd spent so much time living in the shadow of the man he'd become, she'd all but buried the man he'd once been. Now, as she saw this new version of him, she remembered the better times, how quickly they'd hit it off and become more than friends. They'd had months of laughs and happy times. She remembered moving in together and how good she'd felt about it.

The waitress brought their drinks. Max noticed the man from the lobby seated at a nearby table and wondered how she'd missed him coming in.

"Max? Are you okay?"

"I'm sorry," she said, realizing she'd zoned out. "What did you say?"

"I didn't think I'd ever hear from you again after—"

Max dropped her eyes, then silently scolded herself for doing it. This was *her* ball game. Treat's voice gave her strength once again. *You took care of you, Max, and that makes you supremely strong.*

She'd thought of all sorts of ways to handle Ryan, and in the end she fell back on her fail-safe. Honesty. "I surprised myself," Max admitted, "but I wanted to…I needed closure."

"I tried to track you down for weeks after you left, Max. Your parents wouldn't answer my calls. You, well, you never answered anything—calls, emails."

She wouldn't apologize for not responding. She wouldn't apologize for *anything.*

Ryan held her gaze and said, "I finally found you in Colorado."

You tracked me down? Every muscle in her body tensed.

"You worked for a small film company, then a festival company. I've written you dozens of letters and emails over the years, but never had the courage to send them."

You stalked me. What if you had shown up in Allure? What would you have done?

"In the end," he said, "I knew it was unfair to reach out to you."

Ryan kept eye contact with her, which she found unsettling and reassuring at the same time. People who had something to hide avoided eye contact. Why wasn't he acting like he'd done something so wrong to her that it had ruined her ability to have a real relationship?

"I would have fled if I'd known you'd found me again," Max said with her chin held high.

"I don't blame you," he said, and this time it was he who lowered his gaze.

Finally. A little remorse?

When he lifted his eyes, they were soft and apologetic. "Max, I owe you an explanation and an apology, which I know will never be enough to fix what I did."

"I don't want to hear your excuses, Ryan. There is no excuse for what you put me through." *Then what do I want?* Tears of anger stung her eyes, and she refused to let them fall. "You stole something from me, and I can never get it back. You stole my dignity, and you stole my trust." Her voice rose despite her effort to remain calm, and the man who had been reading the newspaper in the lobby looked perched to come to her defense.

"I know I did," Ryan said, "and I've regretted it every day since."

Max didn't hear him. She was too busy formulating her next accusation. "You made me fear relationships and turned me into someone who…" What was she doing? She didn't come here to tell him what he'd *achieved*. She'd come here to prove to him— to herself—that she was fine even though he'd tried his best to tear her down.

"Max—"

"No, Ryan. I honestly don't want to hear your excuses. They're meaningless."

"Max, I was sick. Okay? It's not an excuse."

Max pulled her shoulders back. She was ready for lies. She'd expected them. "Right, Ryan. I was there, remember? You weren't sick. You just changed. You stopped talking to every-one, stopped talking to me. You'd look at me with this cold stare sometimes, and it was like you had been hiding your meanness, or your hatred for me, for all those months, and then you just released them."

"Max—"

"I'm not stupid. I took the hint. I just took it one night too late," she seethed. "And I know it had to do with agreeing to move wherever I got a job instead of where you did. I've finally figured it all out—"

"Max!"

His deep, loud voice startled her out of her rant.

"Max." He lowered his voice and said, "I'm schizophrenic. They missed all the signs over that year or so. We all did. After you left, I fell apart. I spiraled out of control so badly at times that I was afraid to even go home."

"Schizophrenic?" Max had not seen that coming. She narrowed her eyes, looking for signs of deceit.

"Think about it, Max. My behavior changed radically. When I look back now, I see it. That night I...hurt you? It wasn't even you I was seeing or yelling at. I was sexually abused when I was little, but I'd blocked it out. I was delusional. In my mind, it wasn't you I was hurting. It was the woman who had molested me."

"Oh, Ryan." All the bravado that had built up in her chest came tumbling down. "How did you figure it out?"

"One night I hurt someone else. Badly. She didn't call the police or anything, but she could have. In fact," he said with his eyebrows drawn together, "she probably should have. That's when I knew something was really wrong. I went home and told my parents that I wasn't going to leave their house because I was afraid of what I might do to someone else."

Max had considered calling the police when Ryan had hurt her, but the shame of willingly allowing him to use that thing on her had held her back. Now she realized she might have saved the other woman from being hurt if she'd filed a police report.

Swallowing past a painful lump in her throat, she said, "You hurt someone else?"

Ryan explained that he'd hooked up with another girl a few

nights after Max had left him, and they'd gone back to her apartment off campus. While they were in bed, she'd taken the dominant role, and Ryan's memories had come rushing back. "It was like I blacked out. I didn't remember hurting her, or calling her names, and by the time I regained control, she had locked herself in the bathroom, bruised and bleeding. She told me that if I left, she wouldn't report me to the police. After I was back home for a week or two, my parents began to notice—or maybe *accept* is a better word—the changes. My father tracked down psychiatrists and psychologists. He took me to just about every doctor he could find. They all made the same diagnosis, but he didn't want to accept it. I didn't want to accept it either, but I also didn't want to be the person who hurt others."

"Should I have seen something in particular? Did I miss a major sign? Was it triggered by the thought of moving with me out of state?" Max asked. *All these years I thought your anger was aimed at me specifically. What else have I misjudged?*

"No. It had nothing to do with that. They don't really know why I started recalling the memories, but I went through an inpatient program, where they assessed and treated and reassessed. You know my mom. She was nowhere near prepared to deal with this. I've gone through years of therapy, and it took forever for them to find the right protocol of drugs to even things out. But it's been a few years since they figured it out and got it right." He shrugged. "And now it's just a part of who I am and who I will always be. Luckily, with medication, I'm not violent, and I don't have delusions anymore. I just kind of live a regular life with all of that hanging over me."

Max's heart hurt for him, and for herself.

He took a drink of water and then said, "Max, I'm not

telling you this to gain your sympathy. I take full responsibility for my illness and for my actions. But I am glad that you got in touch with me. I have been wanting to explain this to you and to apologize. I know you, Max, and I know you probably blamed yourself all these years. You're so sensitive. It's one of the things I loved about you. I'm so sorry for those weeks, that night, and for all the nights since that you've relived it. If I could erase it all from your mind and add your burden to mine, I'd do it in a heartbeat."

It wasn't me. It wasn't because he was going to move with me. The thoughts of her misplaced blame were quickly pushed aside and replaced with thoughts of Ryan, the boy she'd known before he changed and the man he was, bravely sitting there with her, exposing the most vulnerable parts of himself.

"You must have been so scared when you were going through it," she said. *As scared as I was that night.*

"Petrified. Imagine not wanting to live in your own skin. That's what it was like," he said with a hefty dose of shame. "When I think back to how I hurt you, the awful things I said, and that night...and then the other woman, who I have since explained my situation to and apologized. I just wish it all never happened."

She saw pain and honesty in his eyes, and beyond that, she saw something that she had never expected to see again. She saw the young man who had been her friend, and she remembered what Savannah had said about forgiveness. Maybe this was just what they both needed.

If someone had asked her yesterday if she'd ever forgive Ryan Cobain, she would have said, *Never,* without hesitation. As she looked at him sitting across from her, not hiding behind his illness, not shirking the responsibility of having done those hurtful acts, but laying his life out for her like an open book, she felt the anger leaving her body, floating out with the words as they rolled off her tongue. "Ryan," she said with a shaky voice. "I forgive you."

He looked down at his lap. A little nag in the back of Max's mind worried that when he looked up again, it would be with the cold eyes she remembered—but he didn't. The same warm man who had apologized only moments before was right there in front of her, looking at her with empathy, honesty, and tears in his eyes.

"I can't tell you what that means to me," he admitted, and then shifted his gaze around the room as he blinked away tears. "I'm sorry I'm so emotional."

"How could you not be? This whole thing is emotional. Those years were emotional. Do you remember what we were like when we first met? Everything had us on an emotional high." She was astonished that she'd said it, much less wanted to remember those better times, but it felt good.

"Yeah, I do." He wrinkled his brow. "Max, I have to ask, why now? After all these years, why are you just tracking me down now? You don't have to tell me. It's none of my business. I'm just curious."

Max touched her shirt. *Treat.* "It's okay. I don't mind telling you. I met someone, and, well, I'm not the same person I was when I was with you. After I left, I grew up and became self-sufficient." *But remained scared, until now.* "He makes me even stronger."

"Wait. Do you take out your own trash?" he asked with a teasing smile.

"Yes." She grinned, remembering how she'd deemed that a *boy job.*

"No way. Do you ask for help in stores?"

"All the time. Gosh, I'd forgotten how shy I was. What a mess I was back then." She covered her eyes briefly and shook her head.

"You were adorable, Max. I always knew how strong you were. I never had any doubt about your strength and courage. You were destined to accomplish everything you dreamed of. So, this guy, is he good to you?"

Max's heart swelled even thinking about Treat. "He's the most incredible man I have ever met, and yes, he's very good to me." Talking to the old Ryan was easy, comforting even. If only she'd learned years ago what she now saw so clearly. How different would her life have been? And if she hadn't come to slay her demons...Well, she couldn't even go there. It was too painful to think of how close she'd come to turning around and going home.

"In case you're worried about your guy changing, what I have is pretty rare, Max. We were right at that age when it shows up. We're past that now. I don't think you have to worry about another guy going crazy on you out of the blue." Ryan wasn't making fun of her. He was being honest, like the old Ryan, thinking of her well-being.

"Thank you for that," she said. "For all these years I thought you hurt me because you resented me. I was pretty certain of it. It's guided my relationships, or maybe I should say my lack of relationships."

"Max, I would have followed you anywhere. That's what relationships are, give and take. Compromises are essential." Ryan watched a petite redhead walking their way, and when she arrived at their table, he reached out to her. "Rachelle, this is Max."

A warmth connected their gaze, and Max knew that Ryan cared for her. She smiled and said, "Hi."

Rachelle put her hand on Ryan's shoulder. "Max, I'm so glad that you finally reached out to Ryan. He's told me a lot about you. I know how much you meant to him. He's been worried about you for a very long time."

"I guess I've worried about me, too," Max admitted.

"Rachelle and I met when I was in the inpatient facility. She was a nurse's aide. She's an RN now, and she works at the hospital in town." He smiled up at Rachelle with pride.

The love in Ryan's eyes brought Max's mind back to Treat and the way he looked at her, touched her, and so wonderfully completed her. She'd done it. She'd faced her worst demons, and she was still breathing.

No, she wasn't *still* breathing—she was breathing like never before.

Chapter Twenty-Seven

TREAT AND SAVANNAH sat beside each other on their father's couch. They'd brought Hal home at nine o'clock, and he was asleep by ten. Now it was nearing midnight, and Treat felt like he'd been treading water for the past twelve hours. He'd heard back from his buddy Brett and had learned the truth about Max's ex well before he'd received the call from Max confirming the same. He'd have given anything to have been in both places at once. To his surprise, Max wasn't upset when he told her he'd hired Elite Security to watch over her in his absence. *Maybe I should be upset, but it shows me just how much you care about me.* She'd been incredibly brave to tackle her worst fears, and now he wanted her back safely in his arms. He'd offered to charter a flight to bring her home tonight, but she'd said she was too exhausted to even think about traveling. She'd be back in Colorado tomorrow, and she said she'd call him when she got to her apartment. It was going to be a very long night.

Rex joined them in the living room. "Where's Josh?"

"In the shower. Want a beer?" Treat asked.

"Nah, thanks. I think we need to have a family meeting." Rex sat in the chair next to their father's recliner.

Josh joined them a few minutes later. "Savannah, do you want a drink before I sit down?"

"Yeah, I'll take some wine. Red, please."

"I'll get it," Treat offered. He went to the kitchen. Anything to stop the pain of staring at his father's empty chair. They'd had a near miss, and it had brought his father's mortality into clear focus. He wasn't about to waste any more years away from his family.

In the kitchen, Josh asked about Hugh and Dane.

"Hugh's on his way," Treat explained. "Got hung up on a layover. And Dane gets in tomorrow. How are you holding up?" Josh was the most sensitive of his brothers, and Treat wanted him to know that he was there if he needed to talk.

"Okay. I'm not going to lie; it scared me. I've never thought of Dad as someone who could get sick."

"Me either." Treat took a swig of his beer. "It scared me, too, but I think Ben knows what he's talking about, and if he thought this was anything other than stress cardiomyopathy he'd tell us."

"Do you believe in it? Broken heart syndrome?"

Absolutely. If anything had happened to Max, I'd have been in the hospital next. "I don't know, but we all know Dad believes he still sees and talks to Mom, and I think he just might."

"Yeah," Josh said. "Me too."

"Really?" Treat asked.

Josh shrugged. "Stranger things have happened."

"Wine, please," Savannah called to them from the living room.

They joined the others, and for a while they sat in silence, nursing their drinks. The door opened, and Hugh started to say something, but they all turned toward him with a *shush* on their lips.

"Dad's asleep," Savannah said as she went to hug their youngest brother. "But he's okay."

Treat waited for Hugh to shed his leather jacket, and then he embraced him. "You okay? Your trip all right?" Hugh could easily pass for twenty-five instead of twenty-nine, with his tousled black hair that was badly in need of a trim and wearing worn Levi's.

"It was long, but I'm here, and that's all that matters." Hugh greeted his other two brothers and headed to the kitchen for a drink.

"Do you want me to make you something to eat?" Savannah asked when he returned with a beer.

"Nah. I grabbed a sandwich on the way." Hugh sat beside Savannah on the couch and kicked an ankle up onto the opposite knee. "So, Dad's okay? What is this BHS?"

Treat explained what the doctor had told them.

"Sounds like it should be called BS to me," Hugh joked, his brown eyes flitting from sibling to sibling.

"Hugh." Treat used the same voice he'd relied upon when his brothers were out-of-control teenagers. It hadn't always worked, but it did right then.

"I just mean that I don't see why they call it that. Call it stress cardiomyopathy. Why does everything have to be about *feelings*?"

Treat leaned forward, and Savannah put a gentle hand on his leg, silently reminding him that they were all on edge. "Leave it alone, Hugh," Treat said. "Who cares what they call it? The point is, he needs to take it easy for a few weeks."

"Which is precisely what I wanted to talk about," Rex said. "I've been thinking. Maybe we should hire another ranch hand or two, or a manager who can do more. I'm swamped and—"

"No need," Treat interrupted. "I'm going to stick around for a while."

"You have your own businesses to run," Josh said.

"Yeah, Treat. You've worked too hard to give them up for this," Savannah added.

"I'm not giving them up. I've thought this through. Rex, you were right. I should have come home sooner. I'll hire someone to do my overseas work and negotiating, so I'll have to travel only a few times a year." Just saying it aloud made him feel much better. His dad's illness had been a wake-up call. Even though Max didn't want him to change his business practices, that's exactly what he needed, and wanted, to do. She wasn't the only one haunted by her past. Treat had fled town to escape his own demons, and it was high time he faced them.

"Treat, man, you don't have to do that. I can deal with it," Rex assured him. His biceps twitched, much like their father's did when he was upset. "I'll just hire a hand or two for a few weeks. We'll be fine."

"I know you can. This isn't about you versus me," Treat said.

"Is this about your girl? Max?" Josh's question didn't hold an ounce of resentment, as it might have if it had come from Rex.

The truth was, this was as much about Max as it was about him. She deserved a man free from the weight of his past.

"I'd be lying if I said this has nothing to do with her. I love her." He paused long enough for that information to sink in. "But I realized I can't be with her, or anyone else, until I get this off my chest. To answer your question, this is really about all of you as much as it's about me or Max. Rex, you've been calling me on this for years, and I've deflected every jab, not because they were untrue, as I claimed, but because they were *too* true, and too shameful, to admit. After Mom died, I failed you guys." This was harder than Treat had imagined it would be.

"What are you talking about? You never failed us," Josh said.

"Come on, Josh. I did. I know I did. When it came time for college, I was relieved to move away. As hard as that is to admit it, I need you to know the truth. The ranch was one big reminder of Mom and everything I couldn't do." He gripped his beer bottle tighter.

"Treat," Savannah said, reaching out to him.

"Let him finish," Rex said, and all their siblings' gazes shifted to him. "He's trying to tell us something. Let him get it off his chest."

"Thanks, Rex." Treat didn't know if Rex was waiting with bated breath for him to admit his failure, or if he was being a supportive brother, but it didn't matter which one was more accurate. He was thankful either way to have his support. "Anyway, I worked my butt off to prove that I was worth something, and I realized today that I'll never be the man Dad is." He pointed to his father's bedroom. "That man in there is the best kind of man, and I'm just a regular guy who never quite measured up to him." He'd said it aloud, and now he waited for the *I knew its* and the *It's about times*.

Savannah's arms were around his neck seconds later. "Treat, you have never let me down. You're everything to me, and you're every bit the man Dad is."

"Dude, you let me sleep in your bed after Mom died. Don't you remember? Dad would never have done that," Hugh said with a shake of his head. "You're anything but a failure. You saved me."

"And me," Josh admitted. "You were there every time I needed anything. You waited up for me at night and never let anyone bother me. You let me climb into your bed when I was scared, too, and you listened to me cry for weeks on end. You even gave me money for field trips."

"I had forgotten about that," Treat said with a smile. He realized that Dane wasn't there. It would have been easier to talk to them all at once, but since he'd already opened the floodgates, he might as well let the rest pour out. He'd have to talk with Dane alone after he arrived.

Treat waited to see if Rex would say anything at all, but Rex just cracked his knuckles, leaned his elbows on his knees, and looked at Treat with a stoic expression. The familiar Braden biceps dance was in full speed.

"I'm not telling you this to fish for compliments. I'm telling you because it's haunted me forever, and I don't want it to anymore. I'm ready to put down roots, and before I do that, I need to know that I've been honest with each of you. Rex, I'm sorry. You were right all along. I bailed on the ranch."

Rex got up and walked out the back door.

Treat clenched his jaw as he rose to follow him out. At some point, with Treat around more often than not, that chip on Rex's shoulder was going to come crashing down. Treat hoped it wouldn't cause an even bigger issue between them.

"Let him go," their father said.

Treat spun around and found his father leaning against the stairs. "Dad, you should be in bed."

"I'll go back to bed when I'm good and ready," Hal said.

"How much of that did you hear?" Treat asked.

"Oh, I reckon I heard all of it. All of it that mattered, anyway."

Savannah and Treat went to his side as he moved toward the living room, and he shrugged them off. He settled into his recliner, looking long and hard at his eldest son.

It was one thing to come clean to his siblings, but a whole other thing to face the man who had poured his heart and soul into raising him. He deserved everything his father was about to unload on him. He lowered himself into the chair beside his father's recliner, never breaking eye contact, and said, "I'm sorry, Dad. You tried so hard to raise me right, and I wanted to make you proud, but…"

His father's mannerisms reflected Rex's, and for a minute Treat feared he might walk out just like his brother had. Instead his father reached for his hand and squeezed it. His father's face morphed to that of strength and conviction.

"Son, you are, and have always been, everything I ever hoped you'd be. You were barely eleven when your mama died, and barely nine when she first became ill."

The pressure in Treat's chest nearly knocked the wind out of him. "Dad…"

"No, son. You were everything this family needed, and there has never been a time that you haven't been. You see the faces of your sister and brothers? Do you see the love in their eyes? They are who they are in large part because of you. You taught them about strength and family. You taught them about love, and even when you let your little scraggly brothers in bed with you—and don't think I didn't know about that." He looked at Josh and Hugh. "You, Treat, and you alone, were giving them what I could not. The truth is, when your mama passed, she took part of me with her. I did what I could. I stepped up in every way I was able, but I'm just a man, like you and Rex,

Dane, Hugh, and Josh. We're all just who we are, and who we are is Bradens. Bradens always do their best. Sometimes our best feels like not enough, but that doesn't mean it truly isn't. Not one of my children has ever let me down." He looked at Hugh. "Not Hugh when he didn't show up for the ranch's first auction." His gaze shifted to Savannah. "Not our beautiful girl, Savannah, when she snuck out of the house when she was fifteen, or you, Treat, when you had to haul her back home. And you never said a word to me about it."

Savannah's eyes widened. "You knew about that?"

Their father nodded with a smile, then looked at Josh, who was listening intently. "And not your brother Josh, when he decided to design dresses for a living."

Treat watched his brother soak in their father's pride, and he knew that Josh had been waiting to hear that for a long time.

"The point is, Treat, you might have needed to cleanse your soul so that you could go on without that gorilla on your back, but you've got to know that it was *your* gorilla. It was a monkey devised by a little boy's frightened mind that grew to a full-size gorilla and tried to weigh you down. It has weighed you down for a long while, but you didn't let it take over completely because it wasn't real. I'm proud of you, son. That gorilla was just a figment of that little boy's imagination, and you finally saw your way clear to climb out from under it."

Treat went to his father and held him longer and tighter than he ever had. He didn't know if his father was right or not, but he appreciated every word he'd said, and he knew that he would never let him down.

"Are you really thinking of putting down roots?" his father asked when they separated.

"Not thinking about it. I'm acting on it," Treat said, and

glanced at the back door.

"Now, that boy out there? He's got an even bigger burden on his back than you did. Give him some time," his father suggested.

"I'm not sure what I did to him, specifically," Treat said.

"He'll let you know when he's good and ready. Just like you did." Hal pushed to his feet and said, "Walk me back to my room, Treat."

When they reached his father's bedroom, his father sat on the edge of the bed and patted the space beside him. Hal Braden wasn't a man who talked just to hear his own voice. He chose his words carefully and rarely doled out unsolicited advice to his children. So when he asked Treat to listen carefully, Treat did just that.

"I've been waiting for you to figure out what was holding your heart back all these years. For a while I wasn't sure if it was something I did wrong when you were growing up. I did my best, but being both mother and father had its trying times. Then I thought that maybe you just hadn't met the right woman yet. But when I looked into your eyes earlier today, I saw the fear in them. And I saw the love, too; don't get me wrong. I knew that the other thing I'd worried about for so long was true. Son, your mama didn't die because of our love for each other. Surely you know that."

He nodded, unable to form a response, as his father had seen his greatest fear. As ridiculous as it was, it had lingered far too long.

"This life we're given is short," his father said. "It'll be gone before you know it, and, son, you're a good man. You're a loving, kind, generous man with so much more to give than flashy resorts. You always have been. Just because you allow yourself to love doesn't mean that some higher power will steal that person away from you—or steal you away from her. If you don't allow yourself to love, to fully saturate yourself with someone else's life, someone else's feelings, if you don't allow your ego to disappear and your heart to beat *for* another person, so that every breath you take is taken *for* that person, well then, I'm afraid you'll be missing out on one of life's only blessings. And besides your family and giving life to children, it's the only blessing that really matters."

His father reached into his bedside drawer and handed him a small velvet bag. Treat felt the circle within his fingers and knew what it contained.

He looked at his father with a tinge of disbelief.

"Your mama wanted you to have this, and somehow, today, she knew it was the right time."

"Dad…" His voice was choked out by emotions.

"It's yours, son, to do with as you wish. I'm just doing what I'm told."

Chapter Twenty-Eight

TREAT'S BEDROOM DOOR swung open at five thirty the next morning, and Rex walked in with a triumphant smile, which promptly faded when Treat stood from the chair in front of the desk where he was working, fully dressed in jeans and a T-shirt, and said, "About time you got your lazy butt out of bed." He'd woken up early, anxious to see Max when she arrived later today, and had tackled the emails he hadn't gotten to yesterday. He picked up his flannel shirt from the back of the chair, closed his laptop, and patted Rex's shoulder as he passed him on his way to the stairs.

Rex didn't say a word as they filled to-go cups with coffee and headed out into the cold morning air.

"You're going to have to get me up to speed," Treat said.

"We've got the hired hands taking care of the horses. You and I are on fence repair. Something got into the back fifty and tore down a thirty-foot strip."

Treat climbed into the passenger side of the truck. "What got to it?"

Rex shrugged as he pulled onto the grass. "It doesn't matter, does it?"

Great, an attitude before six a.m.

The truck ambled over the fields, and Treat waited for Rex to bring up what he'd said the night before. The silence between them was not particularly uncomfortable, but as it stretched on, he tried to break the ice. "I checked on Dad. He seemed to be okay."

"Good. Savannah's got him covered for the day, and Josh said he'd monitor his meds." Rex's cowboy hat was tugged down low. He kept his eyes on the field, never once glancing at Treat.

"You mind that I'm staying on for a while?" Treat asked.

Rex shrugged. He parked the truck and they began unloading the wood, wire, and supplies.

"Put 'em over there." Rex pointed to a grassy area on the other side of the broken fence. "We'll set up the sawhorses here and use that area there for waste."

Treat did as he asked, while Rex picked up long pieces of wood and threw them over his shoulder like they were toothpicks. Treat was a strong man, but even he had to admit that his brother had the bigger brawn and bulk. Beneath his Henley, Rex's body rippled with muscles in places that Treat wasn't even certain a body should have them.

Instead of feeling envy toward the brother who was clearly angry with him, Treat was proud of him. He'd spent his life taking care of the family ranch—and their father. That was something Treat hadn't been strong enough to do, and now, he realized, he was able to admit that to himself without feeling shame in its wake.

"You gonna help or watch?" Rex asked.

Treat grabbed his hammer and followed his brother's cursory instructions to a tee. He'd grown up helping his father with everything from mucking stalls to fixing the siding on the barn.

He was a bit out of practice, but it was all coming back to him, including cherished memories of his mother playing nearby with any number of his siblings while he and his father worked.

Working beside Rex also brought out Treat's competitive side. His need for instructions quickly fell away as he sawed the wood to the perfect length, secured wires into place, and pounded poles into the ground. By lunchtime, his chest and arms felt battered and bruised. He gritted his teeth against the annoying pain rather than let his brother, who was no worse for wear, see it.

"Doing all right?" Rex asked as they drove toward the house.

"Just fine." After spending the day doing hard physical labor, Treat expected to feel a longing to return to his fast-paced, professional career, where he was surrounded by creature comforts and a hard day meant securing a purchase for another property. At the minimum, he'd expected to feel a strong amount of trepidation over changing the way he did business. But as they pulled up to the house and he mulled over the suggestions from his attorney to hire more of a front man or woman and handle negotiations via Skype, he found that his longing wasn't to be in the thick of acquisitions at all. He wanted to help out for a while on the ranch until they got a handle on things, and he longed to be with Max. The decision he'd made to put down roots in Colorado, and the suggestion from the attorney, both felt right.

"Looks like Dane's arrived." Rex nodded in the direction of the forest-green Land Rover in the driveway, Dane's go-to rental.

They headed inside, and Savannah called out to them from the kitchen, "Hey, I made you guys lunch."

They kicked off their work boots, and Dane intercepted them in the hall.

"You made it," Treat said, embracing his brother. He'd spent much of the night thinking through how he was going to tell Dane what he'd told his other siblings. He was sure that Dane had already heard it at least three times from them by now, but no matter how uncomfortable it made him, Treat was going to do it himself, in person, man to man. And what better time than the present?

"It was a painfully long flight with one delay after another," Dane said. "But we tagged some nice sharks while we were down under."

"Sorry about the flight, but that's good news for your research, and I'm glad you're here. Come with me for a sec." He led the way outside, and they settled into chairs facing the fields.

"I hear you're staying for a while," Dane said.

"Yeah. It's time."

"What about your businesses?"

"Nothing's going to change except the amount of travel I'm doing and the way I acquire new properties." He looked at his brother relaxing in the chair beside him. His skin was tanned and his eyes were bright. Treat had never really thought about his age before, but after his father's medical trouble, it was on his mind. How had the years passed so quickly? One day they'd be gathering like this for their father's funeral, and it would most likely be in far fewer years than they'd all like to imagine. That large dose of reality came with another. Treat definitely wanted a family. He'd love to see his father spending time with his grandchildren.

"We met Max. Did she tell you?" Dane asked.

"Yeah." Treat smiled. Only a few more hours and she'd be

in his arms again.

"She's really cute. Seems smart, a little shy maybe? But I can see why you like her."

Treat's body went rigid. *She's mine.* He gave Dane a *back off* stare.

"Dude, you *really* like her, don't you?" Dane asked.

"I love her, Dane," he admitted.

Dane nodded. "I've never heard those words come out of your mouth before."

"I've never felt them before." The truth tasted almost as sweet as Max's kisses. "Listen, Dane—"

"Before you tell me, can I just say something I've been wanting to say for a long time?"

"Sure." Treat braced himself for heaven only knew what.

"It's about Mary Jane."

Treat narrowed his eyes.

"Right, well…" Dane took a deep breath. "The truth is, I wasn't as hammered as I told you I was that night. I knew what I was doing."

"Why on earth are you telling me this now?" He couldn't stop his hands from flexing.

"Because the others told me what you said last night, and you need to know. I slept with her to feel like I was at least as good as you, Treat." Dane shifted his eyes away. "Do you have any idea what it was like growing up in your gigantic shadow?"

"My shadow isn't that big, Dane."

"You have no idea. Anyway, it didn't work. I felt even smaller afterward than I had before, and I know that has always undermined our relationship." He looked at Treat. "I'm sorry, bro. I've regretted it ever since."

Treat had never expected to hear anything even remotely

close to what Dane had admitted, and because of that, he was at a loss for words.

"I know that you worry about me and, well, any woman you're interested in. You don't have to. I'm not that stupid kid anymore. I'd never do something as low or as demeaning as that to you or to myself. Or to another woman. Mary Jane was a pawn to me, and I'm sorry for you and her."

"She wasn't a pawn to me." Treat's chest tightened at the memory. He hadn't been in love with Mary Jane, or at least not like he was with Max. But she'd been special to him.

Dane looked down. "I know, and I'm sorry. I apologized to her shortly after it happened."

He appreciated the courage it took for his brother to slay his own dragon, and in an effort to lighten the moment, he teased, "Are you trying to tell me that you won't try to tag Max with your giant spear?"

"Not an inch of it." Dane laughed. "Seriously, though, I'd never make the same mistake twice. Besides, there's a certain someone I can't seem to get off my mind these last few months, so I might not be on the market too much longer myself."

"Yeah?" Treat asked.

Dane leaned back in his chair and looked out at the majestic mountains. "Oh, yeah."

"So, they ratted me out to you already?" Treat asked, nodding toward the house.

"I had three calls by two in the morning."

Typical Braden hotline. "Who didn't call?"

"Who do you think?" Dane nodded toward Rex's truck.

"Right. I'm not sure what to make of things with Rex, but I'll just take Dad's advice and let him be. He'll talk when he's ready."

Dane got up to go inside and Treat held him back. Letting his siblings handle his admission was a cop-out. He needed to deal with things himself if he was truly going to move forward with no regrets.

"I just wanted to say I'm sorry about how things went down when we lost Mom. I was the oldest, and I should have been there more. When you were so mired down in anger, I should have tried harder to help you find ways to deal with it." After their mother died, most of his siblings had fallen back on tears and had crawled into their own shells for a while, but Dane had exploded. He'd gone from being sweet and even-tempered, like he was now, to an angry, petulant boy. Treat had tried to talk him through it, but there were times when he'd let Dane spew his fury far too loud, and he'd always wished he hadn't.

"I was a little off my rocker, huh?" Dane said with a troubled look in his eyes.

"I think we all were. You know how much I love you, right?" There had never been any embarrassment wrapped around his love for his family, and today was no different.

"Never had any doubt." Dane stood and embraced Treat. "We cool?"

"Always."

Treat watched him walk inside, and then he looked out over the property, thinking about his mother. He could still envision her waving from horseback in the field. *Treaty!* He hoped she'd have been proud of him, even with his faults. He remembered the day his mother had come home from the hospital for the last time. Even as a boy he'd known she wasn't going to last very long. She'd become terrifyingly frail. Her cheeks had lost their rosy glow months before. They'd become hollow, her arms and legs atrophied from extended bed rest. He used to stand in her doorway when she was sleeping and just look at her, memorizing every feature as she slipped farther and farther away. One afternoon, when his father was in the field and the other kids were out horsing around, she'd reached for him. He hadn't even known she was awake. He still remembered the roughness of the hardwood floor against his bare feet as he crossed the room and the feel of each slender bone beneath her nearly transparent skin when he held her hand. She opened her eyes and smiled, and in that breath, he saw the mother she had always been, strong, loving, beautiful. She was too weak to keep her eyes open, and they'd fluttered closed. He held on to her hand long after it had gone limp, hoping and praying she'd open her eyes again. He clung to her until his father took him by the shoulders and dragged him away. *Mom! Come back! Please! I'll do better! I'll help you more with the kids! I'll help Dad on the ranch!* Even now his body struggled and fought against the memory, just as he'd struggled and fought against his father's mighty grip until every fiber of his being was exhausted beyond repair and he'd collapsed into his waiting arms. When he'd woken up the next day, he'd run to his mother's room hoping it had been a nightmare. He'd pushed the heavy wooden door open.

All these years later he remembered the long, ominous creak as the door came to a stop and the grief that had consumed him at the sight of his mother's empty bed.

Chapter Twenty-Nine

"KAYLIE, I NEED you," Max said into her Bluetooth. She was almost back to Allure when she realized she had some legwork to do. She'd spoken to Treat early that morning but had held off on calling him when she'd gotten an early flight, wanting instead to surprise him.

"Why, Max, I never knew you were into women," Kaylie joked.

"This is serious. I need help, and I need it now. *Please?*"

Kaylie's voice softened. "Of course. What's wrong? Did something happen?"

"No. Well, something did. Something big. But I can't get into it now." She'd never told Kaylie about what happened with Ryan, and she didn't want to try to go over it now. She was too excited and nervous to waste another second thinking about the past. "Can you meet me at the mall?"

"You hate shopping."

"No kidding. That's why I need you. Please, Kaylie? I hate myself for sounding like a needy woman, but I am. So will you meet me before I change my mind?"

The situation with Ryan could not have been anticipated, and as Max had traveled home, she'd realized it couldn't have gone any better. The pieces of her past were falling into place, clearing a path for her to understand what she had misconstrued years earlier. Although she felt horrible for what they'd both gone through, the fact that Ryan hadn't been in control of his actions when he'd hurt her released her from the guilt she'd been harboring. She could no more take responsibility for causing his actions than she could for Treat wanting to change the way he ran his business in order to make their relationship work.

She'd spent years burdened with guilt she didn't deserve and fearing the worst in the wrong people. Now she was dead set on making things right.

"Be there in thirty minutes," Kaylie said.

"Meet me at Victoria's Secret."

"WHO ARE YOU and what have you done with Max?" Kaylie asked, peering around her.

"Shut up before I change my mind." Max had purposely never stepped foot in a Victoria's Secret store before. She'd stayed away from places that encouraged the idea of women being seen as *playthings*. But now, as she walked through the brightly lit, far-too-pink shop, with half-naked mannequins donning barely there, sexy lingerie, she saw it through the eyes of an undamaged woman. Or at least through the eyes of a woman who was coming out from under the cover of clouds, and she began to understand how sexy lingerie was about owning—and enjoying—her sexuality, not exploiting it or asking to be hurt.

If meeting Ryan was a big step, this was a giant hurdle, and she felt like she had springs on her feet. She was bound and determined to own Treat-worthy, seductive, take-me-all-the-way attire.

"Max, I'm scared," Kaylie teased.

"I want a wardrobe that will turn Treat on. All of it, from my head to my toes." She looked at Kaylie with a serious face and said, "Kaylie, make me *hot*."

"Girlfriend, just saying that makes you hot." Kaylie dragged her to the rear of the store, where she fingered through racks of lacy lingerie, holding up corsets and camisoles, lace bras and barely visible thongs. "What are we talking here, a few nights, a weekend? Seasonal?"

Max held up her credit card. "Whatever it takes. Whatever you would wear, I want to wear. Um, maybe. Be a little careful with that suggestion." She laughed. "Then we're going to buy clothes to go on top of the naughty bits."

"Max, you're talking about a lot of cash. Are you sure? Being sexy is expensive."

Max rolled her eyes. "I've never been more sure of anything in all my life. Besides, I've had the same jeans and shirts for years, and a five-digit savings account that I'll never spend. For Treat? *Definitely* worth it."

"But you can buy a few nights' worth and just use those over and over."

"I want to be sexy *all* the time. I don't mean that I'll stop wearing jeans and T-shirts, but I want to know that what I have on underneath, seven days a week, is appropriate for making him lose his mind. I want to walk into my closet and find something that begs me to pull myself out of *efficient Max* and morph into *seductress Max*. I want *options*. And you know me well enough to realize that this is my one shot. I'm not suddenly going to turn into a woman who loves to shop. I'll probably have whatever we buy today until I'm fifty. Besides, Treat has a major social calendar, and I want to make him proud with nice feminine dresses."

"No, you want to make him horny. Because what you wear to elite social events will not show what we're buying here."

Max grinned. "I want to make him hot and bothered, *and* proud."

That's all Kaylie needed to hear to let loose. "We'll have to go shopping another day for those social-event outfits. You can't find the right dresses for black tie situations at the mall. Right now let's focus on knocking his socks off tonight."

Max tried on so many outfits that her head was spinning. She stood in front of the mirror in a pink lacy baby-doll nighty. "Wow." She turned to the side. "Look at my butt. And look at these." She grabbed her breasts and lifted them up. "They're kinda hot, huh?"

"*Scorching* hot." Kaylie pulled the elastic from Max's hair, and her hair billowed around her shoulders. "You're always gorgeous, Maxy, but now you're too insanely delicious for him to turn away."

"Oh, turning away hasn't been an issue," she said with a coy smile.

They left Victoria's Secret with several large bags and sexy lingerie for every occasion. Kaylie took her hand and dragged her into Hot Allure, a trendy clothing store known for upscale and sexy clothing.

Kaylie and Max picked through the racks and carried enormous piles of clothes into the dressing room.

"You don't know how long I've been wanting to do this," Kaylie said. "This is like every girl's makeover fantasy come true."

"I feel like Julia Roberts in *Pretty Woman*. I really appreciate your help. I would never pick out half these things. I'm still not sure they'll fit." She held up a red clingy dress that looked too small to fit over one leg, much less her whole body.

"It stretches. Trust me," Kaylie said. "I have an eye for fashion and figures and, girlfriend, we're going to feature your figure in fabulous fashions."

"What are you, on a shopping *high* or something?" Max laughed.

An hour and a half later, they collapsed onto a bench in the center of the mall, surrounded by bags of dresses, slacks, sexy skinny jeans, heels, lingerie, and accessories.

"Your man is going to be so excited every night of the week!" Kaylie squealed.

"Uh-oh. Kaylie."

"What? Oh no. You look like something awful happened. Did you spend more money than you meant to? I've done that. Should we return some of it? Not the baby-doll nighty. Every girl needs a baby-doll nighty."

Max shook her head. "I have no idea where Treat is. I know he was at his father's ranch, but what if he went out? I want to surprise him."

Kaylie took out her cell phone and started texting.

"What are you doing?" Max asked.

"I have an idea. He's Blake's cousin, so I'll text Danica. She'll ask Blake, and he'll know how to find out where he is."

"Thank goodness for the sister network," Max joked.

Kaylie's phone vibrated, and she checked the message. "She said hold on a sec."

Max sighed and threw her head back. "How can I be so

together at work and so bad at surprises?"

Her phone buzzed again. "It's part of being a woman. We can't be perfect all the time." She read the text and said, "Fate is on your side! He's at his father's ranch."

Max jumped to her feet. "It really is fate."

"Settle down, doe eyes. Now what?"

Max gathered as many bags as she could carry and started for the exit.

Kaylie scrambled to pick up the remaining bags and hurried after her. "Max!"

Max held up her bags and said, "Home. Shower. Sex it up. Get my man!"

Chapter Thirty

BY DINNERTIME TREAT was exhausted. His father was feeling infinitely better and practically needed to be tied to his chair to follow Ben's order to rest. Every time Treat and his siblings turned around, their father was trying to get outside to the barn. Josh finally lured him back inside by offering to watch a rodeo with him. Now Treat was relaxing on the front porch as Rex parked the tractor in the barn. They'd worked from sunup to sundown, and they still had evening chores to take care of. He had to give Rex credit. He was still running on full steam while Treat was sucking down coffee just to get a second wind.

The screen door opened behind him. "You still alive out here?" Savannah sat beside him on the top step.

"Barely. I had forgotten how labor intensive it was to run the ranch. I don't know how Rex does it."

"He's pretty tough. So are you, you know. Everyone is tough in their own way."

"I guess," Treat said. The spark in his sister's hazel eyes had dulled. He'd assumed it was from his father's health issues, but he remembered what his father had barked at him in the hospital. "Everything okay with you? What was Dad saying about Connor? Do I need to take care of him for you? Because

I'm wondering if Rex might be a better person for that job."

She linked her arm through his and rested her head on his shoulder. "No one is better for that job than you. You've always been my protector."

The weight of her against him made him miss Max even more. "Way to skirt the question, Vanny."

She sighed. "It's complicated."

"Isn't everything?" he said, thinking of Max.

"Yeah, I guess. Do you remember what Mom and Dad's relationship was like before Mom got sick? I don't remember much more than what you've told me."

Treat had always tried to keep their mother's memory alive for his siblings. "I remember some of it, but as a kid, you don't focus on your parents' relationship. You know what I mean? They're Mom and Dad. That's it. Mom was beautiful. She had this light about her that's hard to describe. She was always happy, but I do remember how she used to yell at Dad when he'd try to toughen you up. I can still hear her." He raised his voice an octave. "*Hal, she's a girl. G-I-R-L. She doesn't need to know how to bang a nail. That's what men are for.*" He laughed at the memory.

"She did?" Savannah smiled. "I wish I could remember that."

"She always treated you like you were precious. She'd want to put you in frilly pink dresses with ribbons in your hair, and Dad would say she was raising a sissy."

Savannah scrunched her nose. "*Pink* dresses? I can't even imagine. I loved growing up as a tomboy. I always thought Dad did such a good job with us."

"He did. So did she. She loved us so much. Even when we were bad, she would give us heck for a minute or two and her eyes would turn fierce, like yours. And in the next minute she was laughing and joking like we were blessed angels who could do no wrong."

"Really?"

"Yes. You know it was Mom who started the whole backyard grilling thing, don't you?" He watched Rex ascend the hill, heading in their direction. His jeans stretched tight across his massive thighs, and his hat was still pulled down low. He looked every bit like the quintessential cowboy he was.

"I never knew why we did it," Savannah said. "It's all I've ever known."

"It was Mom."

Rex stepped onto the porch and sat beside Savannah. "What was Mom?"

"She was the one who started the barbecue tradition," Savannah answered.

Rex took off his hat and ran his hand through his thick hair. He set his hat back on his head and wiped his face with his hand. "Remember that? She said we were only nourishing our bodies if we ate inside all the time and that we also had to nourish our souls."

A warmth softened Rex's hard exterior, and for a brief moment Treat saw the gentler little boy Rex had been before their mother became ill. Had he changed too? Was there a before-and after-Mom-was-sick Treat? If so, he had no recollection of that person.

"'Because that's what the sun, wind, snow, and rain are for,'" Treat added, quoting their mother.

"I wish I'd known her the way you guys did." Savannah tried to mask her frown, but she fell short.

Treat put his arm around her.

"You're just like her." Rex pushed to his feet and headed for the door. "You doing night chores with me?"

"Wouldn't miss it," Treat answered.

"Why isn't Max with you?" Savannah asked. "Dad said you haven't brought her over at all."

"Because I'm selfish," Treat admitted. "I wanted every second I could have with her without the pressure of the family." He picked up a rock and tossed it into the yard. "She had to take care of a few things out of town and Dad got sick, so..."

"She *really* likes you." She scooted closer to him again. "I want that for you. I want you to be with someone who adores you. Someone who would go anywhere to be with you, like she did."

"That makes two of us. I want that for you, too." Remembering what Savannah had said about reading between the lines, he asked, "Do you want Connor to follow your bread crumbs?"

A breeze swept her long auburn hair away from her face, and for an instant she was the spitting image of their mother.

A shadow passed over her eyes, and she said, "I'm not sure. Most of the time I think I do. Sometimes, though, I'm not sure if I'm setting myself up to be hurt."

"Please tell me you don't mean physically hurt, because I'd hate to be known as the guy who killed Connor Dean."

"He's a butterfly, really. He's not a fighter."

"Well, you are a *feisty* thing. Is that the problem? That he's not a fighter?"

"It's just schedules and craziness." Savannah put a hand on his shoulder. "Let's analyze you instead."

"Let's not." He'd done enough analyzing for a lifetime. All he wanted was for Max to call and say she was safely back at her apartment. If it weren't for her, he might never have dealt with the guilt that had hung over him for too many years.

He stood and reached for her hand, helping her to her feet. "We'd better help get dinner on the table."

They helped get the food ready, and Treat carried a jug of apple cider out to the table, stopping when he caught sight of his father and Rex walking down by the barn. Rex had a pinched look on his face. Their father put his hand on Rex's shoulder. Treat could practically feel that secure weight on his own flesh. He knew the look his father was giving Rex, and he would bet the discussion had something to do with him.

He'd better go face it head-on.

Savannah touched his arm before he could take two steps. "Leave them," she said.

"I'm sure it's about what I said last night."

"No, it's not. Let them be."

Treat narrowed his eyes at his sister. "How do you know?"

Savannah took the cider from his hands and set it on the table, ignoring his question.

"Savannah?"

"Leave it alone, Treat," Hugh said as he approached from behind. He set plates and silverware on the table. "Rex seems tough, but he's not as tough as you might think. He's having a hard time with Dad's health issues."

Treat shot another glance at Rex, who was looking everywhere except at his father, while his father's attention never wavered from Rex's face.

"Why wouldn't he tell me? We worked in the field together for hours and all he did was snap at me."

Hugh shrugged.

"Would *you* tell you?" Josh asked. He brought the burgers to the table and motioned for everyone to sit down. "Think about it, Treat. He's here every day, slaving to help keep the family business alive, and suddenly you sweep in and expect him to just accept it. Meanwhile, the one person he loves the most lands in the hospital. It's a lot to deal with."

I failed him again? "So, what? I should have asked his permission to come back to my own family's ranch and help out? I thought it was what he wanted all these years."

His three siblings exchanged a look that said perhaps that's *exactly* what he should have done. "All right. I get it. I'll talk to him." He started for the barn.

"Treat!" Savannah hollered. "He's hurting. Please don't push him. You know Rex. When he's ready, he'll open up to you. He always does."

When it came to his siblings, hurting them was the last thing he ever wanted to do. His father and Rex headed toward them, and Treat turned away. Was he doing more harm than good by being there?

A few minutes later Rex and Hal joined them at the table. Rex snagged a burger and bun, eyeing the rest of the food.

"Dad, you have a follow-up with Ben next week. I'll take you," Treat offered.

"I've got it covered," Rex said gruffly.

"Rex'll take me. Tell me what's happening with that pretty little gal I met," his father said, clearly trying to steer clear of the whole Rex situation.

He'd stirred the hornet's nest with Rex, and now it was his turn to wait it out—just like Rex had for the past fifteen years.

"Not much to tell. She's on her way back into town, and every minute she's away feels like a frigging year." He stabbed at the steak Savannah had dished onto his plate, anxious to see her.

"So take that lame behind of yours and go get her," Rex

said, and followed it up with a big bite of his burger. "What are you afraid of?"

"Nothing scares me, little brother. I'm here fighting the demons that have strangled me for years, which is more than I can say for you." He knew he shouldn't push Rex, especially with his entire family watching them, but he was agitated and sick of playing games.

Rex rose to his feet. "What's that supposed to mean? I'm here every single day, taking care of the family business, while you're out doing whatever you please. At least I didn't abandon Dad."

Treat felt his father's eyes on him. Their siblings watched without a hint of stress, and Treat realized that they must have known what was eating at Rex the whole time. His father slowly rose to his feet but made no move to come between them.

"I *apologized* for leaving last night. Remember? You walked out on me. And while you were building your life here, I built mine." Treat pushed to his feet, too, meeting his brother's angry glare.

"Right. You travel endlessly. You live a life of leisure while I hold down the *real* job."

"I'm not going to get into a pissing match with you about my career versus yours. What's this really about?" Treat closed the distance between them.

"You *left*, leaving me to figure out how to hold things together."

Treat had the urge to grab his brother's enormous shoulders and shake him until he spit out whatever he was holding back. "Dane's older than you—it wasn't *your* job to hold them together."

"Dane was a mess, and he had no interest in working on the

ranch. I was fifteen! How was I supposed to watch over the other three kids *and* take care of the ranch—and Dad? Fifteen, Treat. *Fif-teen!*" His eyes flashed with a rage.

Treat stared down at him. "I went to school, Rex. It was what I was *supposed* to do. That was *Dad's* plan for me." He stilled as the truth of his own words sank in. *It was Dad's plan for me. It's true.* He looked at his father, and confirmation shone in his eyes. He'd known all along what Treat was struggling with, but as always, he'd let him come around to it on his own. *Holy sh...How could I have repressed that for so long?*

Rex twisted out of his grip, and Treat planted his feet in the ground, readying for the blow that was sure to come as Rex's hands fisted.

"I came home every time you called, Rex."

Rex's nostrils flared. "No, you didn't."

"What are you talking about?"

"I called you a few weeks after you went to school and said I couldn't do it." Rex's eyes shot darts; every word was laced with venom. "Hugh was pulling away, and Savannah had disappeared for the weekend with her friend. I didn't know what to do."

"What? When?" He vaguely remembered a call about Savannah. It seemed like a hundred years ago. "Was that the time when you said Savannah went to a party and you couldn't find her? I left my date and went back to my dorm and called every one of her friends' parents. I was going frigging crazy looking for her from a million miles away, and you called me a few hours later and said she was back home, that her friend had lied about it to get her in trouble." Treat took a breath and tried to bring his anger down a notch. "I thought it was fine after that."

Rex huffed, rage simmering in his eyes. "Nothing was fine."

"How could I have possibly known? I was a kid, too, Rex. What would you have had me do? Quit college? Give up everything Dad said I had to accomplish? Is this what you've held over my head forever? Isn't this exactly what I apologized for last night?"

They stared at each other, posturing, silently banging chests and measuring feathers. And then, with the force of a bullet train, Treat realized what this was really about. Rex was younger than Dane, but even as kids, after they'd lost their mother, Rex had watched over Dane just as Treat had. And when the pressures of trying to be something neither he nor Treat could became too great, he'd fall apart and Treat would put him back together. *It's no wonder you felt abandoned. And no wonder I felt like I abandoned you.*

"Boys!" Hal's stern voice broke their match. "You want to blame someone? Blame me. I wanted Treat to excel. He was too academic and had too much to accomplish in life to run the ranch. He'd have had me buying up more ranches by the time he was fourteen if I'd let him, and maybe if I had listened to him, we'd all be even richer. And, Rex, you were born to ranch and you know it. The day you started walking, you wanted to follow me all over this place. You'd sit with me while I ran the finances and rode with me on nearly every ride. The ranch is a heck of a lot of responsibility, and I don't blame you for resenting your brothers—all of them—for taking off." He put a hand on Rex's shoulder and spoke calmly. "But, son, I gave you the same choice I gave them. How many times did I say, 'Go out there and get your own ranch, or find something else that you want to call your own?'"

Rex looked away.

"When I'm talking to you, son, you keep your eyes on

mine."

Rex met his gaze. "I didn't want my own ranch. This is family. This is where Mom is." He slid an angry look to Treat.

To a stranger, the two angry men staring each other down would mean fists were going to fly. But Treat knew what they looked like to his family. Two brothers fighting to find their way back to each other.

His father placed a hand on each of their shoulders and said, "Now that you've had your say, let me tell you how it's gonna be. You want to blame someone for all of this? Blame me. I'm the one who led you all those years. Grief is a terrible and powerful thing. I thought you'd each grow out of missing your mama, but that was a fairy tale. If anyone knows that, it's me, and I'm sorry. We all did the best we could." He looked around the table, and then he settled compassionate eyes on Rex and Treat. "We did better than any family could. If Treat had stayed, I'd have felt guilty for not cutting him loose. And, Rex, you've always been the cowboy, not the rodeo clown. I guess I always knew you could handle it, and yes, I knew you were carrying the weight of the world on your shoulders, but you were unwilling to part with it."

Rex's gaze shifted away.

"I'm sorry," Treat said to both of them. "I was a kid trying to keep my own head above water. It's true I abandoned everyone because I felt guilty, but, Rex, you have to believe that if I had known you felt that lost, I'd have come running back. After Savannah came home, I figured it was just more of the same confused, angry kids that I'd left when I went away to school."

Rex continued looking away for the longest time, and when he finally brought his attention back, it was his father's eyes he met, not Treat's. "Sorry I ruined the afternoon, Dad. I've got to go check on Hope." He headed for the barn.

Treat took a step toward him, but his father held him back. "Leave him. This is how Rex operates. You remember this pattern, don't you? He'll work out his frustration. It'll take time, but now you know what's what. It may not be today, and it may not be next week, but at some point this'll come out in the wash."

Treat sat at the table, but he couldn't eat. He knew Rex would eventually come around. There was no avoiding it now that Treat was home. He might buy a place nearby, and he might have to travel and set up an office, but he wasn't going to abandon anyone ever again. And he was done waiting for Max. It was time for him to set his future in motion.

"Sorry I was such a jerk when I was a kid," Dane said.

"You were just a kid." Treat pushed to his feet again. "I've got to go take care of something." Without another word from his family, he headed into the house.

A few minutes later, he was in the car, pulling down the driveway when Rex rode up on Hope and stopped in his path. Treat slammed on the brakes and jumped from the car. "What are you doing? Trying to get Hope killed?"

Rex settled Hope from her startled shuffle and said, "I know all that crap you said back there. I'm not an idiot."

"No. You're not," Treat said.

They stared each other down again. Treat had a feeling they'd be doing that a lot.

"Just like you've been carrying that baggage around with you all these years, so have I."

Treat nodded. Honesty was difficult, and he wasn't about to get in Rex's way.

"I know you didn't abandon me. Or Mom or Dad. I get that," Rex admitted. "The truth is, I wouldn't have wanted you to give up what you were destined to do. I was just..."

"As messed up as the rest of us?"

Rex held on to Hope's reins, and Treat had the overwhelming urge to hug him, but he was afraid to move. Rex had a shell that was thick as a brick, and Treat knew just how much this breakthrough meant to their relationship, which might not be anywhere near normal for years to come, but this was a start.

Rex nodded. "I'm glad you're home, but I'm still running the ranch."

"Okay."

"You're far from in shape for this kind of grueling work," Rex said gruffly. "It'll take you months to get back up to speed—physically anyway."

"Agreed." Every muscle in Treat's aching body could attest to that, though it was his pride that was taking a beating at the hand of his kid brother.

"All right, then."

"All right."

"Where are you going?" Rex backed the horse from in front of the car.

"I've got to get my girl. I'll be back to help with the evening chores."

Rex nodded. "Take your time, bro. Believe it or not, I'm glad you're staying."

Treat ran a hand down the side of Hope's face and swore he saw his mother's beautiful reflection in the horse's eyes, a smile of approval on her lips.

Chapter Thirty-One

MAX SURVEYED HERSELF in the mirror one last time. Her hair was shiny and full. The skinny leather pants she wore might not be perfect for showing up at a ranch, but they were perfect for getting Treat's attention. She told herself that chaps were leather, so her pants weren't so far off. Although the knee-high, stiletto boots were definitely *not* appropriate, which made them perfect. She wanted Treat to stand up and take notice of the changes she felt bursting from within.

She turned to the side to inspect her silhouette. Kaylie was right about the push-up bra. Who knew her boobs could look so perky? Or that a bra could make her torso look longer and slimmer? Wow, she could actually pull off *hot*.

Max tried her best to remain upright on the heels, but as she reached for the doorknob, her confidence began to fade. *I look ridiculous. He loves how I look no matter what I wear. What am I doing?* What was her goal? *Treat.* No, he wasn't her goal. Being the woman he deserved was her goal. Being *whole*, accepting the sides of herself she'd thought she had to ignore for so long. She wanted Treat to see her as an unbroken woman and to know her past no longer owned her. Even if there might be times she slipped up or became insecure, she wanted him to see the confidence she held *now*. And if he wanted to go to Thailand, she'd find a way to be there with him.

She opened the bedroom door, and a bright flash sent her reeling backward as Kaylie snapped a picture.

"What the…?" She'd been so wrapped up in getting ready that she'd forgotten Kaylie was waiting for her.

"I couldn't help it!" Kaylie squealed. "I wanted to come in so badly, but I knew you would never let me help you dress after letting me pick out all your clothes." Her eyes widened. "Oh, Max, you are sinful! Look at you. Not that you need to dress like this, but *look* at you! No man could ever turn you away looking like that."

She smiled at Kaylie's supportive, overly enthusiastic comment. "Can I please carry you on my shoulder? I'm so nervous. What if he thinks I look ridiculous?"

"Max, take a deep breath, because I have a really important question to ask you."

Max did as she was asked and blew her breath out slowly. "Okay, what?"

"Are you really ready for this?"

Max chewed on the worries she'd been trying not to think about. Was she making a mistake? No, she was sure she wasn't. "My whole life I believed that compromising to make a relationship work would lead to resentment, but if Treat wants to change how he does business, that's up to him. And if he doesn't, then I'll tell Chaz I need to telecommute."

"*What* are you talking about? I was talking about the sexy clothes and the way they say *take me seven ways to heaven*."

"Oh." Max looked down at her outfit. "I wasn't talking about that. Am I ready to be taken seven ways to heaven? Yes, please, if it's by Treat."

"Clearly." Kaylie smiled and said, "Now, what were *you* talking about? All relationships require compromise. You know that, don't you? Who's living where? Who's watching the kids so one of us can do something else? Who's on top? Who gets to finish first in be—"

"Kaylie! I'm trying to be serious." Max huffed.

"I know. I'm thoroughly confused right now, but just as long as you don't have any reservations about his love for you."

Max's cheeks warmed. She put her hand over her heart and said, "He'd give up anything for me, and I want to show him I'll do the same for him."

"I hope I was never this swoony-eyed over Chaz, because you're talking in tangents. Okay, go. I'll lock up for you." She glanced at the bedroom, which looked like it had thrown up clothes. "I'll even *unexplode* your closet for you."

Max kissed her on the cheek. "You're the best." On her way out the door, she turned back and said, "Thanks for asking me if I was sure. You're a great friend."

"Yeah, I'm the best," Kaylie said with a toss of her hair. "Now get out of here."

Max ran down the stairs in her stiletto heels like she'd been running in them all her life. Her mind clung to one singular goal—reaching Treat.

Chapter Thirty-Two

TREAT SPED THE whole way to Max's apartment. Traffic was light, and he made it there in record time. He flew into the parking lot and took a cursory glance for Max's car as he ran for the steps, taking them two at a time and feeling lighter on his feet than he had in years.

He knocked on her door twice, then twice more without waiting for her to answer. He had no idea what he'd say, but knew he'd figure it out when he saw her beautiful eyes.

Treat held his breath as the door swung open.

"What did you forge—"

"Kaylie?"

"Treat?"

He looked over her shoulder. "Where's Max?"

A smile spread across Kaylie's lips. "She's heading toward your father's ranch."

"My father's—"

"Yes! Go! She just left ten minutes ago. *Go!*"

He bolted down the stairs and then sped toward the highway.

248

BY THE TIME Max pulled up in front of Treat's father's house, she was so nervous she could barely see straight. She watched one of his brothers riding a horse across the field, toward the driveway. As he approached, she saw it was Rex, the one with the big muscles. Not that all of them weren't cut from some incredibly sexy fabric that she'd never known existed, but Rex's biceps were the size of footballs.

He pulled up on the reins as Max stepped from the car. She realized he was riding Hope and took that as a good sign.

"Max?" He ran an appreciative gaze down her body.

Ugh! She had forgotten what she was wearing, and now, with the swell of her breasts saying hello to the world and her leather pants leaving nothing to the imagination, she felt like a fool.

"Rex, right?" she asked.

"Yeah, that's right. You just missed Treat. He took off to find you."

"Me?" *Oh gosh!*

Rex shrugged. "That's what he said."

His gaze returned to her breasts and Max cleared her throat. His eyes darted up to hers again. "Thank you," she said curtly and climbed back into her car, vowing never, *ever*, to try to surprise Treat again. She was the worst at pulling off surprises. Her surprises needed to be preceded by a bright red neon sign alerting Treat—SUCKY SURPRISE GIVER COMING YOUR WAY! STAY PUT! She snapped on her seat belt thinking about the way Rex had ogled her. She'd come out looking to entice Treat, and now Rex probably thought she was a tramp!

Ugh! She jerked her car into reverse and slammed the pedal to the floor—she couldn't get out of there fast enough.

She felt the impact that sent her flying chest-first into the steering wheel before she heard the crunching of metal on metal. *No, no, no, no, no.* Dazed and shaken, she blinked away her tears and saw the rest of the Braden clan running toward her car. What had she done now?

Rex yanked open the door. "Are you okay?"

"Is she okay?" Max heard someone yell.

"Get away from her."

Treat?

"I've got her," Treat said.

And then he was yanking Rex from beside her door and gathering Max in his arms. *Treat. My Treat.* Max registered voices, but she was too shocked from the accident to think beyond being in Treat's arms.

"I'll call an ambulance."

"Wait. Let's see if she's okay first."

"What happened?"

"Max?" Treat's gentle voice was shaken. "Sweetness, look at me."

She looked into his eyes as he helped her to her feet.

"Are you okay?" he asked.

She saw his car behind hers, the front end smashed by the rear of hers.

"I think so," she whispered. Then, amid the shock, the worry, and his family members pawing at her, unexpected words fell from her lips. "You said you'd love me through it." *What happened to my voice? Why am I whispering?*

"What, sweetness?" Treat asked.

"You said you'd love me through anything," Max said, a little louder this time. "I asked you, that night in Wellfleet, when I told you that if I got scared or insecure and my walls went up, I'd need you to love me through it." *Why am I crying?*

"And you said you'd love me through anything, Treat. *Anything!* You promised."

"Uh-oh," Dane said.

"Of course, Max." He tightened his hold on her.

His siblings stared at her. His father watched him like a hawk. Max looked from Hal to Treat and then back again. She didn't care if she was making a fool of herself, or if his father was sending him telepathic messages that she was a freak. She needed him to know how much his promise meant to her.

"Max, I always keep my promises. You must be really shaken up. Try to hear me, sweetness."

"I hear you! You did what you promised, and it means the world to me that you loved me even though I was broken."

"Broken?" Dane uttered.

Savannah shushed him.

"You've never been broken, baby. Not in my eyes." Treat's voice was a tender caress to her shaken-up heart. "And I know you worry, so please hear me. I'm not giving up my life for you. I'm not giving up Thailand or anything else."

"I don't understand." Tears brimmed in her eyes.

"I'm rearranging how things are done, not giving them up. I'm coming back to help my father on the ranch—for a while, anyway—and I want to put down roots. But I don't care where, as long as you're with me." He wiped her tears with a whisper of his finger across her cheek. "I slayed my demons, Max. All of them. Just like you did. We're fated to be together."

Max was shaking all over. She closed her eyes to try to calm herself down.

"Open your eyes, sweetness," Treat urged. When he had her attention, he said, "The world can test us, but I'm not budging. It's enough already. This is who we are. Treat and Max. Not

Treat Braden and Max Armstrong, two separate people. It's not you and me; it's *us*."

Us. She swiped at the river of tears streaming down her cheeks as she tried to remember all the things she wanted to tell him. "I'll travel."

"What?"

"Whatever we need to do for your business. I'll travel with you. I can work from anywhere."

"Max, we'll figure all that out," he said.

Between her sleepless nights, the craziness of the last twenty-four hours, and the accident, she couldn't think straight. Everything was blurring together. Treat loved her. He loved her! She was in his arms. This was real. This wasn't a dream.

Then Treat released her, and for a moment the world stood still. Her gaze bounced from Savannah's to Josh's, and a smile tugged at his lips. Dane put a hand on Hugh's shoulder, and Rex was grinning like a fool. It was the tears in Hal's eyes that drew Max's gaze back to Treat, only he was no longer standing before her.

"Max." He took her hand in his as he perched on one knee.

She gasped. "Treat?"

"Max, I would be honored if you would let me love you through the rest of your life. Through every insecurity, every argument, and every incredible moment until I take my last breath. And then I'll be waiting for you on the other side of this crazy life." He stood and gazed deeply into her eyes. "I love you with all of my heart and soul, Max. I want to make your dreams come true and to see your belly round with our babies, and when we're old and gray, I want to see you wearing that scarf we bought in Wellfleet and remember making out behind the bushes. Will you marry me, sweetness? Be my wife, and let me be the husband you deserve?"

Savannah grabbed Josh's arm, and that little movement pulled Max from her stupor.

"You're sure?" she asked again.

"You are one careful, beautiful woman. Yes, I'm positive."

Max launched herself into his arms. Her chest ached with the constriction of her muscles, but she didn't care. He lifted her, and she wrapped her legs around his waist and said, "Yes! Yes, yes, yes!"

"I cannot wait to design her gown!" Josh exclaimed.

Treat's laughter filled the air, mixing with the cheers from his family and Savannah's giddy squeal. He smiled as he brushed his lips over hers and said, "I adore you, Max Armstrong." He lowered his mouth to hers, kissing the ache right out of her.

"Looks like we're gonna have a wedding!" his father said.

"I love you," she said as Treat lowered her feet to the ground and withdrew a velvet bag out of his pocket.

Looking her in the eye, with a tease in his own, he said, "Max, just to be clear, will you marry me?"

"Absolutely, one hundred percent yes."

He slid the most gorgeous canary diamond ring on her finger, stealing the remainder of her breath from her lungs.

TREAT HELD MAX'S trembling hand, wanting to never let it go. In all the business dealings he'd ever handled, in all the resorts he'd acquired, he'd never once felt the elation he did at that very moment. It was as if the universe had righted itself, and he and Max were in the perfect place at the perfect time.

Rex pushed past Treat to hug Max, taking a full-body glance at her before pulling her into his arms. That was when Treat finally noticed what Max was wearing. His body reacted instantly to seeing her in such a formfitting, sinfully sexy outfit. Unfortunately, with the way Rex was holding on to her, he assumed her figure had his brother reacting in the exact same way. He tugged him away from Max by his collar.

"Okay, back off. Get your own fiancée." He loved the feel of that word on his lips. *Fiancée.*

Savannah pushed between them and wrapped her arms around Treat, whispering, "Finally! I love her!" Then, louder, she said, "She'll keep you on your toes." She turned to Max with a wide smile and said, "I've wanted a sister for so long," and then she hugged her.

Treat held Max's gaze over his sister's shoulder, and they were passed from sibling to sibling. He couldn't wait to get Max's hand back into his own, where it belonged.

Hal embraced Max. "That was my wife's ring. She and I could not be happier than we are to see it on your finger. Welcome to the family, darlin'."

Max touched the gorgeous stone. "Thank you for the honor of allowing me to wear it and share in the joy of one day being a Braden."

He glanced at Hope and said, "It was my wife's doing."

Savannah shook her head, but her beaming smile remained.

When congratulations had been doled out and Treat and Max finally came together again, he whispered in her ear, "That outfit is going to make me do dirty things to you right here and now."

Max smiled and said, "Then it fulfilled its purpose."

Chapter Thirty-Three

WHILE THEIR FATHER went inside to grab a bottle of champagne and the others inspected the damage to the cars, Treat took advantage of a few quiet moments to make out with his fiancée. They were midkiss when the sound of hooves on pavement called everyone's attention past the crunched vehicles, where a woman riding a black stallion slowed to a halt at the end of the driveway. She wore a flowing white dress, hiked up and bundled across her thighs. She slipped her cowgirl boots from the shiny stirrups and flipped her long black hair over her shoulder, giving Treat a better look at her face.

Treat sidled up to Rex, who was standing a few feet away, holding Hope's reins, and said, "Is that Jade Johnson?"

Rex spun around, practically salivating at the sight of her. "Holy…" He mounted Hope and looked over his shoulder at Jade. When Rex was in high school, he'd had an enormous crush on Jade. But Earl Johnson was the object of their father's grudge, and Treat had written that crush off as Rex wanting the forbidden fruit. But from the way Rex was looking at her now, Treat had a feeling he was very wrong.

"Jade Johnson was our neighbor," Savannah explained to Max. "She moved away quite some time ago."

"Looks like someone got the best of your cars!" Jade hollered.

Rex's eyes narrowed. He fisted his hands tighter around Hope's reins. Hugh looked up from where he was crouched by the crunched fender and shot an uncomfortable look at Treat. Treat glanced back at the house, scanning the porch for their father. If he caught them talking to a Johnson, they'd never hear the end of it.

"Nice to see you, Jade," Hugh said in a low, tethered voice.

"Not quite a Ferrari, is it?" Jade teased their race-car-driving brother. She looked at Rex and said, "Good thing y'all weren't on horses, huh?"

Rex's jaw muscles jumped double-time. He climbed off Hope muttering under his breath.

"I think she's talking to you, Rex," Max said.

In Rex's silence, Hugh said, "We'll be sending this wreck to your neighbor's garage." Jimmy Palen owned the best body shop in Weston, and he lived on the other side of the Johnsons' property.

"Jimmy'll be glad to hear that." Jade's smile promptly disappeared when she glanced at Rex, who was now glowering at her. "See y'all around," she said with a wave, then galloped down the road.

Once she was out of earshot, Treat smacked Rex's leg. "What's with you? You didn't have to be so rude."

"I'll talk to a Johnson when pigs fly." Rex turned away.

"What was that all about?" Max asked, still touching her engagement ring. She hadn't stopped since Treat slid it on her finger.

"Hatfields and McCoys," Savannah teased. "Rex loves her." She lowered her voice and said, "He just doesn't know it yet.

Braden boys are thick that way."

"Not this Braden," Treat said as he swept Max into his arms.

Max whispered, "You're thick all right, but not in the head."

Her cheeks flushed, and he said, "Have these clothes turned my sweet girlfriend into my naughty fiancée?"

"It's what's *under* the clothes," she whispered naughtily.

Heat soared through his veins. "What's under your clothes?"

Her gaze turned sinful, and she put her finger over her lips. "It's a secret. I'd take you to my apartment and show you, but we don't have a vehicle to drive and I'm pretty sure you can't charter a plane for this."

He grabbed her hand and headed for Rex and Hope. He lifted Max up in one fell swoop and planted her on the horse, earning the sexiest squeal-giggle he'd ever heard, then climbed on behind her.

"Where are we going?" she asked with a beautiful smile.

"I may not be able to charter a plane, but I can sure as heck hijack a horse."

He wrapped his arm around her, and she turned, pressing her lips to his. As he deepened the kiss, his siblings cheered them on.

They both came away breathless, and Max said, "Take me away, cowboy."

With a gentle nudge of his heels, he urged Hope to carry them off to celebrate their engagement properly, and Treat thanked his lucky stars that he'd chartered that plane and gotten his girl.

Please enjoy this preview of the next Sweet with Heat novel
Our Sweet Destiny

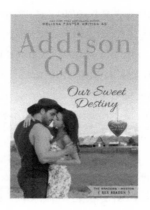

Chapter One

REX BRADEN AWOKE before dawn, just as he had every
Sunday morning for the past twenty-six years—since the
Sunday after his mother died, when he was eight years old. He
didn't know what had startled him awake on that very first
Sunday after she'd passed, but he swore it was her whispering
voice that led him down to the barn and had him mounting
Hope, the horse his father had bought for his mother when she
first became ill. In the years since, Hope had remained strong
and healthy; his mother, however, was not as lucky.

In the gray, predawn hours, the air was still downright cold,
which wasn't unusual for May in Colorado. By afternoon they'd

see temps in the low seventies. Rex pulled his Stetson down low on his head and rounded his shoulders forward as he headed into the barn.

The other horses itched to be set free the moment he walked by their stalls, but Rex's focus on Sunday mornings was solely on Hope.

"How are you, girl?" he asked in a deep, soft voice. He saddled Hope with care, running his hand over her thick coat. Her red coat had faded, now boasting white patches along her jaw and shoulders.

Hope nuzzled her nose into his massive chest with a gentle *neigh*. Most of his T-shirts had worn spots at his solar plexus from that familiar nudge. Rex had helped his father on the ranch ever since he was a boy, and after graduating from college, he'd returned to the ranch full-time. Now he ran the show—well, as much as anyone could run anything under Hal Braden's strong will.

"Taking our normal ride, okay, Hope?" He looked into her enormous brown eyes, and not for the first time, he swore he saw his mother's beautiful face smiling back at him. The face he remembered from before her illness had stolen the color from her skin and the sparkle from her eyes. Rex put his hands on Hope's strong jaw and kissed her on the soft pad of skin between her nostrils. Then he removed his hat and rested his forehead against the same tender spot, closing his eyes just long enough to sear that image into his mind.

They trotted down the well-worn trail in the dense woods that bordered his family's two-hundred-acre ranch. Rex had grown up playing in those woods with his five siblings. He knew every dip in the landscape and could ride every trail blindfolded. They rode out to the point where the trail abruptly came to an end at the adjacent property. The line between the Braden ranch and the unoccupied property might be invisible to some. The grass melded together, and the trees looked identical on either side. To Rex, the division was clear. On the Braden side, the land had life and breath, while on the unoccupied side, the land seemed to exude a longing for more.

Hope instinctively knew to turn around at that point, as they'd done so many times before. Today Rex pulled her reins gently, bringing her to a halt. He took a deep breath as the sun began to rise, his chest tightening at the silent three hundred acres of prime ranch land that would remain empty forever. Forty-plus years earlier, his father and Earl Johnson, their neighbor and his father's childhood friend, had jointly purchased that acreage between the two properties with the hopes of one day turning it over for a profit. After five years of arguing over everything from who would pay to subdivide the property to who they'd sell it to, both Hal and Earl took the hardest stand they could, each refusing to ever sell. The feud still had not resolved. The Hatfields' and McCoys' harsh and loyal stance to protect their family honor was mild compared to the loyalty that ran within the Braden veins. The Bradens had been raised to be loyal to their family above all else. Rex felt a pang of guilt as he looked over the property, and not for the first time, he wished he could make it his own.

With a gentle nudge, Hope trotted off the path and along the property line toward the creek. Rex's jaw clenched as they descended the deep hill toward the ravine. The water was still as glass when they finally reached the rocky shoreline. Rex looked up at the sky as the gray gave way to powdery blues and pinks. In all the years since he'd claimed those predawn hours as his own, he'd never seen a soul while he was out riding, and he liked it that way.

They headed south along the water toward Devil's Bend. The ravine curved at a shockingly sharp angle around the hillside and the water pooled, deepening against the rocky lip just before the creek dropped a dangerous twenty feet into a bed of rocks. He slowed when he heard a splash and scanned the water for the telltale signs of a beaver, but there wasn't a dam in sight.

Rex took the bend and brusquely drew Hope to a halt. Jade Johnson stood at the water's edge in a pair of cutoff jeans shorts, cut just above the dip where her hamstrings began. He'd seen her only once in the past several years, and that was weeks ago, when she had ridden her stallion down the road and stopped at the top of their driveway. Rex raked his eyes down her body and swallowed hard. Her cream-colored T-shirt hugged every inch of her delicious curves, a beautiful contrast to her black-as-night hair, which tumbled almost to her waist. Rex noticed that her hair was the exact same color as her stallion, which was standing nearby with one leg bent at the knee.

Jade hadn't seen him yet. He knew he should back Hope up and leave before she had the chance. But she was so impossibly beautiful that he was mesmerized, his body reacting in ways that had him cursing under his breath. Jade Johnson was Earl Johnson's feisty daughter. Jade Johnson was off-limits. She always had been and always would be. But that didn't stop his pulse from racing, or his body from heating up at the sight of her. Fifteen years he'd forced himself not to think about her, and now, as her shoulders lifted and fell with each breath, he couldn't stop himself from wondering what it might feel like to tangle his fingers in her thick mane of hair, or how her body would feel pressed against his bare chest. He felt the tantalizing stir of the forbidden wrestling with his deep-seated loyalty to his father—and he was powerless to stop himself from being the jerk of a man that usually resulted from the conflicting emotions.

JADE JOHNSON KNEW she shouldn't have ridden Flame down the ravine, but she'd woken up from a restless, steamy dream before the sun came up, and she needed a release for the sexual urges she'd been repressing for way too long. *Stupid Weston, Colorado.* How the heck was a thirty-one-year-old woman supposed to have any sort of relationship with a man in a town when everybody knew one another's business? She'd thought she'd had life all figured out; after she graduated from veterinary school in Oklahoma, she'd completed her certifications for veterinarian acupuncture while also studying equine shiatsu, and then she'd taken on full-time hours at the large animal practice where she'd worked a limited schedule while completing school. She'd dated the owner's son, Kane Law, and when she opened her own practice a year later, she thought she and Kane would move toward having a future together. How could she have known that her success would be a threat to him—or that he'd become so possessive that she'd have to end the relationship? Coming back home had been her only option after he refused to stop harassing her, and now that she'd been back for a few months, she was thinking that maybe returning to the small town had been a mistake. She'd gotten her Colorado license easily enough, but instead of building a real practice again, she'd been working on more of an as-needed basis, traveling to neighboring farms to help with their animals without any long-term commitment, while she figured out where she wanted to put down roots and try again.

She heaved a heavy rock into the water with a grunt, pissed off that she'd taken this chance with Flame by coming down the steep hill. She knew better, but Flame was a sturdy Arabian stallion, and at fifteen hands high, he had the most powerful hindquarters she'd ever seen. Flame's reaction time to commands, and his ability to spin, turn, or sprint forward was quicker than any horse she'd ever mounted. His short back, strong bones, and incredibly muscled loins made him appear indestructible. When Flame stumbled, Jade's heart nearly skipped a beat. He'd quickly regained his footing, but the rhythm of his gait had changed, and when she'd dismounted, he was favoring his right front leg. Now she was stuck with no way to get him home without hurting him further.

She bent over and hoisted another heavy rock into her arms to heave more of her frustration into the water. Her hair fell like a curtain over her face, and she used one dusty hand to push it back over her shoulder, then picked up the rock and—she dropped the rock and narrowed her eyes at the sight of Rex Braden sitting atop that mare of his.

The nerve of him, staring at me like I'm a piece of meat. Even if he was every girl's dream of a cowboy come true in his tight-fitting jeans, which curved oh so lusciously over his thighs. She ran her eyes up his too-tight dark shirt and silently cursed at herself for involuntarily licking her lips in response. She tried to tear her eyes from his tanned face, peppered with stubble so sexy that she wanted to reach out and touch his chiseled jaw, but her eyes would not obey.

"What're you looking at?" she spat at the son of the man who had caused her father years of turmoil. When she'd first come back to town, she'd hoped maybe things had changed. She'd ridden by the Bradens' ranch while she was out with Flame one afternoon. Rex and his family were out front, commiserating over an accident that had just happened in their driveway, resulting in two mangled cars. She'd tried to see if they needed help, to break the ice of the feud that had gone on since before she was born, but while his brother Hugh had at least spoken to her, Rex had just narrowed those smoldering dark eyes of his and clenched that ever-jumping jaw. No way would she accept that treatment from anyone, especially Rex Braden. Despite her best efforts to forget his handsome face, for years he'd been the only man she'd conjured up in the darkest hours of the nights, when loneliness settled in and her body craved human touch. It was always his face that pulled her over the edge as she came apart beneath the sheets.

"Not you, that's for sure," he answered with a lift of his chin.

Jade stood up tall in her new Rogue boots and settled her hands on her hips. "Sure looks like you're staring to me."

Rex cracked a crooked smile as he nodded toward the water. "Redecorating the ravine?"

"No!" She walked over to Flame and ran her hand down his flank. *Why him? Of all the men who could ride up, why does it have to be the one guy who makes my heart flutter like a schoolgirl's?*

"Taking a break, that's all." She couldn't take her eyes off of his bulging biceps. Even as a teenager, he'd had the nervous habit of clenching his jaw and arms at the same time—and, Jade realized, the effect it had on her had not diminished one iota.

"Lame stallion?" he asked in a raspy, deep voice.

Everything he said sounded sensual. "No." *What happened*

to my vocabulary? She'd been three years behind Rex in school, and in all the years she'd known him, he probably hadn't said more than a handful of words to her. She narrowed her eyes, remembering how she'd pined over each one of his grumbling syllables, even though they usually came after a dismissive grunt of some sort, which she had always attributed to the feud that preceded her birth.

"All righty, then." He turned his horse and walked her back the way he'd come.

Jade stared at his wide back as it moved farther and farther away. *What if no one else comes along?* She looked up at the sun making its slow crawl toward the sky, guessing it was only six thirty or seven. No one else was going to come by the ravine. She cursed herself for not carrying her cell phone. She wasn't one of those women who needed to be accessible twenty-four-seven. She carried it during the day, but this morning she'd just wanted to ride without distraction. Now she was stuck, and he was her only hope. Getting Flame home was more important than any family feud or her own conflicting hateful and lustful thoughts for the conceited man who was about to disappear around the corner.

She shook her head and kicked the dirt, wishing she'd worn her riding boots. The toes of her new Rogues were getting scuffed and dirty. *Could today get any worse?*

"Hey!" she called after him. When he didn't stop, she thought he hadn't heard her. "I said, *hey!*"

He came to a slow stop but didn't turn around. "You talking to me? I thought you were talking to that lame horse of yours." He cast a glance over his shoulder.

Jerk. "His name is Flame, and he's the best horse around, so watch yourself."

His horse began its lazy stroll once again.

"Wait!" She gritted her teeth against the desire to call him a nasty name and shot a look at Flame, still favoring his leg, softening her resolve.

"Wait, please."

His horse came to another stop.

"I need to get him home, and I can't very well do it myself." She kicked the dirt again as he turned his horse and walked her back. He stared down at Jade with piercing dark eyes, his jaw still clenched.

"Can you help me get him out of here?" Up close, his muscles were even larger, more defined than she'd thought. His neck was thicker, too. Everything about him exuded masculinity. She crossed her arms to settle her nerves as he waited a beat too long to answer. "Listen, if you can't—"

"Don't get your panties in a bunch," he said, calm and even.

"You don't have to be rude."

"I don't have to help at all," he said, mimicking her by crossing his arms.

"Fine. You're right. Sorry. Can you please help me get him out of here? He can't make it up that hill."

"Just how do you suppose I do that?" He glanced at the steep drop of the land just twenty feet ahead of them, then back up the ravine at the rocky shoreline. "You shouldn't've brought him down here. Why are you riding a stallion, anyway? They're temperamental as a baby with a bee sting. What were you thinking? A girl like you can't handle that horse on this type of terrain."

"A girl like me? I'll have you know that I'm a vet, and I've worked around horses my whole life." She felt her cheeks redden and crossed her arms, jutting her hip out in the defiant stance she'd taken up throughout her teenage years.

"So I hear." He lowered his chin and lifted his gaze, looking at her from beneath the shadow of his Stetson. "From the looks of it, all that vet schooling didn't do you much good, now, did it?"

Ugh! He was maddening. Jade pursed her lips and stalked away in a huff. "Forget it. I can do this by myself."

"Sure you can," he mused.

She felt his eyes on her back as she took Flame's reins and tried to lead him up the steep incline. The enormous horse took only three steps before stopping cold. She grunted and groaned, pleading with the horse to move, but Flame was hurt, and he'd gone stubborn on her. Her face heated to a flush.

"You keep doing what you're doing. I'll be back in an hour to get you and that lame horse of yours."

An hour, great. She was aching to tell him to hurry, but she knew how long it took to hook up the horse trailer, and she had no idea how he'd get it all the way down by the ravine. She watched him ride away, feeling stupid, embarrassed, angry, and insanely attracted to the ornery jerk of a man.

To continue reading, please buy
Our Sweet Destiny

Have you met the Seaside Summers crew?

Fall in love with Kurt and Leanna in **_Read, Write, Love at Seaside_**

(Offered **free** in digital format at the time of this printing. Prices subject to change without notice.)

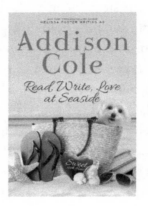

Chapter One

THE TIDE LAPPED at the sandy shore beyond the deck of the cedar-shingled bungalow where Kurt Remington sat on the deck of his cottage, fingers to keyboard, working on his latest manuscript. *Dark Times* was due to his agent at the end of the month, and Kurt came to his cottage in Wellfleet, Massachusetts, to hunker down for the summer and complete the project. He lived just outside of New York City and he wrote daily, sometimes for ten or twelve hours straight. In the summers, he liked the change of scenery the Cape offered and was inspired by the Cape's fresh air and the sounds of the sea.

He'd bought the estate of a local painter a few years earlier with the intent of renovating the artist's studio that sat nestled among a grouping of trees on the far side of the property. Initially, Kurt thought he might use the studio as a writing retreat separate from where he lived, with the idea that leaving the cottage to work might give him a chance to actually have a life and not feel pressure to write twenty-four-seven. What he found was that the studio was too far removed from the sights and sounds that inspired him, and it made him feel like even more of a recluse than he already was. He realized that it wasn't the location of his computer that pressured him. It was his internal drive and his love of writing that propelled his fingers to the keyboard every waking second. The idea of making the studio into a guest cottage crossed his mind, but that would indicate his desire to have guests, which would mean giving up his coveted writing time to entertain. So there it sat, awaiting…something. Though he had no idea what.

The cottage was built down a private road at the top of a dune, with a private beach below. A curtain of dense air settled around him. Kurt lifted his eyes long enough to scan the graying clouds and ponder the imminence of rain. It was seven twenty in the evening, and he'd been writing since nine o'clock that morning, as was his daily habit, right after his three-mile run, two cups of coffee, and a quick breeze through the newspaper and email. Once Kurt got into his writing zone each day, other than getting up to eat, he rarely changed his surroundings. The idea of moving inside and breaking his train of thought was unsettling.

He set his hands back on the keyboard and reread the last

few sentences of what would become his thirteenth thriller novel. A dog barked in the distance, and Kurt drew his thick, dark brows together without breaking the stride of his keystrokes. Kurt hadn't risen to the ranks of Patterson, King, and Grisham by being easily distracted.

"Pepper! Come on, boy!" A female voice sliced through his concentration. "Come on, Pepper. Where are you?"

Kurt's fingers hesitated for only a moment as she hollered; then he went right back to the killer lurking outside the window in his story.

"Pepper!" the woman yelled again. "Oh geez, Pepper, really?"

Kurt closed his eyes for a beat as the wind picked up. The woman's voice *was* distracting him. She was too close to ignore. *Get your mutt and move on.* He let out a breath and went back to work. Kurt craved silence. The quieter things were, the better he could hear his characters and think through their issues. He tried to ignore the sounds of splashing and continued writing.

"Pepper! No, Pepper!"

Great. He was hoping to squeeze in a few more hours of writing on the deck before taking a walk on the beach, but if that woman kept up her racket, he'd be forced to work inside—and if there was one thing Kurt hated, it was changing his surroundings while he was in the zone. Writing was an art that took total focus. He'd honed his craft with the efficiency of a drill sergeant, which was only fitting since his father was a four-star general.

More splashing.

"Oh no! Pepper? Pepper!"

The woman's panicked voice split his focus right down the center. He thought of his sister, Siena, and for a second he considered getting up to see if the woman's concern was valid. Then he remembered that his sister often overreacted. Women often overreacted.

"Pepper! Oh no!"

Being an older brother came with responsibilities that Kurt took seriously, as had been ingrained in him at a young age. That loud woman was someone's daughter. His conscience won over the battle for focus, and with a sigh, he pushed away from the table and went to the railing. He caught sight of the woman wading waist deep in the rough ocean waves.

"Pepper! Pepper, please come back!" she cried.

Kurt followed her gaze into deeper water, which was becoming rougher by the second as the clouds darkened and the wind picked up a notch. He didn't see a dog anywhere in the water. He scanned the empty beach—no dog there, either.

"Pepper! Please, Pep! Come on, boy!" She tumbled back with the next wave and fell on her butt, then struggled to find her footing.

Come on. Really? This, he didn't need. He watched her push through the crashing waves. She was shoulder deep. Kurt knew about the dangers of riptides and storms and wondered why she didn't. She had no business being out in the water with a storm brewing.

Drops of water dampened Kurt's arms. He swatted them away with a grimace, still watching the woman.

"Please come back, Pepper!"

The rain came in a heavy drizzle now. *For the love of…* Kurt spun around, gathered his computer and notes and took them inside. He checked to see that he'd saved his file before pushing the laptop safely back from the edge of the counter, then turned back to the French doors. *I could close the doors and go right back to work.* He eyed his laptop.

"Pepper!"

She sounded farther away now. Maybe she'd moved on. He went back out on the deck to see if she'd come to her senses.

"Pep—" Another wave toppled her over. She was deeper now and seemed to be pulled by the current.

"Hey!" Kurt hollered in an effort to dissuade her from going out any deeper. She must not have heard him. He scanned the water again and saw a flash of something about thirty feet away from her. *Your stupid dog.* Dogs were smelly, they shed, and they needed time and attention. All reasons why Kurt was not a fan of the creatures.

The rain picked up with the gusty wind. *Good grief.* He grabbed a towel from inside and stomped down the steps, *Dark Times* begrudgingly pushed aside.

LEANNA BRAY WAS wet, cold, and floundering. Literally. She'd been floundering for twenty-eight years, so this was nothing new, but being pummeled by rain, wind, and waves, chasing a dog that never listened? That was new.

"Pepp—" A wave knocked her off her feet and she went under the water, taking a mouthful of saltwater along with her. She tumbled head down beneath the surface.

Now Pepper and I will both drown. Freaking perfect.

Something grabbed her arm, and she reflexively fought against it, sucking in another mouthful of salty water as she broke through the surface, arms flailing, choking, and pushing against the powerful hand that yanked her to her feet.

"You okay?" A deep, annoyed voice carried over the din of

the crashing waves.

Cough. Cough. "Yeah. I—" *Cough. Cough.* "My dog." She blinked and blinked, trying to clear the saltwater and rain from her eyes. The man's mop of wet, dark hair came into focus. He held tightly to her arm while scanning the water in the direction of where she'd last seen Pepper. His clothes stuck to his body like a second skin, riding the ripples of his impressive chest and arms as he held her above the surface with one arm around her ribs.

"Come on." She coughed as he plowed through the pounding surf with her clutched against his side. She slid down his body, and he lifted her easily into his arms, carrying her like he might carry a child, pressing her to his chest as he fought against the waves.

She pushed against his chest, feeling ridiculous and helpless...and maybe a little thankful, but she was ignoring that emotion in order to save Pepper.

"My dog! I need to get my dog!" she hollered.

Mr. Big, Tall, and Stoic didn't say a word. He set her on the wet sand and tossed her a rain-soaked towel. "It was dry." He pointed behind her to a wooden staircase. "Go up to the deck."

She dropped the towel and plowed past him toward the water. "I gotta get my dog."

He snagged her by the arm and glared at her with the brightest blue eyes she'd ever seen—and a stare so dark she swallowed her voice.

"Go." He pointed to the stairs again. "I'll get your dog." He took a step toward the water, and she pushed past him again.

"You don't have t—"

He scooped her into his arms again and carried her to the stairs. "If you fight me, your dog will drown. He won't last in this much longer."

She pushed at his chest again. "Let me go!"

He set her down on the stairs. "The waves will pull you under. I'll get your dog. Please stay here."

Her heart thundered against her ribs as she watched him stalk off and plow through the waves as if he were indestructible. She stood in the rain on the bottom stair, huddled beneath the wet towel, squinting to see him through the driving rain. She finally spotted him deep in the sea, wrapping his arms around Pepper—the dog who never let anyone carry him. He rounded his shoulders, shielding Pepper as he made his way back through the wild waves.

She ran to the edge of the water, shivering, tears in her eyes. "Thank you!" She reached for Pepper and the dog whined, pressing his trembling body closer to the guy.

"You have a leash?"

She shook her head. Her wet hair whipped across her cheek, and she turned her back to the wind. "He doesn't like them."

He took her by the arm again. "Come on." He led her up the stairs to a wooden deck, opened a French door, and leaned in close, talking over the sheeting rain.

"Go on in."

She stepped onto pristine hardwood. The warm cottage smelled of coffee and something sweet and masculine, like a campfire. She reached for Pepper. Pepper whined again and pressed against the man's chest.

"He..." Her teeth chattered from the cold. "He must be scared."

"I'll get you a towel." He eyed the dog in his arms and shook his head before disappearing up a stairwell.

Leanna scoped out the open floor plan of the cozy cottage,

looking for signs of *crazy*. How crazy could he be? He'd just rescued her and Pepper, and Pepper already seemed to be quite attached to him. *He went into the water in a storm without an ounce of fear. The man was crazy.* It dawned on her that she'd done the same thing, but she knew *she* wasn't crazy. She'd had no choice. To her right was a small kitchen with expensive-looking light wood cabinets and fancy molding. A laptop sat open beside two neatly stacked notebooks on the shiny marble countertop. The screen was dark, and she had an urge to touch a button and bring the laptop to life, but she didn't really want to know if there was something awful on there. He could have been watching porn, for all she knew, although he hadn't checked her out once, even with her wet T-shirt and shorter-than-short cut offs. She couldn't decide if that was gentlemanly or creepy.

She shifted her thoughts away from the computer to the quaint breakfast nook to her left. Her eyes traveled past a little alcove with two closed doors and a set of stairs by the kitchen to the white-walled living room. There was not a speck of clutter anywhere. A pair of flip-flops sat by the front door, perfectly lined up against the wall beside a pair of running shoes. She located the source of the campfire smell. A gorgeous two-story stone fireplace covered most of the wall adjacent to an oversized brown couch. There was a small stack of firewood in a metal holder beside the hearth. The cottage was surprisingly warm considering there wasn't a fire in the fireplace. Dark wood bookshelves ran the length of the far wall, from floor to ceiling, complete with a rolling ladder. The room was full of textures—a chenille blanket was folded neatly across the back of the couch, a thick, brown shag rug sat before the stone fireplace, and an intricately carved wooden table was placed before the couch.

Leanna had a thing for textures, and right now she was texturing the beautiful hardwood with drops of water. She snagged a dishtowel from the kitchen counter as the man came back downstairs with Pepper cradled in his arms like a baby and wrapped in a big fluffy towel.

The possibility of him being crazy went out the door. *Crazy people don't carry dogs like babies.*

He shifted Pepper to one arm and handed her a fresh towel. "Here. I'm Kurt, by the way."

Pepper sat up in his arms, panting happily. *Show-off.*

"Thank you. I'm Leanna. That's Pepper." She tried to mop up the floor around her. Every swipe of the towel brought more drips from her sopping-wet clothing. "I'm sorry about this. For the mess. And my dog. And..." She frantically wiped the floor with the dishrag in one hand, using the fisted towel in the other to scrub her clothes, trying desperately to stop the river that ran from her clothes to his no-longer-pristine floor. She lifted her gaze. He had a slightly amused smile on his very handsome face. She rose to her feet with a defeated sigh.

"I'm so sorry, and thank you for rescuing Pepper."

He glanced at his laptop, and that amused look quickly turned to pinched annoyance. His lips pressed into a tight line, and when he glanced at her again, it was with a brooding look, before stepping forward and closing his laptop.

"You should have"—Pepper barked in his ear; he closed his eyes and exhaled—"had the dog on a leash."

The dog.

"He hates it. He hates listening, leashes, lots of things." Pepper licked Kurt's cheek. "Except you, I guess."

Kurt winced and set Pepper on the floor. "Sit," he said in a deep, stern voice.

Pepper sat at his feet.

"How did you do that? He never listens."

He dried Pepper's feet with the towel, apparently ignoring the question.

"Labradoodle?"

You know dogs? She was intrigued by the dichotomy of him. He was sharp, brooding, and maybe even a little cold, yet Pepper followed him to the fireplace as if he were handing out doggy biscuits. Leanna couldn't help but notice the way Kurt's wet jeans hugged his body. *His very hot body.* He crouched before the fireplace, his shirt clinging tightly to his broad back, his sleeves hitched up above his bulging biceps, and she made out the outline of a tattoo on his upper arm.

"Yeah, Labradoodle. How'd you know? He looks like a wet mutt right now."

He shrugged, expertly fashioning a teepee of kindling, then starting a small fire. "Where's your place?" He slid an annoyed look at Pepper and shook his head.

"Um, my place?" she said, distracted as much by Pepper's obedience as by Kurt's tattoo. *What is that? A snake? Dragon?*

He looked at her with that amused glint in his eyes again. "House? Cottage? Campsite?"

"Oh, cottage. Sorry." She felt her cheeks flush. "It's about a mile and a half from here. Seaside. Do you know it? My parents own it. I'm just staying for the summer. I've known the other people in the community forever, and Pepper likes it there."

He looked back at the fireplace, the amusement in his expression replaced with seriousness. "Come over by the fire. Warm up."

She tossed the towels on the counter and joined him by the fire, shivering as she warmed her hands.

He kept his eyes trained on the fire.

"Did you drive here?" He picked up a log in one big hand and settled it on the fire.

"No. I biked."

"Biked?"

"I bike here a couple times each week with Pepper, but we usually go the other way down the beach. Pepper just took off this time. I left my bike by the public beach entrance."

His eyes slid to Pepper, then back to the fire. "I don't know Seaside, but let me change and I'll drive you home." He headed toward the stairs with Pepper on his heels. Kurt stopped and stared at the dog. Pepper panted for all he was worth. Kurt looked at Leanna, as if she could control the dog.

Fat chance. "He's not really an obedient pet." She shrugged.

Kurt picked up Pepper and brought him to Leanna. "Hold his collar."

Okay, then. She looped her finger in Pepper's collar and watched Kurt go into the kitchen and wipe the floor with the towel he'd given her. Then he wiped the counter with a sponge before disappearing into the alcove by the kitchen. He returned with a laundry basket, tossed the dirty towels in, and then returned the basket to where he'd found it and climbed the stairs.

"Guess he doesn't really like dirt…or dogs after all," she said to Pepper.

Pepper broke free and ran up the stairs after Kurt.

Leanna closed her eyes with a loud sigh.

Just shoot me now.

To continue reading, please buy
Read, Write, Love at Seaside

More Books By The Author

Sweet with Heat: Seaside Summers

Read, Write, Love at Seaside
Dreaming at Seaside
Hearts at Seaside
Sunsets at Seaside
Secrets at Seaside
Nights at Seaside
Seized by Love at Seaside
Embraced at Seaside
Lovers at Seaside
Whispers at Seaside

Sweet with Heat: Bayside Summers
(Includes future publications)

Sweet Love at Bayside
Sweet Passions at Bayside
Sweet Heat at Bayside
Sweet Escape at Bayside

Sweet with Heat: Weston Bradens
(Includes future publications)

A Love So Sweet
Our Sweet Destiny
Unraveling the Truth about Love
Sea of Sweet Love
Promise of a New Beginning
And Then There Was Us

Stand Alone Women's Fiction Novels
by Melissa Foster (Addison Cole's steamy alter ego)
The following titles may include some harsh language

Chasing Amanda (mystery/suspense)
Come Back to Me (mystery/suspense)
Have No Shame (historical fiction/romance)
Megan's Way (literary fiction)
Traces of Kara (psychological thriller)
Where Petals Fall (suspense)

Acknowledgments

There are so many people to thank for helping me bring this book to readers. There's a community of bloggers, reviewers, authors, readers, and friends that each deserve to be listed here, but I simply don't have space. My sincere gratitude goes out to everyone who has inspired, helped, and encouraged me though this exciting journey. I hope we can continue to inspire each other. Thank you all so very much.

My dedicated and efficient editors and proofreaders deserve a chocolate sculpture ten feet high for their energy and skills. Thank you, Kristen, Penina, Lynn, Juliette, Marlene, Elaini, and Justinn. I'm so lucky to have you on my team.

To all my besties and assistants who have supported my whirlwind journey to bring Addison Cole to readers, thank you! You are the best friends a person could hope for, and I treasure every moment of our laughter, whining, wining **wink wink**, and trouble-making time together—virtual and otherwise. Sisters at heart…forever.

My writing life would not exist if not for the support and understanding of my mother, my husband, and my children. You rock my world and I love you all.

Meet Addison

Addison Cole is the sweet alter ego of *New York Times* and *USA Today* bestselling and award-winning author Melissa Foster. She enjoys writing humorous and deeply emotional contemporary romance without explicit sex scenes or harsh language. Addison spends her summers on Cape Cod, where she dreams up wonderful love stories in her house overlooking Cape Cod Bay.

Visit Addison on her website or chat with her on social media. Addison enjoys discussing her books with book clubs and reader groups and welcomes an invitation to your event.

Addison's books are available in paperback, digital, and audio formats.

www.AddisonCole.com
www.facebook.com/AddisonColeAuthor

CPSIA information can be obtained
at www.ICGtesting.com
Printed in the USA
LVHW012340250619
622381LV00001B/160

9 781948 868129